THORN

CARTER KIDS #2

CHLOE WALSH

Thorn,
First published, February 2016
All rights reserved. ©
Cover Designed by Bee @ Bitter Sage Designs.
Edited by Nouvelle Author Services.
Proofread by: Brooke Bowen Hebert.

DISCLAIMER

This book is a work of fiction. All names, characters, places and incidents either are products of the author's imagination or are used fictitiously. Any resemblance to events, locales, or persons, living or dead, is coincidental.

The author acknowledges all songs titles, song lyrics, film titles, film characters, trademarked statuses, brands, mentioned in this book are the property of, and belong to, their respective owners.

Chloe Walsh is in no way affiliated with any of the brands, songs, musicians or artists mentioned in this book.

PREFACE

The man who loved me was a fighter.
He had blood on his hands.
He was dangerous, treacherous, and he called me his Thorn.
I was his strength and his weakness, all rolled into one.
He was trained – bred – to play a pivotal part in an underworld
concocted of violence and destruction.
The question was could I love him in spite of the danger he
represented to my life?
Could I love him in spite of the danger he represented to my
soul?

1

THE PAST

SEVEN YEARS AGO

Noah

*T*eagan was safe.

I could handle the whole damn world falling down around me just as long as she was safe – alive and breathing. My little Thorn was okay, and that made this whole damn mess worth it.

I knew I was facing prison time because of my role in the quarry. I knew I was going away for a while – up to five years for GBH.

Three if I didn't fuck up again, Kyle's suit had assured me at the station tonight. That didn't sound too fucking bad to me. Hell, three square meals a day, and a long ass rest sounded like heaven to my body. I might even get lucky and score a cell of my own.

To be perfectly honest, the only reason I was handling this so calmly was because I had Teagan. I didn't think she realized just how much I loved her crazy ass. That girl was everything to me and I didn't say that lightly.

She'd seen the worst of me and she loved me through it.

Fuck, she was prepared to keep me even when we thought I'd killed Gerome Javi.

Jesus Christ, what that girl did for me tonight – running into the Hub all guns a-blazing.

I never realized a man's heart could love as hard as this.

This was an insane kind of love.

One I never thought I would have.

Fuck, my whole world had pretty much burnt to dust tonight. I knew shit was going to be a hell of a lot different in the morning.

I had a family now.

Kyle was my brother, Lee was my sister-in-law, and the triplets and Hope were my niece and nephews.

Kyle had bailed me out. I was back on Thirteenth Street because of the guy and his big fucking heart. I couldn't resent that. Besides, I knew what kind of upbringing my older, half-brother had, and it wasn't fucking pretty. The man was self-made. I could only aspire to be like him one day. Maybe that's why I had always felt so damn comfortable in the Carters' house?

It was because I was one of them.

Well shit...

Just a few short hours ago, I was the only child of a murdered ex-con and a schizophrenic heroin addict. And now? Now I had brothers, and more family than I'd ever dreamed possible.

I should be losing my shit right about now, but the meds flushing their way through my bloodstream kept me highly sedated and extremely drowsy.

My body was in pieces. Everything hurt. My back, my face, my fucking chest; hell, even my dick was throbbing. But I was alive, breathing, and I hadn't killed anyone.

Pain was smothering my senses, my ribs were burning like vinegar seeping into an open wound, but I knew I would sleep easy tonight.

Because I was free.

Free from George Dennis, and free to live my life.

Free to be with Teagan.

Inhaling gingerly, I allowed my eyelids to flutter closed, comforted by the knowledge that my Thorn was safely tucked up in her bed next door.

Fuck it, a bright future was actually attainable for a guy like me.

"Mmm...Yes!" A female voice mewled, startling me awake.

The sudden weight that slammed against my pelvis was fucking fantastic.

"Thorn?" My voice sounded groggy and slurred.

So sweet and soft and warm.

So damn snug and tight.

A nervous tingle shot up my spine and I heard myself groan in pleasure.

"Shh," was the last thing I heard before unconsciousness claimed me.

WHEN I CAME TO I WAS ALONE ON MY BED, NAKED, AND FEELING more satisfied than I had in days.

Even though I couldn't remember jack shit from the night before, the wet patch on the mattress assured me that a late night visit from my girlfriend was the reason I felt so sated.

Slightly dazed and feeling like a freight train had mowed me down, I shrugged on a pair of sweatpants, climbed unsteadily to my feet, and made my way over to my bedroom window.

My eyes immediately honed in on Teagan standing on her front porch and my heart flipped inside of my chest.

I needed to get used to looking at her from behind a pane of glass, I thought to myself as I studied her beautiful face. Her face that was *crying*?

Confused as hell, I watched in a mixture of surprise and anxiety as my girlfriend walked toward a cab with a suitcase.

What the...

I tapped on the windowpane and tried to get her attention, but she didn't look back.

That caused the anxiety inside of me to multiply rapidly.

"Teagan!"

I could barely breathe from the pain in my side, but the slicing in my chest watching Teagan, followed by Hope, climb into the cab was fifty million times worse.

Fuck, I would rather take a knife than feel this.

"Teagan!"

I rapped my knuckles harder against the window.

"Thorn!"

And then the car pulled away.

Fuck no...

Frantic for answers, I grabbed my phone off my nightstand and swiped my thumb across the screen. Immediately, a message thread opened up.

NOAH: NEED 2 SHOW U SOMETHING. FRONT DOOR'S UNLOCKED. *I'M in bed. Come straight up.*

Teagan: Be there in 2.

"WHAT THE..." GAPING AT THE SCREEN OF MY PHONE IN confusion, I slowly worded out the messages under my breath as I tried to make sense of the texts I knew I hadn't sent.

Forcing my legs to move, I shuffled clumsily out of my bedroom and down the staircase. Leaning against the hallway wall when I reached the bottom step, still woozy from the pain meds, I shook my head and tried to clear my vision.

Raw anxiety was eating at my gut.

What the hell was happening?

"Good morning, sexy."

My entire frame froze the second my eyes landed on Reese, in the doorway of my kitchen, with a mug of coffee in her hands, dressed in nothing but my blood-stained t-shirt.

"What the fuck." It wasn't a question. I already knew the answer – it was smeared all over my dick. No doubt it was the reason Teagan had torn off in that cab quicker than a bat out of hell.

Jesus Christ.

A million different emotions were coursing through me. I couldn't think straight. I couldn't believe my fucking eyes. "You fucking rapist," I snarled, feeling violated and furious.

"Calm down," Reese cooed, holding out the mug for me to take.

I took it from her and plastered it against the opposite wall. She yelped when it shattered and coffee sprayed everywhere.

"You raped me." Three words I never thought would come out of my mouth, but there they were. "You fucking forced yourself on me, didn't you?"

When she didn't deny it, I let out a roar. "You sent Teagan that text from my phone, didn't you?"

Reese's eyes welled up with tears as she nodded her head.

My heart sank. "Did she see?" I managed to choke out. "Did my girlfriend see you fucking me?"

"Noah please," Reese protested. "Let me explain –"

"Don't you dare goddamn *Noah* me," I roared into her face. "You took advantage of me." My voice sounded strange even to me. "And now Teagan's gone because of you!" Violent and wholly enraged. "Was shaming her with that CCTV footage not enough for you?" I demanded, "You had to do *this*?"

"I'm sorry, okay?" Reese shook her head in despair. "I didn't expect you to behave like this. I thought you would –" she started to say, but I cut her off.

"What?" I stalked past her towards the front door. "You didn't expect me to feel violated?" With the front door open, I glared once more at the girl in my shirt. "You better get suited with a good fucking lawyer," I warned her. "There's a special place in the state penitentiary for women like you. Don't think you'll get away with this because I'm the one with the dick."

It was freezing when I stepped outside, wearing only a pair of black sweatpants, but I didn't let it stop me. I was like a crazed man on a rampage.

I needed to stop Teagan from leaving me.

I *needed* her, period.

I wouldn't survive the next few years without her.

Staggering across the yard, I stumbled up her porch steps and thrust my elbow against the panel of glass in her uncle's front door.

The sound of the house alarm went off, almost deafening me, and I knew I was burying myself under another lawsuit, but I was desperate.

The glass shattered, as I knew it would, and I slipped my hand inside, feeling the nicks of razor sharp shards as they sliced at my skin.

Twisting the doorknob, I let myself inside and grabbed Teagan's car keys from the desk table in the foyer.

Racing outside, I didn't think twice about unlocking her little, red, Honda Civic and climbing inside, ignoring Reese's screaming protests that I was on house arrest and couldn't leave. With my foot to the floor, I tore out of the driveway in the direction the cab had gone.

I was less than a mile from The Hill when red and blue sirens alerted me to the fact that I had company.

Cursing like a sailor, I threw the car into fifth and gunned it. Praying for a miracle but preparing for the worst, I continued driving like a madman; driven by desperation – by fucking love.

In the end, I wasn't sure if it was the meds, or the actual pain that caused me to veer off the road, but for the life of me I couldn't keep control of the car.

I took the corner too sharply and stuck the nearby ditch.

The car flipped twice before settling on its roof.

Game over.

TEAGAN

I had to admit that it wasn't my brightest idea, running home to Ireland with nowhere to go, but my ex-boyfriend's family had taken us in when we arrived at their door at the crack of dawn last Saturday. They had been more than hospitable, all things considered.

"Are you okay, pet?" Sheila Harte asked me for the twelfth time in the past hour through the door of the toilet, and for the twelfth time I had to repeat the words 'I'm grand, Sheila,' as I clung to the toilet bowl in her downstairs bathroom like it was my very own personal lifeline.

The whole flight all I could do was cry, puke, scream, and die inside. I was fairly certain I wouldn't be welcome back on an Aer Lingus flight anytime in the foreseeable future. And even though we had arrived at the Harte's home almost a week ago, I was still vomiting and seriously considering taking the valium Liam's mother had offered me last night.

Noah had never been mine.

I knew that now.

How could I even be sure that he was *ever* faithful to me?

I couldn't be sure.

I couldn't believe anything.

Our whole relationship had been a lie.

I had wasted my heart and my virginity on a gangster whore.

Goddammit.

This was the worst pain I had ever felt in my eighteen years.

I was dying.

I was sure of it.

And there was nothing anyone could do to take it away for me.

Angry was an understatement. Fury wouldn't hold my coat. I was pissed off and heartbroken. An ugly combination for an emotionally unbalanced teenager.

Hope was in the sitting room with her phone glued to her hands when I finally finished dry heaving and rinsed my mouth out. Liam sat in the armchair opposite her, looking uncomfortable but curious.

"I'm sorry about this," I repeated when I reached them, sinking down on the arm of the chair Hope was occupying. "If we had anywhere else to go we would be there," I added. *Trust me.*

"It's fine, Teegs," Liam replied. Rising from his chair, he moved towards me with his arms outstretched. "I'm glad you came to me."

Actually, I had come to his mother, but I decided not to correct him. It seemed to be a rude thing to do. "Right," I mumbled, embracing him in an awkward half-hug. "Uh, thanks again."

Hope's phone continued to vibrate in her hands as she stared blankly at the lit up screen. Mine on the other hand, was void of messages and calls.

I wasn't being chased after or worried about because I had made the foolish decision to put all of my eggs in Noah Messina's basket and the bastard had betrayed me in the worst way.

I burned my bridges with Uncle Max.

I didn't think he would ever forgive me.

And I didn't blame him.

I chose Noah over him, over my own flesh and blood.

I was a shitty niece.

All I had was Hope and I was secretly terrified her father was going to arrive at any moment and sweep her back to Colorado with him. And then I would be totally alone, because there was no way in hell that I was ever facing Thirteenth Street again.

"Are you going to answer that?" Liam asked Hope, releasing me from his grasp. "Could be important."

"It's not," Hope replied coldly, not taking her eyes off the screen of her phone.

"You should just answer him and get it over with, Hope," I said wearily. I knew it was her dad. He wasn't going to lie down over this. "He won't stop calling until you speak to him," I added after a pause.

I watched Hope deliberate with herself before finally swiping her thumb across the screen and putting the phone to her ear. "Dad," she acknowledged in a tone void of any emotion. "What's up?"

Taking a few steps back from us, Liam hovered awkwardly by the sitting room door. When our eyes met, he inclined his head, gesturing for me to follow him, before stepping out of the room.

I didn't want to know a damn thing about Thirteenth Street, I couldn't cope with it, so I was glad for the escape Liam was offering me.

Sliding off the arm of the chair, I followed Liam down the hallway of their bungalow, stopping when we reached the last door at the end of the hall on the right.

When I stepped foot in his bedroom, years' worth of memories bombarded me. I had spent most of my life in this room. It had been a sanctuary for me after Mom died.

"Are you going to tell me what happened?" Liam asked when he sank down on his bed.

The same bed I'd given my first blowjob in.

He patted the mattress, beckoning me. "Come on, Teegs. You look like you've gone ten rounds with Tyson."

I stifled the scream that was forcing its way up my throat at the thought of rounds and rings and fucking fighters.

"I don't think I can," I admitted, flopping down on the bed next to him. "Talk about it, that is," I reiterated. "Everything is so screwed up, Liam." Throwing myself back, I lay motionless, looking up at the ceiling. "I'm in so much trouble."

Liam leaned back and rested on his elbows before letting out a heavy sigh. "I'm guessing a fella is behind this."

I turned my face to look at him. "What makes you think that?" He was right. One hundred percent. But I wasn't about to tell him that. "Well?"

Now Liam was the one to flop onto his back. "Because you've been puking your guts out in the bathroom for the past hour." Liam closed his eyes and I watched as a vein ticked in his neck. "How far gone are you?"

"What?" I rolled my eyes in disgust, ignoring the nervous flutter in the pit of my stomach. "You think I'm pregnant?"

He blinked rapidly. "You're not?"

"Liam, I'm nursing a broken heart," I choked out, "not a fucking baby." There was no way in hell Noah Messina had knocked me up. I refused to believe that the period I had been waiting on to arrive for the last ten days was down to anything other than stress.

"Oh." Liam seemed to consider this for a moment. "Is your friend pregnant?"

"Seriously?" Jerking off the bed, I turned to glare at my former flame. If he could just stop talking about babies for one freaking minute. "No one is pregnant, Liam. Jesus!"

"I'm sorry, alright." He held his hands up in defense. "I just presumed..."

"I caught my boyfriend cheating on me with the school slut, okay?" I hissed angrily. "And now he's going to prison for almost killing a man at an illegal fighting ring."

Liam's cheeks reddened and his mouth fell open. "The next-door neighbor?" He asked, winning major brownie points for remembering the emails I had sent him last year. "The tattooed fighter guy – what was his name again?"

"Noah," I whispered, nodding, feeling physical pain when I spoke his name.

Liam opened his mouth to say something, but his bedroom door swung inward, causing him to pause.

We both turned our heads to look at Hope.

"That was my dad," she announced, sliding her phone into her jeans pocket. Her face was pale and her eyes were bloodshot as she leaned against the doorframe. "He's at the airport."

"What?" I deadpanned. "In the states?"

"In Shannon, but it doesn't matter because I am *not* going back."

"Hope, be realistic," I mumbled. I felt like weeping. Kyle was in Ireland and he was going to kill me, and then he was going to take Hope away.

I secretly wondered if he could also take my memories?

The man was a millionaire, surely he knew people that could open my brain and toss Noah Messina out?

"I am," Hope shot back. "I am not going back there, Teagan, and the only way my father is going to make me, is if he takes me home in a body bag."

NOAH

*M*y mother was schizophrenic and in some small part of my mind – the part I tried not to listen to – I was afraid that what had happened to her would eventually happen to me.

It wasn't my mother's fault.

Her illness just was, and I understood that, but I was afraid of becoming her.

No, screw that. I was fucking petrified.

And even though her drug habit was the reason I had been dragged into the underground, I *couldn't* hate her.

She had never been much of a mother to me – not really. What I felt for her was more pity than love because in truth, since I was fifteen years old, Lee Carter had been more of a mother to me than my own ever had. She had been there for me, cleaning my cuts and broken bones, and driving me to the hospital whenever I had come close to bleeding out.

Out of all the people to arrive at the jail, I should have known it would be Lee.

I felt like shit – like I'd let her down. I was scum, I always knew it, but now Lee did too and that filled me with shame.

I watched Kyle's wife like a hawk as an officer ushered her into the room I was being held in.

"Oh Noah," Lee whispered when we were alone.

Lowering herself into the chair opposite me, she reached across the table and covered my hand with both of hers. The feel of her skin on mine was almost my undoing and I had to look away and clench my jaw shut to stop myself from crying like a pussy. "I'm sorry," I managed to squeeze out, looking anywhere but her direction. "For fucking up my bail," I added, "I'll pay Kyle back...someday."

"Forget about the money," Lee drawled in her soft southern accent. "I don't care about it and neither does Kyle. We care about you."

"Why?" The question was laced with sarcasm and out of my mouth before I could think.

"Because we love you," Lee replied quickly and without an ounce of hesitation. "You're like a son to me and to Kyle," she told me. "We want to help you."

"Except I'm not his son, am I?" I tossed out, clenching my jaw again. "I'm his fucking *brother*."

"True," Lee shot back, not missing a beat. "All the more reason to let us help you. Noah, look at me. Please."

Inhaling a sharp breath, I looked at her. The warmth and motherly love I saw in her eyes touched something deep inside me. "We know about Max Jones pressing charges on you for breaking and entering and grand theft auto."

"Yeah." I let out a heavy sigh. Teagan's uncle loved this. "Asshole couldn't wait to press charges."

"Kyle has arranged the best defense attorney in the state to fight in your corner," Lee told me. "They've already made a bargain plea on your behalf, and the prosecution has accepted – bringing your sentence from twelve years down to five and a half."

I had always known I was going to do time.

I had done it, and committed the crimes. I pulverized Gerome Javi to within an inch of his life. I broke into Max Jones's house. I stole Teagan's car.

It was all on me.

In a sick way, I had spent my entire life preparing for this moment. It was fucking inevitable. I had been living on the edge for so long; a pawn in a gangster's world, that in one sense it was a relief.

But I was only eighteen; five and half years behind bars was a lifetime to me.

Leaning forward, Lee squeezed my hand, as she said, "Don't give up hope, sweetheart." Her big gray eyes were full of unshed tears. "Five years isn't forever. I promise you that. You'll get through this, Noah."

"Teagan's gone," I groaned, addressing the only thing that mattered to me. Jerking my hand away from her, I bowed my head when my voice cracked. "She fucking bailed on me, Lee." I closed my eyes, forcing the dampness to remain behind my eyelids.

Twisting around in my chair in real, honest-to-god physical fucking agony, I fought the urge to lose my shit. Something was breaking inside of me and I was losing myself in the process. "The girl I love more than every damn soul on this planet thinks I fucked her over. And worse, she thinks I invited her to watch it unfold!" My brain was like a fucking broken projector, tormenting me with image after image of my girlfriend's heart-broken expression when she climbed into that cab.

"Noah," Lee whispered in a worried tone of voice. "What on earth are you talking about? What do you mean 'she thinks you invited her to watch it unfold'?"

"It doesn't matter, Lee," I choked out. "Not anymore." Resting my elbows on the table, I dropped my head in my hands, tugging at the ends of my hair in agitation. "I'm here and she's...gone." Teagan was the most frustratingly stubborn girl I'd ever met. I didn't want to think about what she thought of me now. "Teagan doesn't trust easily – it took me *months* to earn it. And even if I get the chance to see her and explain, she'll think the worst of me." *She always does...*

"Talk to me, Noah," she begged. "I can help you."

How could I explain what Reese did to me that night with a straight face?

Who the hell was going to believe a skinny little thing like Reese could force me into anything?

The cop I told sure as hell didn't. Asshole cracked laughing when I tried to explain what she had done to me that night. His reaction had told me all I needed to know, so I kept my mouth shut from that point on.

The officer arrived back into the room then, letting us know visiting time was over.

Pushing her chair back, Lee got to her feet and, with a determined look on her face, she said, "I'm going to help you, Noah Messina. Not because you're my husband's brother, or my children's friend. I'm going to help you because you *deserve* to be helped. You deserve *better* than the life you've been forced into. Have faith," she added before she was led from the room.

TEAGAN

*K*yle Carter was like a hurricane, I decided as I watched him pace the Harte's kitchen floor, dominating the room and causing the air to crackle with electricity.

To be honest, my heart went out to Sheila as she pottered uneasily around the two huge American men in her kitchen, offering tea and brown cake – a typical Irish mammy.

The attractive, blonde-haired man who had arrived with Teagan's father was unfamiliar to me, but Hope called him Uncle Mike.

Apparently, he was another one of Hope's grandfather's offspring, though he was the one that had been claimed and carried the surname Henderson.

From what I could gather, Mike Henderson lived in London, and was due to fly back to the states to discuss the newest member of the family when Kyle told him to meet him at Shannon.

"This is bullshit, Hope," Mr. Carter all but roared, pulling at his tie and then ruffling his hair with his free hand. "You're not staying here. I forbid it... oh thank you, Sheila," he added, taking a tiny china teacup from Liam's mother.

Sheila blushed scarlet red before excusing herself from the kitchen, leaving us alone with Mr. Carter and his brother.

"You can't forbid me to do anything, Dad, I'm eighteen," Hope reminded him as she leaned against the doorframe. "And you can't force me to do anything either." She crossed her arms and narrowed her eyes at her father. "I'm not Mom."

That comment earned a chuckle from the uncle, who was much calmer than his brother.

"Help me out here, Mike," Mr. Carter begged, clearly distraught.

"Technically, she's right, brother," Mike announced, clapping him on the shoulder. "Hope is legally an adult."

Mr. Carter growled, shrugging Mike's hand off to resume his pacing. "I knew I should have brought Derek. You're fucking useless to me."

Mike grunted and Hope screamed.

"Don't you dare," she snapped, eyes wide and glowing with anger. "Keep anyone with the last name Porter far away from me."

"Good girl," Mike chimed in. "Those Porters are bad news."

"Shut the hell up, douche," Mr. Carter grumbled, glaring at his brother before turning his attention to his daughter. "What the hell did that little shit do to you?"

Hope's cheeks turned bright pink. "Nothing."

"And what about your mother?" he accused, hands on his trim hips, as he towered over her. "Do you think Mom needs this kind of stress in her life; especially considering the circumstances?"

Hope narrowed her eyes. "What circumstances?"

"Well..." he muttered, rolling up the sleeves of his shirt. His cheeks reddened as he started to backtrack. "I didn't want you to find out like this."

"Find out about what, Dad?" Hope asked. The blood seemed to drain from her face and she roared, "Tell me you didn't!"

"I did," her father muttered with a grin, causing Hope to scream. "Mom's pregnant."

"Again?" Mike chuckled, patting his brother on the shoulder. "Congratulations, man."

"Thanks," Kyle replied proudly, "She is three months." Turning his attention to his daughter, he said, "We wanted to sit all the kids down and tell them *together*."

"Ugh, you complete freak," she wailed, holding her head with her hands in sheer dismay. "You guys are too old to be parents again," she groaned. "This is sick."

"I'm forty-one, Hope," Kyle shot back, wounded. "Your mother's only thirty-eight. We're hardly over the hill."

"You need to be sterilized!" Hope retorted angrily. "How many this time?" she added sarcastically. "Because we all know you don't shoot singles, Dad."

A laugh escaped my mouth and I had to smother it with a cough.

"Sorry," I mumbled, covering my mouth with my hand when she glared at me. There was no way I was getting on Hope's bad side, not while she was in this mood.

"Angel. Just come home with me," her father said with a sudden vulnerability in his voice – a vulnerability that made Hope flinch. "And I promise you that I will fix *everything*. Just come home. *Please*," he added in a desperate tone.

"I can't go back there, Dad," she whispered. Her eyes welled up with tears. "Please understand."

Kyle Carter stared at his daughter for what felt like forever before turning his attention to me. "What about you, Blondie?"

I swallowed deeply. "What about me?"

"You're just gonna leave the kid to rot?" He demanded, and the accusatory tone in his voice caused my hackles to rise. "After all he's been through?"

"No offense, Mr. Carter," I seethed, grinding my teeth. "But what I do with my life is absolutely none of your business."

"Noah's my brother," he declared proudly. "The kid loves you, Teagan. He's going out of his mind worrying about you."

"Then you take care of him," I hissed, forcing myself not to flinch. "He's not my problem anymore." Not since he stuck his dick in Reese fucking Tanner. I forced down the bile that was threatening to spill out of me. "And you can tell your brother that I am done!"

Noah didn't love me.

He didn't give a damn about me.

If he did, he wouldn't have thrown everything we had away for a quick fuck.

"So it's like that?" Mr. Carter asked in a tone laced with disgust. "You're just going to carry on with your life and pretend your boyfriend isn't sitting in a jail cell right now?" He shook his head and shrugged. "I thought you were made of tougher stuff than to run at the first hurdle."

"He's *not* my boyfriend," I managed to choke out, feeling winded and completely broken. "I am protecting myself, Mr. Carter, from getting even more hurt than I've already been. So stop trying to make me feel bad for doing nothing wrong."

He shook his head in defeat. "You're making a mistake, Teagan," he told me wearily. "I may not know the ins and outs of what happened between you two, but if you loved the boy, you would be standing by him now and not hiding out here like a coward."

"You're right about one thing, Mr. Carter. You don't know a damn thing about me!" I hissed before stalking out of the room. Stopping in the doorway, I turned and glared back at him. "You don't know what happened between us, but if you go and ask Reese Tanner, I'm sure she'll be more than happy to tell you everything."

Swinging around, I bolted from the kitchen and didn't stop moving until I was inside Liam's room.

Slamming the door shut, I rushed over and threw myself down on the bed. Tears burned behind my eyelids, but I refused to let them fall.

What if I'm wrong about Noah? The niggling voice inside my head asked, but I shut that bitch up swiftly.

It wasn't true.

They were making a fool out of me.

Aside from the fact that Noah had slept with Reese, he had also lied to me. He left me that night to go to the quarry.

I gave up everything for him and he threw it all away for a fight and a fuck.

Memories flooded me, visions of us on the flat screen TV fucking in the elevator – of Noah taking away my innocence.

I was such a fool.

For all I knew, he and Ellie had planned this whole thing – making me fall in love with him just so that he could break me and then kick me when I was down.

A sudden pain, intense and throbbing, hit me directly in my lower belly and I had to dive across the hallway for the bathroom. When I saw the blood tinged stain on my underwear I laughed and cried simultaneously.

All that worrying had been for nothing. All those sleepless nights that had been filled with anxiety and fear about the future had been pointless. Stress had been the reason for my late period. I wasn't pregnant, and that was that. There would be no unfinished business between us. No messy confrontations or reluctant phone call in nine months.

Noah was really gone from me.

Cleaning myself up, I went back to Liam's room and, curling up in a ball on his bed, I let my mind drift back to that night...

CLIMBING NOAH'S STAIRCASE, I WALKED STRAIGHT TO HIS BEDROOM *and knocked lightly before twisting the knob and pushing the door inward.*

My heart dropped the moment I saw him lying there.

My stomach churned and a painful cry tore my throat.

Skin – naked skin –limbs and long red hair invaded my vision.

That's all I could see.

The blood rushed to my brain so fast everything became cloudy, and when I was eventually able to focus, the image that laid before me caused my stomach to churn.

Noah and Reese fucking like rabbits, right in front of my eyes.

Reese was straddling Noah, screwing him like a fucking Duracell bunny, bouncing up and down, grinding her naked body on top of my naked boyfriend.

"Noah," I cried out as disgust churned inside of me.

He didn't even incline his face in my direction. He kept his eyes closed, grunting softly as Reese fucked him.

"I'm leaving," I screamed, frantic. "I can't...I...I... how could you do this to me?" I was losing control of myself.

Tears were spilling from my eyes, I needed to get a grip, but every time I tried to grab onto the ledge of something rational, their sweat-soaked naked bodies fused together impaled me and I felt like bursting into flames.

I could forgive a lot of things, and maybe I had my priorities all wrong, but I couldn't forgive this.

I could never forgive this.

Noah didn't respond.

But she did.

Twisting her head to one side Reese glanced at me with a smirk. "Bye now," she sneered before lowering her mouth and claiming Noah's.

"BASTARD!" I SCREAMED, BEATING MY FIST AGAINST THE mattress. My throat felt like it was closing in on me. "You ruined everything," I roared into the duvet, gasping for air. "You ruined *me*..."

I heard the door creak open and quickly close, but I didn't look up. I didn't care who was there. I felt the mattress dip beside me, and then warm hands pulling me onto a lap.

Liam's lap, I realized when I heard him whisper words of comfort in my ear – telling me that I would be okay again.

Except I wasn't comforted, and I wasn't okay.

Truthfully, I didn't think I would ever be *okay* again.

TEAGAN

*Y*esterday was one of the lower points in my life.

Having Kyle Carter tear strips out of me and hashing up my personal life in front of a roomful of people was something I didn't care to experience *ever* again.

Even though a small part of me understood where he had been coming from, I was still feeling hurt and hugely resentful.

When I woke up this morning with a stuffy nose and puffy eyelids, I had decided I needed to take control of my life. It was because of the emotions that had poured out of me last night that I found myself lying on my stomach, as a tattoo artist drew on my body with needles.

I welcomed the throbbing burn as the needle penetrated my flesh. This tattoo was a symbol of my freedom, and a warning of how close I had come to destruction.

Noah Messina was bad for me – he was treacherous.

I needed to remember that, and this tattoo would be the perfect reminder.

I wouldn't cry over him again.

It was pathetic and I was *not*.

Not another damn tear would I shed.

When I arrived back at the Harte's home later that evening, I spent a good twenty minutes standing in front of the bathroom mirror, ogling my back.

Getting a tattoo was so unlike me.

It felt sort of surreal.

"What the hell have you done to your body?" Hope's yelp of outrage quickly turned into a squeal of excitement when she rushed into the bathroom for a closer examination. "Oh my god, Teegs, it's huge." She trailed her fingers over the black lettering that trailed in a vertical line down the entire length of my back.

"Ouch, Hope, don't freaking touch it," I groaned, flinching from Hope's touch.

"Why did you do that, Teegs?" Hope asked me in a voice full of concern.

Letting my loose t-shirt drop back down and cover my back, I spun around and faced my friend. "I needed a reminder," was all I replied and it was the truth.

"Of Noah," she said quietly.

"Yeah," I croaked out, forcing down the turbulence of emotions threatening to spill out. "Of Noah."

NOAH

I wasn't surprised when the judge passed my sentence.

I didn't bat an eyelid.

I just stood slowly, with my hands in chains, and let the officers lead me away.

I purposefully ignored every damn person in the courtroom.

I didn't care anymore.

To the outside world, I was emotionless.

Inside, I was dead.

My one consolation lay in the knowledge that George Dennis was gone.

Fucker had a stroke three days ago and never pulled through.

That piece of news was the only good thing that had come out of his daughter's mouth during her visit the other day. I had thought Ellie wanted to visit to gloat or pass on a message from her father.

When she cried over her dead daddy and apologized and then cried some more, I felt something break free inside of me. It was like the shackles that had held me down for so many years had been torn off.

George's son and right-hand man, JD, was still out there

somewhere. He'd managed to escape arrest that night, but with his father dead, and his gang either in prison or in hiding, he was weakened. I knew JD wouldn't forget about me, not by a long shot, but right now I was taking one small victory at a time.

I would sleep soundly tonight because the grudge I had feared George was holding had died with him.

The man who knew my weakness was dead.

And my Thorn was safe.

TEAGAN

*T*he remainder of spring passed in a hazy blur, and by the time summer arrived, Hope and I were settling back into Irish culture and lifestyle. We had found ourselves a nice little bedsit, close to Salt Hill where we had lived contently for the past three months, but one visit from Hope's parents last week, and it was decided that our living quarters weren't close to being good enough for their only daughter.

Mr. Carter made a few phone calls and one night's packing, plus a four-hour drive later, we found ourselves standing in the swankiest bachelorette pad *ever* in the Rebel County.

I wasn't friends with Hope for the money, but the fact that her dad was loaded with cash didn't hurt. Personally, I would have preferred to stay in Galway, but I was homeless and the Carters' had the money, so it was their call.

"I can't believe you actually own this place," I told my best friend as I unpacked a box of towels. "This is insane." It wasn't a huge apartment– two bedrooms, with one bathroom and a kitchen/lounge – but it was beautiful and in a really safe part of the city. This place made our bedsit look like a cow shed. "Most nineteen-year-old girls get hair straighteners for their birthday, Hope. *You* get a property."

"You know what my father says," Hope huffed as she balanced a gigantic box against her thigh, lowering it onto our brand-new coffee table, matching our brand-new L shaped couch. "Rent money is dead money." Dropping the box on the table, Hope stretched her back and let out a sigh. "This isn't a freebie, Teegs, and I'm not accepting this place as a birthday gift either. I'll pay him back."

"I don't think he minds, Hope," I assured her, holding back on the sarcasm. Being in debt to her dad was a touchy subject for Hope. She hated getting handouts. For a daddy's girl, she was unusually independent and incredibly self-sufficient.

"I mind, Teagan," Hope shot back, "I..."

Hope's phone went off and she dropped everything she was doing before bolting down the hallway towards her bedroom.

Of course, I knew why she was rushing to get to the phone. It was the same reason Mr. and Mrs. Carter had flown back to the states instead of helping us move.

Noah was being sentenced today.

When I thought about Noah locked away in some shitty penitentiary halfway across the world, my chest squeezed so tightly I could barely draw a breath.

A huge chunk of me wanted to board the next flight just to be there for him, to support him and love him; but then I remembered what he had done to me and I shut those feelings down. I couldn't feel sorry for him, it would break me, and I couldn't cry for him because if I did, if I let myself mourn, I would never stop.

"Teagan, look at me. Look at me." Noah's eyes were red and pained. "This is not your fault. Do you understand me? This is my fault, baby, and you're not going down for it."

The sound of sirens blasted through my ears and panic tore through me.

Noah hissed out a sharp breath. "The second this belt cracks, I want you to get out of this car and run." He caught my chin between his fingers. "Do not stop running. Do not wait for me."

I ran and ran until every breath left my body – until I couldn't run any further.

Hiding behind a boulder on the side of the dirt road, I sank to my knees and wept.

Noah...

What was going to happen to him?

Oh god, I shouldn't have left him there. I was a horrible person.

Every fiber of my being demanded I go back there and help him, do something, anything... but I couldn't move.

I was frozen in fear.

In shock.

I MUST HAVE STOOD IN OUR KITCHEN FOR HALF AN HOUR, FROZEN to the spot; waiting, wishing, hoping and praying until, finally, I couldn't take anymore.

Walking down our short hallway, I opened the first door on the right and let myself inside. Hope was sitting on her bed, looking as numb as I felt. When she noticed my presence, she wiped her eyes and smiled brightly. "Hey babe," she whispered, patting her bed.

Walking over to Hope's bed, I climbed up and sat cross-legged, facing her. Then I asked the question I had been telling myself I didn't need to know. "How long did he get?"

Hope stared at me for a long moment, chewing on her lip in deliberation, before finally answering me. "Five and a half years."

I swear to god, the moment those words came out of Hope's mouth, my heart shriveled up and died in my chest.

"That long?" I managed to squeeze out, as my breath came in short, fast puffs. "But I thought the lawyers were going to–"

"It didn't work out that way," she interrupted quickly. Taking my hand in hers, Hope smiled sadly. "Noah got himself into some more trouble and broke the conditions of his bail," she told me. "He's been in custody since we arrived here."

"Is...is he okay?"

"Honestly, I don't know, Teagan," Hope replied. "He stopped

all contact with my family over a month ago – says it's easier that way. They went to court today, but he won't see my father. He won't even let Logan visit, and they were best friends."

"I don't know how to deal with this," I admitted, voice torn. "I want to be there for him. I don't want him to go through all of this on his own. I want...him, but I can't get past what I saw," I confessed, my words barely more than a whisper. "In my dreams it still haunts me, Hope. The image of her naked, sweat soaked body pumping my boyfriend, grinding her pussy all over him, taking him into her body... Oh god, saying the words out loud makes me feel physically sick."

"Don't," Hope ordered, reaching out and grabbing my hand. "Don't you dare torture yourself like this."

"I'm still in love with him, Hope...even though he's dangerous and wrong for me and broke my heart for kicks," I choked out. "He's the love of my life." Tears spilled down my cheeks. "He is everything and I love him...all the time. It *won't* go away. I am stuck in a never-ending cycle of loving him, losing him, missing him, hating him, mourning him, waiting for him, and caring. It won't stop and I can't claw my way out. I feel like I am dying."

And then I admitted to my best friend my darkest thought – the thought that made me hate myself more than I hated him. "Sometimes I regret leaving him." Clasping the back of my head with my hands, I fought to catch my breath. "Sometimes I think that I would have been better off staying *with* Noah and letting him treat me the way he did – letting him cheat on me. Because at least then I would still *have* him and not this empty fucking hole in my life." Shaking my head in self-loathing, I looked straight into her eyes. "How pathetic does that make me?"

"Noah fucking Messina," Hope muttered after a long pause.

"Yeah," I half laughed, half cried, "Noah fucking Messina."

NOAH

*T*ime in prison passed by a lot differently; long, fucking hard days. The only thing I took comfort in was my anger and the only thing that kept me company was my thirst for revenge.

Today marked my first month down out of a five-and-a-half-year prison sentence, and the third month since I'd been remanded in custody for breaking my bail conditions.

Four of those years were my punishment for my involvement in the Ring of Fire. The remaining eighteen months were courtesy of the man in front of me, who in true asshole fashion, had pressed charges on me for breaking and entering.

"I must say, Messina, the orange jumpsuit becomes you."

I clenched my fists and fought the urge to lunge across the table to rip Teagan's uncle's throat out.

That bastard loved this.

"What are you doing here, Max?" I ground out through clenched teeth. Everything about the man pissed me off. His crisp, gray suit. His face. His fucking attitude.

Since my sentencing last month, I hadn't seen a soul from the outside world. I had warned them not to come here. I needed to get used to my new life and having the Carters visiting me was just too fucking painful. I didn't want their pity.

Having this dipshit here only added salt to my wounds. The fact that he had added eighteen months onto my sentence with his stupid fucking claims enraged me.

"Besides reveling in the fact that you're behind bars?" Max taunted as he leaned back in his chair and smiled. "I'm here to discuss my niece."

"What about her?" I found myself straightening in my seat, edging forward, perking up. "Is she okay?" I couldn't pretend I didn't care about Teagan. She had been my every thought for the last three months and hearing her name ruined me. Jesus Christ, I missed her so much. I was dying in here. I was dying without her. But my reaction gave Max exactly what he wanted.

Power over me.

"You were never good enough for her," Max told me, setting a stack of envelopes on the table before pushing them towards me. "And you never will be."

I knew the poorly written scrawl on each envelope. They were my pathetic attempt at contacting my girlfriend.

I clenched and unclenched my fists, trying to stop my hands from trembling, before reaching forward and taking the half a dozen letters.

I felt like a fool for mailing them to Thirteenth Street, but I didn't have any other option. That was the only address I had for her, and I guess deep down I had hoped that Teagan would somehow get them, read my truth, and come back to me.

I was used to being let down – fucking thrown to the wolves – but with Teagan, it was different. She wouldn't leave me here to rot. She would come back. I had to believe she was coming back; if I didn't, I wouldn't fucking survive this.

"You can't keep her away from me," I said vehemently, fucking desperately, as I balled the envelopes in my hand. Lee had told me to have faith. Well, I was trying. Problem was, all my faith was tied up in Teagan Connolly changing her mind about me. "She'll come around," I hissed, as rage bubbled inside of me. "What we have is real."

"What you *had*," Max corrected with a smirk. "And do you

see her anywhere? No, of course you don't. Because she saw your true colors and has come to her senses." Smiling, he added, "Forget about my niece, Noah. By the time you're out of this place she'll be married with children."

I watched numbly as Max shoved his chair back and stood. "Enjoy your stay," he told me, plucking at the sleeves of his jacket. "You're exactly where an animal like you belongs. In a cage."

———

Max said that I had lost Teagan and she was gone from me forever, but I refused to believe that.

There had to be a way back for us.

Back in my cell, I tossed the poorly written letters on my table with too much force and watched as they scattered onto the floor. Then I proceeded to grab the mattress off my bed and drag it over to the wall.

Setting the piece of shit against the cold stone of my cell, I pummeled it, executing precise blows, pretending I was rearranging that asshole's face.

I hated that bastard.

I fucking *hated* him.

Max was right about one thing though – I was a fucking animal.

But I didn't have to be.

I could change my ways, make things right. Get an education and find a trade. I was never going to be a doctor, but surely I could fucking do something with my life? A construction worker or a plumber – something with my hands.

I just had to make it out of this place in one piece.

"Well I've heard some folks like to fluff their pillows, but I think you're taking it to an extreme, Messina."

I swung around when the sound of my cellmate's voice infiltrated my mind.

Lucky Casarazzi stood in the doorway of our cell with his

shaggy blonde hair pulled back in its signatory man-bun, a cigarette hanging from his mouth, and his tattoo covered arms crossed over his chest. He had a deep frown set on his face as he studied me with wary, ice blue eyes.

In truth, the guy looked like he belonged on a stage somewhere, headlining a rock concert, rather than slumming it in a prison cell with me.

But from the limited conversations we'd had since my arrival, I knew better than to judge him based on his appearance. He had shed the blood of a man, the same as me, and at the age of twenty-three, had served my entire five-and-a-half-year sentence already. The guy was the best kind of bad you could find in a place like this.

"I'm working something out here, man," I snarled, turning my attention back to my target, continuing my rampage. "Just give me a damn minute."

Holding his hands up in the air, Lucky shook his head and muttered, "Have at it, man." Stepping around me, he pulled himself onto the top bunk and settled down on his back. Tucking his arms behind his head, he let out a contented sigh. "So, is she a blonde or a brunette?"

Stopping what I was doing, I turned to face him. "What?"

"The girl you're losing your shit over," he replied calmly, staring up at the ceiling. "Is she a blonde or a brunette?"

Suddenly all the fight left me. Dragging my mattress back onto the bunk, I sank down on the edge and let out a heavy sigh. "Blonde."

Lucky chuckled. "Thought so." Swinging his legs off the top bunk, he jumped down and sat down beside me. "Brunettes make you lose your head," he went on to say, offering me a smoke first and then a light when I accepted. "Reds break your bed." He inhaled a deep drag of his cigarette before exhaling a large cloud of smoke. "But blondes? Blondes land your ass in a place like this." Lucky shook his head. "Blondes steal your soul, Messina."

I grunted in response, taking a deep drag. "You get fucked

over by a blonde or something, Lucky?" Flicking my ash on the floor, I rubbed my boot on it, smudging it away.

"Something like that," he responded, eyes darkening, as he stared straight ahead.

TEAGAN

"*S*ay that again?" I asked Hope – begged. "Please, just say it again, and tell me you're not joking."

"George Dennis is dead, Teegs," she repeated. "He had a stroke last month and didn't pull through. Apparently, Dad forgot to *mention* it. You know, with all the baby preparations and all," she shuddered.

I sank down on the bed with a thud and just sat there for a moment, taking it all in.

My first thought was Noah.

"Thank god," I finally whispered, when my voice found me. Relief flooded my body: dominant, pungent and incredibly welcoming.

He was safe now.

He was free from their clutches.

The big bad wolf was dead.

Looking up at my best friend, I noticed the tears shining in her eyes and realized that this was affecting her too. Noah was her uncle after all, and she cared about him.

"He's free now," I managed to choke out, wrapping my arms around my stomach. "They can't control him anymore."

"I know," she replied, sitting down on the bed next to me. "And so are you."

"What do you mean so am I?" I asked, twisting my face to gape at her.

"Haven't you been worried about them, you know, coming after you?" she asked, squirming uncomfortably.

"No," I gasped, jumping off the bed to pace the bedroom floor. "But I am now!"

"It's fine, Teegs," she coaxed, climbing to her feet to follow after me. "The ring of fire is gone. Problem solved." Grabbing my shoulders, she forced me to stand still and look at her. "No one is going to come looking for you," she said. "George is dead, Teegs, *dead*; as in vamoose, poof, no more. It's over."

"But his son isn't dead." Fear clawed at my gut as I thought about Noah's evil step brother chasing us down that night, causing us to crash. He was a bad man – worse than his father ever was.

Oh god, I didn't want to think about J.D Dennis being out there – anywhere on this planet was too close for comfort. I didn't want to believe it, but what if he *was* waiting for us. Waiting to seek his revenge. Was I living on borrowed time?

Clutching her arms tightly, I whispered, "JD wasn't arrested that night, Hope. What if he's out there somewhere...waiting?"

"He is not going to ever come looking for you," Hope assured me. "My father has one of the best private investigators in the country out hunting that prick down," she added, "and that's not to mention the police and his own enemies."

"He does?" I never knew that. "Wow, I'm liking your dad a little more now, Hope."

"You are nothing to J.D," she told me, wrapping her arm around my shoulders. "Just a kid. Another blonde. That's all."

"Gee, thanks," I muttered.

Laughing, Hope led us over to the bed before sitting down. "What I mean is J.D would *never* risk coming out of hiding just to get revenge on Noah. It would be insanity of the highest order," she added after a pause.

"Do you really believe that?" I asked quietly, sinking down beside her.

"Absolutely." Hope nodded. "My guess is J.D is somewhere

far away, skulking and hiding from the cops and the gangs he messed around with."

"Yeah..." I whispered, letting her words sink in. "I guess you're right."

"I'm always right," she shot back with a grin. "Besides, do you honestly think Gonzalez and his men are going to go down without their pound of flesh? Hell, no! They will chase that little turd to the ends of the earth."

"Oh my fucking god," I groaned, as Gonzalez's face entered my mind. "I totally forgot about yellow teeth." Gonzalez had escaped arrest that night, but from what I had heard, George sold out several members of Gonzalez's men to save his own ass.

"Before you get your panties in a twist, Gonzalez never had an issue with Noah," Hope declared. "There's no beef there, so you have nothing to be worried about."

Hope was right about that. In that weird gangster way, Gonzalez had always been sort of fond of Noah. Me, not so much, but he always had a soft spot for Noah.

"Noah's fine," she continued to say. "You are fine. Everyone is fucking fine. I promise." Jumping to her feet, she stretched and said, "Now stop freaking out because I'm getting a little antsy just watching you. Let's go get something to eat. I'm freaking starving."

"Fine," I replied, standing up and following her out of the room. But I couldn't seem to shake the feeling that J.D wasn't finished with us.

Not by a long shot.

TEAGAN

I had only visited my father a handful of times since mom's funeral.

The last time I saw him was over a year ago, when Uncle Max took me to visit him in prison before we left for the states. Back then, he was a broken mess, and in some ways I had felt incredibly sorry for him; but a huge chunk of me felt it was only fair he still suffered.

After all, he was the one who decided to take the risk and drive under the influence. He was the one who'd taken my mother away from me. I couldn't get over that part, and a four-year prison sentence wouldn't bring my mom back.

Sitting here now, in the middle of a crowded cafe and looking at the shaken man before me, it was clear that he was still the same.

"I've missed you, Teagan," my father told me, voice slurred. My father had been released from prison last week, and already I regretted accepting his invitation to meet up.

His thinning, gray hair was disheveled. His eyes were bloodshot, and the stench of alcohol wafting off him was so strong that it was making me feel lightheaded.

I guess it was clear that some things never changed.

"How have you been?" he added, reaching over to take my hand.

"Fine," I replied coolly, pulling my hand away from his. I didn't want his touch, and he had no right to expect anything from me. Not after what he did. "You?"

"You know me," Dad chuckled. "I'm the same as always."

"Yeah," I ground out, fiddling with a paper sachet of sugar. "It sure smells that way."

"I'm quitting," he told me. "I just...needed a little something to get me through today. Dutch courage."

"You're always quitting, Dad," I shot back, both disappointed and unsurprised. "Until you don't."

"That's not fair," he muttered, his pale, mottled skin turning an even whiter shade of death. "I've been through hell and back."

"And I haven't?" Straightening in my chair, I dropped the teaspoon I had been using to stir my coffee and glared at the pathetic creature opposite me. "What do you want from me, Dad?" I asked him coldly. "Why did you want to meet up?"

"I'm going away," Dad managed to slur before burping loudly. "Back to Galway."

"And?" I folded my arms across my chest and stared impassively at him. "You're telling me this because?"

"I thought you would want to come with me?"

"No thanks," I snorted in disgust. "Is that all?"

"I thought you'd be happy to see me." Dad shook his head as if he couldn't quite understand my coldness towards him. "Teagan, I'm your father and I..."

"You haven't been my father since I was fourteen years old," I snapped, furious at the audacity of this man. "You *killed* my mother – you almost killed me! You weren't there for me when I needed a father, and I sure as hell don't need you now." Throwing my chair back, I grabbed my bag and stood up. "Have a nice life, Patrick."

I RAN ALL THE WAY HOME AS FAST AS I COULD, DESPERATE TO RID my body of the rage churning inside.

What the hell did my father expect me to do?

Drop everything to go home with him and live in an unstable environment again?

Did he honestly think I could forget about what he'd done?

Maybe I was a heartless bitch, but I couldn't forget it, and I knew in my heart and soul that I would never let it go.

I would *never* forgive him.

When I got back to the apartment and saw who was sitting on our couch next to Hope, I could have cried. Like big, fat, raindrop sized tears.

"I'm not in the mood for you," I warned him, closing the flat door behind me. "I'm having a really bad day, so if you could refrain from the insults, I'd appreciate it," I added, moving towards the kitchen to get a glass of water.

Mr. Carter stood up and seemed to dominate the room with his presence alone. "Nice to see you too, Teagan," he acknowledged coolly.

"Sure it is." I rolled my eyes and fought the urge to poke my tongue out at him. Kyle didn't like me, and he didn't hide it well. He tried to be civil for the sake of his daughter, but I was fairly certain he thought about throttling me on more than one occasion. We tended to stay out of one another's way whenever he visited. I was still struggling to get past the crap he'd spewed that night when he arrived at the Harte's home, and Mr. Carter? Well, I guess I was a big fat reminder to him as to why his daughter was living abroad.

Turning his attention back to Hope, Kyle asked, "Have you thought any more about coming home for Christmas?"

She shook her head and sighed wearily. "We've already talked about this, Dad. I'm staying here with Teegs."

"I know," Mr. Carter grumbled. "But Christmas is a time for being with your family, and the twins haven't met their big sister."

"How are the little guys?" Hope gushed and I couldn't help but smirk. She had been dead set against her parents having another child, but when her twin baby brothers were born three months ago, she had gone straight out and gotten a picture of them blown up. That photograph was now pride of place on the wall in our lounge.

"They'd be a lot better if they met their sister," Kyle grumbled. His gaze flickered to me and I reddened in embarrassment. I could feel the anger radiating off him in waves – directed towards me.

"Hey, don't look at me like that," I found myself saying, dropping my glass in the sink before holding my hands up in defense. "You can blame Jordan 'the dickhead' Porter for this."

Mr. Carter's brows shot up in surprise and then he did something I didn't expect him to.

He actually cracked a smile.

"Jordan the dickhead Porter," he snickered, "I knew there was a reason I liked you, Blondie."

Having Kyle Carter actually compliment me was a strange feeling. I wasn't stupid though. I knew full well the only reason he wasn't throwing jibes or snotty comments at me was because we shared a hatred for Jordan Porter.

Hope's ex boyfriend was number one on Kyle's shit list.

I was a close second.

"Thanks...I think?" I replied uncomfortably before returning my attention to making a sandwich.

"How long are you staying this time, Dad?" Hope asked, and I was as eager to know the answer to that particular question as she was.

Kyle checked his watch and sighed. "I fly out later this evening."

"Oh, that soon?" I piped up, sarcasm evident in my voice

Purposefully ignoring my comment, he focused on Hope. Pacing around the sitting room area, he began to speak. "Your brother called me earlier," I heard him say in a hushed tone, "Logan's worried about Noah's frame of mind. He declined his visit – *again*."

That was where I checked out.

Leaving them to talk about Noah, I left my untouched sandwich on the countertop and headed in the direction of the short hallway toward my bedroom.

I couldn't listen to this.

I couldn't deal with *him*.

"You should hear this too, Teagan," Kyle called out, stopping me in my tracks. "Oh wait, I forgot, you don't give two shits about Noah anymore."

See, this was *exactly* why I didn't stick around when Hope's father visited.

He held a grudge against me.

Because of *him*.

"I'm not doing this again," I warned him. "I've told you a million times, what goes on with Noah is none of my business."

"Hope told me what you saw that night; what you *think* you saw," he countered steadily. "But I'd bet every dime I have that you're wrong."

I froze, unblinking, as I registered what Kyle had just said to me. "Are you calling me a liar, Mr. Carter?"

Kyle folded his arms across his chest and shook his head. "No, Teagan, I'm not calling you a liar. I'm telling you that you are wrong about him."

"Dad, shut the hell up," Hope snapped, her voice a tone of pure disgust, as she leapt off the couch and stood in front of her father. "Don't do this to her. She's been through enough already."

"She needs to hear this, Hope," her father replied evenly. "Lee went to see him before the sentencing – before he banned everyone who cares about him from the fucking prison – and the kid was a total mess." Straightening his spine, Kyle looked over Hope's head and directly into my eyes. "My guess is that somehow that Tanner girl played you both, and you fell for it- hook, line and sinker."

A wave of hysteria burst to the surface, causing me to laugh humorously. "Are you trying to ruin my life?" I demanded, delirious with a raging mixture of rage and heartbreak.

My whole body shook violently.

I couldn't seem to stop.

"It takes two to tango, Kyle, and from what I remember, Noah was more than a willing participant," I snarled, refusing to believe the bullshit dripping from his mouth. "He fucked her. Right in front of me."

"I know how it looks, Teagan," Kyle shot back heatedly. "I know how it sounds too, but come on. That's not Noah. You *know* him. He wouldn't do that to you."

"Why are you doing this to me?" I whispered, paling. "It's been nine months. Why bring all of this up again?"

"Look," Kyle sighed, rubbing his face with his hand. "I'm not intentionally trying to upset you here. But if you could just visit the guy...talk to him."

"No," I refused, backing all the way down the short hallway to my bedroom. "I won't do it."

As soon as the door was closed behind me, I threw myself down on my bed and cried like a baby.

LATER ON, WHEN MR. CARTER HAD LEFT FOR HIS FLIGHT, HOPE came into my room.

"I'm not going to ask you if you're okay," she told me, coming to sit on the edge of my bed. "Because that's a stupid question when it's obvious that you're not." Stroking my head, Hope sighed heavily. "I'm so sorry about my dad, Teegs."

Leaping off my bed, I began to pace. I couldn't sit still and take her pity. I couldn't fucking sit on this pain. Swinging around to face Hope, I begged, "Please tell me I did the right thing."

I closed my eyes and fought back the voice inside of me telling me that I had been wrong about him. I never wanted to break away from my life more than I did at this moment.

Was it pity making me feel like I was wrong?

Wrong for jumping to conclusions without hearing him out?

Was I a huge fool for even contemplating that my eyes had deceived me?

I was so confused.

"Tell me I didn't misjudge the situation," I blurted out,

unable to handle the emotions churning inside of me. "Please, Hope, tell me your dad is wrong."

"I don't know, Teagan," she groaned. Climbing to her feet, she walked over to my bedroom window and looked out through the curtains. "I want to believe you misjudged him," she told me after a long pause. "My heart is telling me you did..."

"But?" I offered, sensing there was a very big but to come.

"It's just too shady," she admitted. Swinging around to face me, Hope scrunched her nose up. "You saw him and Reese with your own two eyes, and it's not like they haven't been together many times before."

"Exactly," I exclaimed wearily. "I *saw* them. I didn't make it up." Even though I wished I had.

Hope sighed. "Look, I've known Jordan my *entire* life," she told me. "And if he could do what he did to me, butcher my heart and betray me, then I'm sorry, Teagan, but I'm not holding out much hope for the rest of the male population."

"Yeah," I whispered, taking in her words, feeling my heart break all over again. "Neither am I."

NOAH

$\mathcal{L}$ights out had been hours ago, and I had been lying in the darkness ever since, listening to the noise coming from the cells on either side of ours. The assholes on our left were arguing over a missing pack of cigarettes. The ones on our right were fighting because they could; because there was nothing else to do in this place.

I remained perfectly still on my bunk, quiet as a mouse, as I racked my brain and tried to come up with a plan that wouldn't get me killed in this place. I'd been challenged to a fight this morning. I refused.

Now, I was biding my time, trying to figure out how the fuck I wouldn't have to use my fists in this place. I was surrounded by assholes, many of which knew my background as a street fighter. That made them curious. It made them want to take me down a peg or two. I wasn't afraid of any dick in this place, but I didn't want the trouble. I was fucking weary.

"What was she like, Messina?" Lucky asked, breaking the eerie silence, and the question threw me. I had thought the guy was asleep.

Rolling onto my back, I folded my arms behind my head and stared up at the metal bars above my head. "Who?"

"Your girl." I heard him twisting around on the bunk above me. "You never told me her name." The sound of a match striking filled the silence followed by the aroma of nicotine wafting through the air.

"Teagan," I whispered, feeling the burn in my chest that came with saying her name aloud. "And she was...different." Teagan was the only one who had ever known me – like really known me. She had gone to the trouble of digging deeper, finding the screw-up inside of me, and loving me anyway. That wasn't normal. *She* wasn't normal. "She was a pain in my ass," I added with a smirk, thinking back to the numerous times Thorn had caused me nothing but trouble.

"She loved you?"

"Not enough."

"You still love her?"

"It doesn't matter anymore," I hissed through clenched teeth. Hell fucking yes I still loved her, but I wasn't the type of guy who talked openly about my feelings. Christ, before Thorn, I wouldn't have thought I had feelings to talk about. "It's in the past."

"It's the only thing that matters," he corrected. "And the past is never in the past. It's always waiting in the wings, ready to swoop in and fuck up the present," he muttered and after a pause added, "I'd bet my last cigarette she's the reason you're in this wonderful establishment."

"It's not her fault," I shot back defensively, tensing up. "I was a fuck up long before I met her." Shaking my head, I let out a sigh and asked, "Why are you bringing this shit up, man?"

"Because when I look at you, it's like I'm looking at the eighteen-year-old version of myself."

Even though I was pissed as hell at him for bringing up my business, I didn't dare open my mouth and say so. Lucky was as closed off as I was. It wasn't an everyday occurrence that the guy spoke about himself, and I wanted to hear what he had to say.

The bunk shifted and squeaked in protest as he climbed down. "I'm gonna tell you a little story, Messina," he announced, "from one lovesick fool to another."

The moonlight flooding in from the tiny, bar covered

window in our cell illuminated his profile, and I watched as he walked over to our small desk and hoisted himself on top of it before taking a deep drag of his cigarette and exhaling heavily. "I fell for this chick from my hometown," he began to explain. "Fell real fucking hard. Her daddy was a cop, one of the good guys. Shit, back then, *I* was one of the good guys," he chuckled, flicking the ash from his cigarette before taking another drag. "We'd dated all through high school and I was in deep, Messina. Real fucking deep..." His eyes glazed over and his voice trailed off.

Exhaling heavily, I sat up and grabbed my cigarettes from under my pillow. "You don't have to tell me shit, Lucky," I told him as I sparked up. "It's cool, man. I understand."

"The night I was arrested, I had the ring in my jeans pocket," he told me in a quiet tone, ignoring my words. "Was on my way to pick her up at her dorm – Hayley was a freshman at the time..." His voice broke off then, it was the first time I had ever heard him quiver, and when he spoke again, I felt like I had been sucker punched in the chest.

"When I let myself into her room all I could hear was the sound of her crying weakly...begging for mercy and calling my name." He took a helluva long time before continuing. "Her blood," he whispered. "It was everywhere. Smeared all over the sheets. The walls. The fucking carpet. Her clothes had been ripped from her body... by the bastard standing over her zipping up his pants."

"Jesus Christ," I choked out, not knowing what to say.

"I killed a man that night, Messina. With my own bare hands," hae growled. "And in doing so, I wasted the last moments I would ever have with her."

"She died?"

"He fucking butchered her," he confirmed coldly. "And I butchered him while my girl was taking her last breath in this world."

"Lucky," I whispered. "I'm so damn sorry."

"I got eleven years," he said after a moment. "Would've been a helluva a lot more, but her father had pull and I was convicted of manslaughter instead. And I've been here ever since." He shrugged. "Existing."

Rubbing a hand down my face, I struggled to take it all in. "Why did you tell me all of that, man?"

Dropping his cigarette butt in the sink, he jumped down from the desk and stretched his arms over his head. "Because my girl's dead, Messina, and I ain't ever getting her back. But it's not over for *you*," he told me passionately. "Look, I've got another six years in this place, so it looks like we'll be seeing this out together. It would be nice to have an ally."

"You want me as an ally?" I asked, watching him climb back up on his bunk.

"I've got a good feeling about you, Noah Messina," he chuckled. "Now shut the fuck up and get some sleep."

I didn't sleep a wink that night.

Instead, my mind went through Lucky's admission over and over until the sun rose and the lights were turned back on.

It's not over for you, he had told me, and Christ, I wanted to believe him.

More than anything.

NOAH

This place was a living, breathing hell.

Even now, twelve months later, I hadn't gotten used to my surroundings; if I was being honest, I didn't think I ever would. Time crawled by. I had too much time to think – to fucking torture myself with what ifs. Like what if I had gotten on that plane with Teagan and never went to the quarry? We'd be in Ireland now, and I would be lying beside her and not four concrete walls.

All I had was myself.

All I could work on was my body.

Growing it.

Strengthening it.

Preparing for the trouble that I knew was lurking behind every damn corner.

I wasn't a virgin to bloodshed, but I'd lost count of the number of times I had a rib busted in this place. Fucking vultures were the reason I kept a blade in my toothbrush.

But I was running out of time.

I followed the line of inmates as the guards rounded us up and led us into the visiting room like a goddamn herd of cattle. I watched, emotionless, as the guys in front of me filed into the visiting room, claiming tables that were filled with people who loved them.

I didn't have any family waiting for me here. I didn't have a disappointed father, or a heartbroken mother to look forward to seeing every Thursday afternoon. I didn't have a horny wife, saddled down with half a dozen of my kids.

I scanned the room for the one person I could stand the sight of these days, and when I found him sitting alone in the far corner of the room, I went straight for him.

"Anything?" I asked the minute I sat down; my hands twitching on the table in front of me and my knees bopping restlessly underneath.

Tommy Moyet stared at me for a long time before letting out a heavy sigh. "Sorry, man," he mumbled. "I've sent over fifty emails, but Hope isn't responding."

I let my head drop forward, my chin almost touching my chest, as I struggled to reign in my raging emotions. The visiting room was packed full of fuckers who didn't need to see me break down. Dammit to hell, one weak moment in this place could cost me my life.

"Tommy, I need you to do something for me," I said in a hushed tone, hating what I was about to ask my only friend to do.

"Anything, man, you know that," he replied without hesitation.

Leaning forward, I kept my voice low enough so that Tommy was the only one who could hear me – and not the bastard at the next table. "I need you to get a message to Logan."

Tommy frowned. "Okay...but can't you just phone him?"

I shook my head. "There are too many eyes and ears in this place," I muttered. "It's not safe."

His blue eyes widened in fear. "What do you want me to tell him?"

I leaned forward and kept my face down when I spoke, so our conversation wasn't lip-read. "Tell him Angelo Javi was transferred to my block last week and he knows who I am – what I did to his brother."

I knew I could count on Lucky to have my back, and if I told him about Javi and his gang, he would back me up without a second's hesitation, but I wasn't involving him in my bullshit.

No fucking way.

Shoving my chair back, I stood up and stared down at my best friend for what could be the last time. "Tell him I need him to call Teagan and tell her I love her and I'm sorry. And tell him... tell him I'm a dead man."

"Noah!" Tommy called out as I walked away from him, but I didn't turn around.

I couldn't.

Angelo Javi had power in this place, and I was a sitting duck.

I needed to get back to my cell before visiting time was over, and I was cornered in a fucking corridor with those guys.

I needed a fucking miracle.

TEAGAN

I felt like a total creeper as I opened the lid of Hope's laptop and scrolled through her emails from her family members – desperate for news. Today was one of the rare days she had left her laptop at home instead of taking it to University with her.

Hell, today was one of the rare occasions Hope actually *left* the apartment.

Most days she remained holed up in her bedroom.

Her reasons for avoiding the real world were always the same old excuses; she was either working on a story she was writing, or she was tired. But I knew better.

Hope wasn't dealing with her breakup with Jordan.

One year on, and she was more withdrawn than ever and avoided contact with everyone. In the beginning, when we first came to Ireland, Hope had been my rock to lean on. But now, the only time she went out was when she had a class.

She hadn't made any new friends at school, and the friends I had made in my Sports, Fitness and Nutrition class at the local PLC had to drag conversation out of her when we all hung out.

Even Liam, who moved down to Cork last September to study SF&N with me, couldn't bring her around. She remained standoffish, uninterested in spending time with anyone other than her imaginary characters and her memories of Jordan.

I scrolled through her inbox and trash until I found an unread email from Tommy Moyet, of all people, in her junk folder.

Bingo.

Clicking the email, I braced myself for what I was about to read.

To: Hope Carter
  Subject: HELLO!!!
  From: Tommy Moyet
  I know you're probably tired of me blowing up your inbox, Hope, but I'm getting pretty sick of sending unanswered mails. Oh, don't worry though, this is the last time you'll hear from me. Forget everything I've said. Doesn't matter now. Have a nice life.

"What are you up to?" A familiar voice called out and I yelped in surprise and ended up knocking a stack of papers off Hope's desk as I scrambled to exit the Internet.

"Liam." I hissed when words found me again. I glared at my former flame as he stood in the doorway of Hope's bedroom, dangling a set of keys in his hand. "You almost gave me a heart attack."

"What are you doing?" he asked, grinning. "Snooping around in your roommate's stuff?"

Closing the lid on Hope's laptop, I grabbed the papers off the ground and set them back where they had been before stalking out with Liam in tow. "You never saw me in here."

I made my way into the kitchen and flicked on the kettle. "What are you doing here?" I checked my watch. "We don't have to leave for work for at least another hour."

Liam and I had both scored a few shifts each weekend at his cousin's gym across town. The pay was worse than bad, but it was a good work experience for us. Besides, I made good money from the part time job I had managed to snag at Griffin's Coffee Dock on the Grand Parade last summer. The owners, John and Andrea, were lovely to work for, but the best part was the place was only a ten-minute walk from our apartment.

"I thought we could grab a bite to eat beforehand," Liam announced, shoving his hands into his sweatpants pockets.

I narrowed my eyes at him in suspicion. "Why?"

"Because I'm a growing boy," he laughed, shuffling awkwardly. "And dinner is important?"

I studied Liam's face for a long moment, trying to figure this whole thing out. For a while now, Liam had been acting a little more like old Liam – as in *boyfriend Liam*.

Getting back together wasn't something I had any interest in. To be perfectly honest, I didn't think I would ever trust another guy again. Like *ever*.

"It's just dinner, Teegs," Liam reminded me, all humor gone from his expression. "As in two friends sharing a meal and paying separately afterwards."

"Right," I muttered, feeling like an overreacting tool. "Well, then I'll definitely go for dinner with you..."

The front door of the flat flew inward and slammed against the wall.

"I can't believe it!" Hope practically screamed as she appeared in the doorway, with her phone pressed to her chest. Her eyes landed on me and widened.

"Teagan," she blurted out, rushing towards me. "Logan's on the phone. He says that Noah has been involved in some sort of incident at the prison again–"

"Don't," I warned her, waving my hand in front of my face. "I *can't* hear about him, Hope. Okay?" One year had passed by since I left the Hill and I was struggling to block it all out; all my thoughts, my memories of him, my guilt for the way his life had turned out. I was getting there. I was rebuilding my life, a life that didn't include Noah Messina. But I couldn't handle another sentence with his name in it. I wasn't strong enough. "Just leave me out of your family business."

"Dammit, Teagan," Hope huffed, as she padded through the flat towards me before thrusting her iPhone into my hand. "You need to hear this."

"I can't," I warned her, clenching my eyes shut. It was too painful and I was feeling weak.

"What's going on?" I heard Liam ask, but his question went unanswered.

"Talk to Logan," Hope demanded. "For the love of god, Noah was *stabbed*, woman."

"What?" I deadpanned.

Dread devoured me.

Fear claimed my heart.

With trembling hands, I dragged the phone to my ear. "Is he alive?" I heard myself ask in a voice so shrill that it didn't sound like mine. "Logan," I heard myself scream louder. "Is he alive?"

Please god, let him be okay...

Please, god, please...

"Yes."

That was the most perfect 'yes' I had ever heard.

"What happened?" I found myself asking. My legs gave out beneath me and I fell to the floor in relief, cradling the phone to my ear.

"Teagan?" Liam dropped to the ground, attempting to comfort me, but I pushed him away.

I couldn't have him near me right now.

"Liam, go," I heard Hope warn him. "She'll call you later."

I didn't listen to their exchange or check to see if Liam had in fact left. I was too busy having my life ripped out from underneath me. "He got into it with Angelo Javi in the yard the other day," Logan announced, getting straight to the point. "The fucker and his posse waited for Noah and jumped him when he was showering later that day, nicked him twice in the side with a blade."

"Angelo Javi? As in..."

"Gerome Javi's brother," Logan said, confirming my worst fears.

"Oh my god." A tsunami of emotions burst through me,

overwhelming me, attempting to strip away my sanity. "Where is he now?"

"He was sent to the hospital, got stitches and what not." I heard Logan sigh. "They sent him back there, Teagan."

"Can they do that?" I demanded, frantic. Climbing to my feet, I began to pace the flat. "It's not safe. Jesus Christ, they can't fucking send him back in there!"

"They can and they have," Logan replied, "It's a joke."

"What can I do?" I heard myself ask.

"Write him a damn letter for starters," Logan shot back. "And if it's not too much trouble, maybe you could get on a plane and come see the guy."

I cringed when I heard the venom in his tone.

Logan wasn't an aggressive person and we were friends; or so I had thought.

Not anymore apparently.

"He's going through hell inside, Teagan," Logan added. "And you checked out on him. Imagine how he feels."

"Logan, he cheated on me," I cried out in defense. "He fucked that girl right in front of me and he didn't bat an eyelid doing it. What am I supposed to do? Run back to him and wait for it to happen again?" I shook my head and wiped my cheeks with my free hand. "He broke me, Logan."

"He knew they were coming for him," Logan hissed in tone of pure disgust. "And do you know the only person Noah was worried about? *You.* He could've been killed in there, and the only thing that concerned him was getting a fucking message to you. You don't deserve him, Teagan," Logan hissed and I paled.

I tried to find the words to defend myself but Hope's younger brother continued before I had a chance.

"This is on you," he added in a deathly, cold voice. "If you hadn't come around and fucked with his head, Noah wouldn't be where he is today. He was protecting you that night, to keep you safe from JD and George, and you betrayed him, Teagan. You fucking buried him and you bailed when it got tough."

"Alright, Logan, that's enough," Hope, who snatched her

phone out of my hand, warned her youngest brother. "Don't even think about putting any of the blame on Teagan."

I didn't hear Logan's reply, but from the way Hope's face reddened and her voice rose, I guessed it wasn't pretty.

Was Logan right?

Was I responsible for this – for Noah being in prison?

"You are *not* responsible for this," Hope growled, reading my thoughts. Tossing her phone on the couch, she knelt on the floor and pulled me into her arms. "None of this is on you, babe."

I nodded and agreed and held onto Hope for dear life, all the while wondering if Noah blamed me too.

Did he go down for me?

Did he hate me?

NOAH

"I have a message for you," Angelo Javi announced when he walked into the shower room, flanked by his goons. "From JD Dennis."

"Tell that asshole that if he wants me, I'm right here," I shot back, not taking my eyes off him. Anxiety churned inside me as I watched them approach. My hands balled into fists on their own accord. "Come and fucking do his own dirty work."

"He wants you to know that he hasn't forgotten about you," he taunted, closing the gap between us, surrounding me. "He wants you to know that if it takes him all the days of his life, he will find a way to make you pay for what you did."

"Like I said," I snarled. "You can tell that piece of shit that I'm right fucking here, Chico."

"This is for my brother," Javi hissed, seconds before ramming the blade into my side. Collapsing on the ground, I fought to drag air into my lungs as his two little helpers held me down. "And consider this a little sample," he added before stabbing me again, "of what you have to look forward to on the outside – if you live long enough to make it out of here."

Crouching down beside me, Javi slapped a folded up piece of paper on my chest and smirked. "Your fate is sealed, Messina."

.   .   .

LAYING ON MY BUNK HOURS LATER, STITCHED UP AND BANDAGED, I was still clutching the note smeared with my own blood. As I held the piece of paper in front of my face, I wasn't dumb enough that I couldn't make out what the two words were – or what they meant.

Tick Tock.

It was inevitable that JD would try and get me for my part in the Ring of Fire being taken down. A criminal mob prince was bound to have contacts in low places, and Angelo Javi was the perfect messenger boy because he wanted the same thing JD wanted.

My blood.

To be honest, I didn't blame Angelo Javi for stabbing me. His brother spent six months pissing through a tube because of me, and I wasn't even badly hurt – just a couple of nicks in the side less than two inches deep. In a sick way I could respect the man for what he'd done. If the shoe was on the other foot, and he had done what I did to Low, Cam, or Colt, I would have reacted exactly the same. Except I would have done a better fucking job than he had. I would have put him in a body bag.

But I would be a liar if I said JD's note didn't unsettle me, and I would be an absolute fool to believe the guy didn't blame me for his father's death and the demise of their family business. JD was weak now, but he wouldn't always be, and knowing he was out there somewhere made me, for the first time, thank god that Thorn was an ocean away.

I might not be free of him, but she was, and that was music to my ears.

Thinking of Thorn caused the burning pain in my side to spread to my chest.

Deep down inside, I'd known she wouldn't come to me; she wouldn't call, and she wouldn't care. But there was this tiny glimmer of hope that wouldn't fade no matter how much time passed, or how badly she let me down. She had burst into my world and thrown it upside down, ruining everything, and making it right all at once.

Disappointment bloomed inside of me. Getting stabbed was the sign I had been waiting for, and now I had to accept the fact that it was over.

She wasn't coming back.

She didn't want me.

My Thorn was gone.

And I was fucking hemorrhaging from the inside out.

TEAGAN

There weren't many things I had done in my lifetime that I regretted.

I was a live in the moment kind of person.

I was passionate and let my emotions guide me through my life.

I didn't do the whole regret thing – I never had.

But not going to Noah that night, leaving him alone to deal with his injuries, well, I regretted that.

I called the prison the night I found out, but that had proved fruitless. I wasn't told a damn thing about him, which I had expected to happen anyway. I wanted to see him, no one would ever realize how badly I wanted to see that boy, but how could I show up after a year of no contact? And what if he refused to see me?

Oh god, my mind was a mess, obsessing and freaking out over the potential possibilities – working myself up about conversations that hadn't taken place.

If he had just listened to me that night. If he had trusted me and come away with me then none of this would be happening now. He wouldn't have cheated, he wouldn't be in prison, and I wouldn't be driving myself out of my mind worrying about him.

But he didn't listen to me that night.

He didn't trust me.
And now I was stuck.
Trapped in his love.
Lost in my misery.
I couldn't get past it.

NOAH

I never had a stable home life as a kid.

My parents were a goddamn disaster, and in many ways, had steered me in the direction of prison life from the day I was born. Every bad thing I had ever done was both for and because of them. I had never really had a chance at normality.

I couldn't read for shit because I had missed a lot of school growing up. I wasn't even sent to a mainstream school until I was seven, and even then, we had moved around so much I never really got a chance to settle down anywhere – not that my folks gave a damn about that.

They weren't concerned with what I could do with my mind, only what I could do with my fists. I remembered the first time I stood in a ring. I was six and up against a boy who was nine. That kid beat me so badly that I cried. I had quickly learned that showing weakness was a mistake, and after taking my beating from my father, I had been tossed back into the ring and told- *fight or die.*

Fight or die.

Three words that had been my bedtime prayers.

After that day, I never cried again. I toughened up. I stopped feeling.

But I knew I had one reason to thank my parents.

Their fucked-up-ness kept me clean.

Experiencing what I had growing up was the reason I was able to keep my head clear in this place. Drugs were as easy to come by as a glass of water, and I'd be a goddamn liar if I said I wasn't tempted.

Fuck, I wanted to forget about shit, just like every other asshole in this place, but I wanted to not be like my parents that much more.

So I used my best attribute and hit the weight room as hard as I could every spare chance I got; fucking working myself to the goddamn bone.

I accepted every fight I was challenged to in here, and I destroyed every single opponent. I was ruthless because I feared nothing, and I was unbeatable because I had *nothing* to lose.

Losing didn't matter to me.

Dying meant even less.

Whoever took me on would have to put me in a body bag or quit like a bitch, because I felt *no* pain and I showed *no* remorse.

I'd had more fights in the last two years than I could remember – broken more bones and spilled more blood – and it did absolutely *nothing* to stem the anger inside of me.

Anger at being abandoned.

Fucking hatred at being let down by the one person I had put my trust in.

Thorn...

Some nights, I forced my mind to pretend that she had never existed in the first place. It was just easier to live in denial than to live with the fucking betrayal, hurt, and goddamn torture of it all.

But then there were other nights.

Nights when I dreamed about kissing my girl; of feeling her body against mine, flesh against flesh, no barriers. Those nights, the memories of being inside her kept me company. Thoughts of Thorn, naked and spread open beneath me, kept me company at night.

Fisting my dick, I would envision fucking her in every orifice in her body, every night from my jail cell. Trapped in the silence, I would mentally paint her image on the ceiling of my cell.

Her hazel eyes.

Those plump fleshy lips.

That long, blonde hair I fucking adored, and her sassy spirit.

There was a time I would have done pretty much anything for that girl. Anything. I would have torn the skin off another man's flesh just to keep her safe. But she betrayed me in the worst fucking way – abandoning me when I needed her most.

It wasn't like I wasn't used to being let down and betrayed.

I was.

Hell, my whole life consisted of disappointment after disappointment, but with Teagan, I always knew deep down in my bones that I had found something different – special.

Something permanent.

She was the polar opposite of every woman I had ever known. She never wanted me for my dick, or my fists, or the popularity that came from being with the local bad boy. Teagan had never been interested in any of that shit. She saw through it – she saw the real me.

That's why it hurt so fucking bad. I swear to god, nothing had ever hurt me like she had.

Now my anger was all I had.

My anger and my thirst for revenge.

"You are moving fucking mountains in this place, Messina," Lucky announced later that afternoon when he sauntered into our cell.

Walking over to where I was lying on my bed, he slipped his hand into his pants before tossing half a dozen packs of cigarettes on my lap. "You did some number on Campbell," he said, grinning. "Poor fucker's still pissing blood."

"He needs to learn how to rein in his emotions," I told my cellmate. "The guy fights with his feelings. That's never a good thing."

"It's a good thing for us," Lucky shot back with a shit-eating grin on his face, as he crouched down and pulled the small bottle of amber liquid out of his sock. "It's a fucking great thing for us."

"I'll be in the weight room," I told him, refusing the bottle when Lucky offered me a sip. Grabbing the packets, I shoved them into the hole in the side of my mattress before climbing to my feet and heading down the corridor to the only release I needed.

TEAGAN

"*You* said in," Noah whispered as he held himself above me, smiling down at me. "You said you're in love with me."

My cheeks reddened. "Yeah, so?"

"That's the most important word." Noah bent his head and pressed his lips to mine. "And for what it's worth, my in belongs to you," he whispered.

"It does?" I asked, barely breathing as my heart hammered in my chest.

"Of course." Noah scorched me with a kiss that ignited a fire that burned a hole right through the center of my heart. "You're my Thorn," he rasped between kisses. "If you leave me, I'll bleed out."

We were lying on my bed in Uncle Max's house. Noah had his arm wrapped around my shoulders and I had never felt so safe.

Twisting onto my side, I curled into him and smiled. "I'm glad you feel that way," I admitted, biting down on my lip to stop myself from grinning like a lunatic. I couldn't help it. He made me that happy. The thuggish boy next door had well and truly won me over. I knew I would never be the same again. Noah Messina would forever own me. Heart and soul. "I want you to need me." Stretching up, I pressed a soft kiss to his lips. "I want to be the one to make you fall apart — to make that hard exterior crack clean open."

"Mission accomplished," he rasped, cupping my cheek. Using his *free hand, he dragged me on top of him. "You own me," he added, kissing me again. "What are you going to do with me?"*

"Keep you forever," I whispered against his lips...

BEEP...BEEP...BEEP...

The shrill sound woke me from the best dream I'd had in months and I could have cried. Stretching out in my bed, I curled and uncurled my toes before reaching underneath my pillow for my phone. "What the heck," I croaked out, voice thick and sleepy when I checked my screen to see who was calling.

Holding my phone between my ear and shoulder, I covered my mouth to stifle a yawn. "It's like..." I glanced briefly at the screen of my phone. "Half past one in the morning, Sean, come on."

He was always doing this. Phoning me at outrageous times of the night even though he lived on the floor below us.

Sean Hennessy and I had struck up a conversation one day when we were passing in the hallway, and in the two months that had passed since he had moved into our building, I had come to know him as very lovable – and very gay. Sean had stepped in as a sort of surrogate Hope for me. Ever since she hit the NYT bestsellers list with one of her books last year, she had been hitting the town hard on the weekends, partying with the newfound *friends* she had found since hitting the big time and drinking her memories away. During the week she still barely left her room.

Sean was fun, and I needed that in my life.

The night I discovered his sexual preference – during an extremely clumsy and surprisingly amatory game of charades on my birthday – I had rushed upstairs to my apartment to drown my sorrows with three bottles of wine and an entire box of After Eights. Not that I would ever admit it, not to a soul.

I had been trying to force myself to move on from Noah. I was feeling so lonely, and in my drunken state, I had thought Sean to be the perfect candidate. He was the polar opposite of

Noah – thin, with baby blue eyes and choppy light brown hair, happy and outgoing. Where Noah was a fighter, Sean was a hairdresser. It should have worked, but it didn't, because I wasn't over Noah and Sean preferred male company.

Ugh, the shame of forcing myself upon my gorgeously gay neighbor would forever haunt me. My heart still hurt a little at the memory...

"Time for you to get your skinny ass out of bed," I heard Sean chuckle down the line. "I'm outside, babe, and I come bearing gifts of the *Foxy Dan* kind."

"It better be some good whiskey," I grumbled, throwing the covers off my legs, and climbing to my feet.

"You're looking a little flushed there, Teegs," Sean announced, studying my face with his brows furrowed, when I let him inside. "Have you got a fella hiding in your room that I don't know about?"

"Oh yeah," I muttered, rolling my eyes. "He's hiding in the closet right now." Grabbing the bottle of Jameson out of his hand, I made my way over to the couch, curling up in a ball as I unscrewed the cap and swallowed a mouthful of whiskey. "I'm all alone, Sean," I told him after I forced down the alcohol, grimacing as it burned my throat. "Same as always."

"Babe," he replied sadly. Sinking down on the couch beside me, he patted my thigh. "Come on."

"It's true," I hiccupped, handing him the bottle. "I wouldn't know what to do with a man anymore."

"Well that makes two of us." Sean slumped back and took a deep draw from the bottle. "I'm going through a serious dry spell, Teagan. Six months."

"Ha," I grumbled, not feeling one bit sorry for Sean. "That's nothing." If six months was classed as a dry spell, then I was living in a drought. "Try going without any for two years and then come back to me."

"You could always have Liam," Sean offered after a moment before bursting out laughing.

"Funny," I shot back crankily. "But no, thanks all the same."

"Why not?" Twisting on the couch, he faced me. "He's crazy

about you, Teagan – always has been by the sounds of it. And you two had that thing back in secondary school."

"Liam and I are just friends," I declared, flustered at the thought of being anything more than that. "Seriously, Sean," I said crossly when he waggled his eyebrows at me. "We are just friends."

"Then you might want to tell him that," Sean scoffed. "That guy has a soft spot for you."

"No, he doesn't," I grumbled, not liking where this conversation was going. "Can we change the subject now? *Please*?"

"Fine. Suit yourself," he replied, holding his hands up in the air. "But I really think you ought to give the guy a chance."

"I can't give Liam a chance, Sean, because I'm still not over the last guy I gave a chance to," I snapped. "So just back off. Okay?"

Sean's mouth curved into a knowing smile. "So that's it," he whispered, as if the whole world suddenly made perfect sense. "You've been burned."

"I guess if you call having your heart annihilated burned, then yes, I've been burned before," I grumbled. "I'm still burning."

"Want to talk about it?" he asked.

"Nope."

"Want to get drunk?"

"Definitely."

NOAH

*a*s time passed by, and my heart grew harder, shriveled up and died in my chest, I allowed myself to forget all about JD Dennis and his threat that night. I knew he was still out there, somewhere, but I didn't care. I had nothing left to lose. All I cared about now was fighting...well, fighting and the sadist sitting on the bunk in front of me.

"Stop moving, man, fuck!" Lucky hissed, shoving me backwards with the palm of his hand.

"I'm trying," I hissed out through clenched teeth, as I wrapped my hands around the metal bunk and braced myself for the pain. "Fuck, Lucky, I thought you said you knew what you were doing?"

"I do," my one friend in this shit hole of a place replied as he inked the side of my ribcage. "So stop crying like a bitch and let the master work his magic."

"Look at me," I snarled, clenching the bars of the bunk when it felt like he was going to cut through my ribs. "I'm fucking bleeding out here."

I wasn't a stranger to pain, but letting Lucky tat me with his fucked up concoction of ink was almost unbearable.

"Fuck!" I hissed, when he nicked me for what had to be the fiftieth time. Throwing an arm forward, I swiped the cigarette that was balancing between his lips, and put it to my mouth, inhaling deeply.

"There," he mumbled, "Done."

Inhaling one final drag, I passed Lucky his smoke and climbed off the bed. "Jesus Christ," I growled, looking down at my tender, bloodstained skin. "You fucking butchered me, man."

"You wanted a thorn in your side, Messina," Lucky drawled, leaning back from where he was perched on the bottom bunk. Chuckling, he admired his handiwork with a shit-eating grin on his face. "And it looks like you've got one."

TEAGAN

oday was Noah's birthday and I found myself, like every birthday before that, standing in front of the postbox at the end of my street with a crumpled envelope in my hands. I had lost count of the number of times I wrote him a letter, only to chicken out before mailing it.

Crowds of people brushed past me, carrying on with their day-to-day lives, oblivious to the turmoil churning around inside of me.

Maybe I had too much pride, or maybe I was a coward, but as the days turned into weeks, and the weeks turned into months and then years, I found myself too afraid to send that damn letter. I wanted to, but I was frightened of what he would say, or worse, what he didn't say if he chose to behave the way I had in the beginning.

My life wasn't like the fucking Notebook. My Noah wasn't at war, he was a criminal serving time for a serious crime, and I sure as hell wasn't anybody's Allie.

I didn't have money or a rich fiancé.

No, all I had was a stack of bills longer than both my arms, and a best friend who was more emotionally fucked up and closed off than I was.

Tucking the envelope back into my coat pocket, I closed my eyes and whispered, "Happy birthday, Noah."

TEAGAN

"*K*ill me now."

The half snarl, half roar that came from Hope's bedroom was my first warning of trouble.

The large stuffed gorilla she slept with at night being hurled halfway across the landing from her room into mine was my second.

"What's wrong?" I dared to ask, unsure if I really wanted to know.

"I've lost sixty thousand words," she hissed, stalking into my bedroom, looking somewhat deranged with her hair in knots and standing up in forty different directions. "Gone, freaking lost. Forever. That's what's wrong."

With a yodel of sheer despair, Hope threw herself down on my bed beside me and grabbed my pillow. "That piece of crap computer just crashed *again* and wiped all of my work *again*. I have a deadline I can't meet, I have obligations I can't fulfill, and now I'm officially screwed," she moaned, covering her face with my pillow as she lay on the flat of her back. "All that work for nothing. Just leave me here to rot. I'm done. I quit. I resign."

I told you to back up your work, was on the tip of my tongue, but I forced myself to refrain.

Hope was right about one thing.

Her computer was a piece of crap.

It had been giving her trouble for months now. "Don't be so dramatic, Hope. You work for yourself and your readers will understand if you need to push the date back a few months. So just calm your shit and buy a new computer," I told her. She really needed an upgrade. "But maybe take a shower before you go into town." I took a quick whiff of my friend and gagged. "I get that you're in your hermit, locked-in-the-house writer mode, but I think you should get out of the apartment for a day." *With me,* I silently added. I knew full well why Hope preferred to hang around with her new friends; they didn't remind her of the past. They didn't know about Jordan, and she could pretend when she was with them. God knows, I understood it, but I didn't like it. Hope was vulnerable and I hated to see her being taken advantage of.

"You don't get it, Teegs," she moaned, ignoring the shower part. "I started on that one – I wrote my very first book on that piece of crap. It holds sentimental value. And I don't want to jinx myself. For all I know I've been incredibly lucky. That computer could be my lucky charm."

I rolled my eyes. "You're not lucky, you're bloody talented." Jumping off the bed, I reached forward and grabbed her hand, pulling her miserable, stinky, overgrown ass off my bed. "The words are in here," I told her, tapping her head, "not in that piece of shit plastic in there."

I was used to Hope's crazy writer mode, and I understood when she needed to dive into a book and stay there, but she was like a dazzled baby bunny when she came back up for air.

This time was more severe than usual. Hope only got *this* bad around the anniversary. It kind of ruined her, and her being ruined kind of saved me from going down that similar spiral.

"I don't know," she mumbled, tugging on the sleeves of her hoodie – the same hoodie she had been wearing since Wednesday.

"Well then, it's a good thing I do," I countered. "Come on," I told her. "Clean your ass up and we'll hit the shops."

"I do need ink cartridges," she offered, slightly optimistic at the thought of our shopping spree. "And some sharpies, too."

"Yes." I nodded, as I shoved her towards the bathroom. "We can get all of those and more. Just clean yourself up first."

"Hey Teegs?"

"Yep?" I looked back at my distraught looking roommate.

"Thanks for taking care of me," she muttered sheepishly, as she poked her head around the bathroom door. The steam rising behind her assured me she was indeed going to clean herself.

"It works both ways, Hope." I told her.

WE SHOPPED UNTIL WE DROPPED, AND WHEN WE WERE FED AND watered, we made it back to the flat to get dolled up for a night out on the town with our friends.

We ended up staying in Reilly's bar, our usual hangout, for karaoke night.

It was going really smoothly, right up until Hope put her hand up for a song.

Liam, noticing my grimace, turned to me and asked, "Is she a terrible singer or something?"

"No." I closed my eyes and braced myself. "She can sing, but she gets a little...weepy after alcohol."

Hope took the microphone and when the background music of Pink's *Who Knew* blasted around me, I knew this was bad.

She sobbed into the microphone, choking out the lyrics of the song and I groaned inside.

This was fucking painful to watch.

I flinched, feeling her pain right down in my bones. Sometimes I wished I could erase Jordan Porter altogether. It killed me watching Hope live this half-life of an existence.

I hoped his conscience kept him up at night.

Bastard.

In many ways it was worse for Hope. With Noah, I knew I

was playing with fire. He was like a ticking time bomb, ready to go off at any moment. But Jordan wasn't like Noah. He and Hope had been together their entire lives, and the guy had let her down worse than anyone I'd known. I'd never seen heartbreak quite like that.

I was *living* my life, miserable as it may be, whereas Hope's life seemed to be on a complete standby. She was on pause and it infuriated me.

I had fair warning with Noah.

Hope never stood a chance with Jordan.

By the time Liam and I had managed to wrestle the microphone out of Hope's hands and get her back to the apartment, I was completely wiped out.

"Happy Valentine's Day to us, buddy," I whispered when I had finished undressing Hope and had gotten her into bed.

Closing her bedroom door behind me, I went back to the lounge to where Liam was standing. Wrapping my arms around his waist, I gave him a drunken hug.

"Thank you for tonight," I whispered. "I wouldn't have been able to get her home without you."

"Whatever you need, Teagan," he replied warmly, enveloping me in his arms. "Always."

"You can stay here tonight," I said against his chest.

"I can?"

"Sure." I nodded, breaking out of his hold. "You'll never get a taxi at this hour. I'll go grab you a blanket for the couch."

"You looked beautiful tonight," Liam told me when I returned with his blanket.

"Thanks," I replied, embarrassed.

Reaching out, he tucked a loose tendril of hair behind my ear and smiled. "You're welcome."

"So...do you want to watch some telly?" I offered, desperate to change the weird, clammy atmosphere that had settled between us. "I have the first three episodes of the new season of *The Walking Dead* recorded."

Liam stared at me for a long moment, almost imploring me with his eyes, until finally he shook his head and sighed. "Sure, Teegs, it's your call," he told me, sinking down on the couch.

Grabbing the remote, I flicked on the television before settling down on the far side of the couch. "Rick Grimes it is," I replied nervously.

NOAH

"**M**erry Christmas, dude." Tommy Moyet slid the packet of cigarettes towards me.

"Ho fucking ho, man," I shot back, smirking. Fucker sure knew how to brighten up an inmate's day.

Tommy and I had been friends since high school, and to be honest, the guy had stepped up when I went inside. He visited frequently, at least once a month, which I had to admit I enjoyed a helluva lot more than I let him know.

Reaching down, I slid the packet into my sock. It wasn't against the rules to have cigarettes in here, but I sure as shit didn't share and Lucky was a chain smoker. "Appreciate it, T."

"Anytime," he replied warmly. "Eight more months, Noah," he added, leaning back in his chair. "You'll be out before you know it, man."

I responded with a grunt.

It might seem that way to Tommy, but anyone who had ever been inside knew that you weren't out until you were out.

A million and one fucking problems could happen between now and my parole, and I wasn't getting my hopes up. Not for one fucking moment. Not when there were assholes inside who could jeopardize my future at the drop of a hat.

This was a dangerous fucking world to live in and the only

reason I'd made it this far as unscathed as I had was because I had been born into it.

I knew the rules of the underworld.

I knew the code of the scum.

Stick to myself, keep my nose clean, and *never* back down.

But I would be a liar if I said I wasn't nervous.

Eight more months.

Two hundred and forty days.

I was on the cusp of freedom.

I could practically smell it... and it was fucking terrifying.

Say nothing bad happened and I *was* released in eight months. How would I make it in the real world? I was only a kid when I came here, eighteen and green. Now I was almost twenty-four. That was a long ass recess from the real world.

"People are talking, Noah," Tommy said in a hushed tone, leaning over the table towards me. "There's more interest in you with the MFA now than back in high-school, dude. Some of the guys are saying that with some training you could go pro –"

"In case it's passed your attention, I'm a criminal, Tommy. I've got a record as long as your arm, dude. I'm not getting signed by any respectable company," I responded wearily, resisting the urge to roll my eyes. My getting signed had been Tommy's wet dream of an obsession since we were in our teens. Back then, before Teagan Connolly had come around and knocked my concentration to shit, the MFA – the fastest growing league for mixed martial arts and street fighting in North America – had shown an interest in me. That was then, before I had a rap sheet to contend with. "You know it and I know it, so why don't you give the whole MFA shit a break, man. Please."

Shrugging my words off like the optimistic bastard I knew he was, Tommy continued planting the seed in my brain.

"Times are changing, Noah," he argued, excitement evident in his eyes. "And the rules are changing too. In your favor, dude. The sport is sluggish, and they're looking for fresh meat – someone with enough personality to draw the crowds back in. Young, skilled, and ruthless." Drum rolling his hands against the table, Tommy grinned. "And you're all of those, man."

"Forget it," I told him. "There's not a company on this side of the continent gonna sign the likes of me."

"You sure about that, man?" Stuffing his hand into his pocket, he dragged out a crumpled sheet of paper and placed it in front of me.

"And this is?" The letter was scribbled out in cursive. I was a fucking terrible reader and I sure as hell wasn't about to embarrass myself by trying to sound it out in a prison visiting room.

"A handwritten letter from Quinn 'The Ripper' Jones himself," Tommy informed me proudly. "Letting your pessimistic ass know there's a place waiting for you in his gym when you're out. In eight fucking months."

"Why?" It was the one question I needed answering. Why the fuck would Quinn Jones write to me? That guy was practically MFA royalty. Two-time heavyweight champion, I'd followed his career back in the day. Hell, come to think about it, I was fairly certain that I'd had a poster on my bedroom wall of him when I was a kid.

Since his early retirement a few years ago – when he broke a bone in his back – Quinn had settled for coaching up and comers. He had his pick of the litter and trained only the best. The elite. The guys with the biggest potential. The guaranteed future heavyweight champions. The fighters that were guaranteed to bring in the big bucks and make a shit ton of cash.

So what in the fuck was he doing sniffing around a waste of space like me?

"Gimme that thing." I snatched the letter out of Tommy's hands and held it up to my face, concentrating my hardest.

Nope, still couldn't make out a damn word, but I believed Tommy.

He wouldn't fuck with me.

The guy was as loyal as they came.

"This is it, Noah," Tommy chuckled, rubbing his hands together. "This is your goddamn meal ticket out."

I leaned back in my chair and sighed.

My meal ticket out?

Well shit.

TEAGAN

*G*od, I loved music.

It was by far my favorite wonder of the world. It was soul searing and wondrous and deserved to be on the list.

How amazing were the writers, poets, and musicians of the world?

They could shove their hands through your chest and pull on your heartstrings with lyrics and melodies.

Okay, so I knew music wasn't listed in the Seven Wonders of the World, but I thought that was a crying shame. Sure, Niagara Falls was nothing short of wonderful, and the Coral Reef was splendid, the Grand Canyon spectacular, but I could easily live without those. What I *couldn't* live without was music, and that had to count for something, right?

Pumping Imagine Dragons' *Radioactive* on my iPod, I pounded the footpath, desperate to rid my body of the tension building up inside of me since I got out of bed this morning and had to spend an entire day ignoring what today represented to me.

I hated New Year's Eve.

It was the worst day of every year for me and this year was harder than others.

As I ran down the path, dodging happy couples and families with smiling children, I couldn't help but think of my mother.

Today was the anniversary of her death and I think I missed her more now than I did when I was fourteen. I missed her voice and her hugs. I missed her advice and the way she could always make me feel better no matter how hard things were.

I wondered what she would say to me now.

Would she be proud of me?

Of the choices I had made?

WHEN I MADE IT BACK TO THE APARTMENT, I LET MYSELF INSIDE and headed straight for a shower, desperate to wash away the icky sensation of windburn and sweat.

When I was finished and dressed, I decided to bite the bullet and call the one person in this world that hated New Year's Eve as much as I did. Sitting cross-legged on my bed, I inhaled a deep calming breath and dialed his number.

"Hello?" The sound of his familiar voice filled my stomach with a flurry of nerves.

"Hi, Uncle Max," I heard myself say in a voice much smaller than normal. "It's me."

"Teagan," he acknowledged slowly. "Are you all right?"

"Yeah," I replied, nodding slowly. "You?"

"I've been better," was his response. "I'm at work, actually," he added, and the sound of machine's beeping in the background suddenly made sense.

Max was a doctor – a workaholic to be exact.

I should have known he would be at the hospital today. He had a tendency to work through his feelings – literally.

"It's been a while," I said, throwing it out there, tackling the big, fat elephant between us. I hadn't spoken to my uncle since I left The Hill.

Not a single word.

All correspondence between us had been done through the Carters.

"It's lonely not having family around – especially today," I admitted, closing my eyes, hating how weak that sentence made me sound.

"That was your choice, Teagan, not mine," Max replied coolly. "But I presume you already know you made the wrong decision by shacking up with that criminal."

"I am *not* shacked up with Noah," I snarled, rising onto my knees.

This was the crux of it all; Max would never get over me choosing Noah over him all those years ago.

"Because in case it hasn't crossed your attention, Noah's in prison." My voice was full of pain and sarcasm. "And it wasn't his fault," I added.

He might be a cheating bastard, but Noah wasn't a criminal – not through choice at least. He had been thrown into a world of crime and had done the only thing he could do. Survive. "Hate Noah if you want, Max," I growled. "But don't call him that."

"I'm simply calling a spade a spade," he replied, not giving an inch.

Sighing heavily, I struggled to rein in my emotions and make the peace. "Look," I coaxed in as reasonable a tone as I could muster. "It's been almost five years. Can't we just bury the hatchet and call a truce?"

"And when Noah gets out?" Max countered, ignoring the olive branch I was offering him. "What happens then?"

"What do you mean what happens when he gets out?"

"How long will this so-called truce last when lover boy gets released from prison?"

Shaking my head in confusion, I opened my mouth to defend myself but Max jumped in before I had a chance.

"I will not condone you being in any sort of relationship with a criminal, Teagan," he told me in that snotty, superior tone I had forgotten he loved to use when talking down to me. "I will have no part in it."

"Oh my fucking god," I hissed, "Max, do you realize how insane you sound right now?" Jumping off my bed, I stalked my floor, feeling angrier than I had in months. "This conversation is pointless because Noah and I are *over*."

"We'll see how over you two are when he gets out, won't we?" he shot back coolly.

"What the hell is that supposed to mean?" I demanded, pinching the bridge of my nose in frustration.

"Don't act so stupid, Teagan," my uncle snarled, finally losing his cool demeanor. "That thug was obsessed with you! Do you honestly believe he's not going to come looking for you when he gets out?" he all but roared down the line. "Bringing with him all the danger and trouble that comes hand in hand with gang members."

"George Dennis is dead," I informed him angrily, reciting the words that had kept me sane since I found out all those years ago. "It's over, Max. The Ring of Fire is gone, and when Noah is done serving his time he will be a free man. And besides, Noah and I have had *no* contact," I choked out. "Not one phone call in all these years." I blinked away the hot tears that were burning my eyes. "For all I know, he's forgotten about me –"

"It will *never* be over for him and you know that," Max interrupted, ignoring my protests. "There is *always* another low life waiting in the wings to swoop in and take the reins in a gang."

"You're wrong," I countered shakily. "It's over."

"Look at what he dragged you into, Teagan," Max snarled, clearly furious. "Illegal fighting rings. Drug lords. Car chases. Police stations. Brothels." I could hear the outrage and disproval dripping from his voice. "You've taken beatings for him. You've been bullied because of him – *he* bullied you, Teagan. For Christ's sake, that man took your innocence and he uploaded it to the Internet for the world and its mother to see."

"He didn't do that."

"Keep defending him."

"I'm not. I'm stating facts."

"And you will go back to him," Max added condescendingly. "Because that's what women like you do."

"Women like *me*?"

"Weak women," Max informed me. "Dependent women. Women who bend their morals and go against everything they've ever believed in for a man. And just like your mother, you will end up getting killed because of that man," Max added, sticking the knife in deeper.

"How dare you bring Mom into this?" I screamed, becoming hysterical. "I am not weak or dependent, and neither was she." Bringing up my mother and father's relationship was Max's favorite party trick. He did it when he wanted to hurt me most.

Well, mission accomplished.

"She fell in love, Max. My mother followed her heart, which is something you will never understand because you don't have one." Squeezing my phone so tightly I was surprised it didn't crack, I roared, "And I am not that kind of woman."

"You were prepared to run away with a murderer," Max protested smugly. "That makes you exactly that kind of a woman."

"Noah is *not* a murderer!"

"Yet."

"At all!" I screamed, reaching my boiling point. "Now stop this. I mean it. Stop it right now!"

"He is the worst kind of wrong for you," my uncle bellowed. "The moment you decided you loved him, you were lost to me. You sold your soul to the devil himself."

"Stop talking about him like that," I sobbed, breaking down, as my emotions overwhelmed me, and my uncle's hurtful words stabbed through my heart. "Noah has done *nothing* to you, Max. Nothing!" Pulling on my hair in frustration, I cried, "This is between you and me... so just leave him alone. Please! Just stop talking about him like that."

"Why?" He demanded. "Why do you care what I say about that piece of scum? I mean, let's be honest here, Teagan, at the end of the day that's all Noah Messina amounts to; criminal scum –"

"Because I love him, that's why!" I slapped my hand over my mouth the second the words fell.

"And there it is," Max said sadly. "Your allegiance to that

man after all he's done to hurt you is as strong as ever." Sighing heavily, he added, "I'm sorry, Teagan, but I would rather cut ties with you now than watch you go down in flames because of your infatuation with that man."

I opened my mouth to respond, to retract my words, but it was too late. The sound of beeping in my ear told me that my uncle had hung up on me.

Rushing over to my bed, I sank down in a heap and cried.

I cried for my dead mother and for my unfixable relationship with my uncle.

But mostly, I just cried for Noah.

NOAH

The minute the warden, surrounded by three guards, approached me in the weight room I knew something was wrong. He didn't come around often. The guy was like the grim reaper. He only brought bad news. Everyone in this place knew that you didn't want to get a visit from the warden. I hoped whatever it was wouldn't fuck with my release date. I only had one month left in this place.

Tense as hell, I continued lifting the dumbbells that were in my hands, ignoring the burning sensation in my muscles and the ache spreading in my chest, as I prepared myself for what I was about to hear. "

Who is it?" I managed to grunt, continuing my set.

Someone was dead.

I could fucking smell it.

There was only one name I was praying didn't come out of the warden's mouth; *Teagan.*

"Your mother," he told me without an ounce of sympathy in his tone.

If he expected me to snivel and cry like a bitch then he was talking to the wrong fucking inmate.

No matter how much pain I was feeling or how badly I was hurting, I sure as shit wasn't going to show it.

"What happened?" I managed to grunt out even though my airways felt like they were closing in on me.

"Overdose."

I took in the warden's words and realized that I wasn't surprised. Not in the least. This was the news I had spent my whole life preparing for. She had finally destroyed herself, like I always knew she would.

"You've been granted one day's leave for the funeral," he added cagily.

"And when is that happening?"

"Tomorrow. You'll be accompanied by officers Smith and Marshall."

In the five years and four months I had been here, I learned Smith was a decent man. He didn't take shit, but he didn't give it out unnecessarily either. Marshall wasn't horrible – a newbie on cell block C and younger than I was, but he wasn't as bad as the other cowboys in this place.

"Fine," I told the warden before he left the room.

———

I STOOD AT THE SIDE OF THE GRAVE, WATCHING AS THEY LOWERED my mother's casket into the ground.

I felt nothing.

I should have felt something, anything, but I didn't.

I was numb, cold to the bone, and emotionless.

Lee and Kyle were at the graveside, two small boys no older than four or five clung to their legs, offering me their unwanted support. Well, Lee was here to offer her condolences.

I knew why Kyle was really here and it wasn't to sympathize.

My *brother* was here to make sure my mother was really dead.

Mom had messed up so much for the guy in the past that I figured this was closure for him.

Satisfaction.

Kyle had his arm wrapped around his wife's shoulder

proudly, guarding her like a soldier, like she was the only thing on this earth that mattered to him, as he stared at my mother's casket lying in the dirt.

I heard the sound of heavy footsteps behind me moments before a hand clamped down on my shoulder.

I didn't turn to see who it was.

I already knew.

"This is not on you, Noah," Logan Carter said in a low tone as he came to stand beside me. "So don't you dare believe otherwise."

"She was never cut out for this world, Low," I heard myself say, eyes locked on my mother's casket. "All that...suffering and pain." I left out a heavy sigh. "Fuck, man, I hope she's in a better place now."

"I believe she is, Noah," he replied. "Someplace good. Somewhere her demons can't chase her."

Nodding slowly, I took in his words. That was the best reply I could have heard in that moment. I didn't need anyone pussyfooting around me or feeling sorry for me. I just needed those exact words.

Somewhere her demons can't chase her.

"I don't know if I'm ever going to be ready for the whole family thing," I told him, admitting for the first time the real reason why I was pushing Logan and his family away.

I had always cared about the Carters, and knowing they were related to me by blood only deepened those feelings, which sent out huge red flags in my brain.

"I'm used to doing this whole life gig on my own," I confessed. From my past experiences, caring about people only brought me pain and suffering. It gave my enemies a way in to hurt me. I had been dragged into the underground because of my duty to my mother. I was in this fucking mess because I had dared to let myself fall in love with Thorn and that love was used against me. "I don't want a family right now," I added gruffly. "I'm not...ready for that, man. I can do this on my own."

"I know you're not ready to play happy families, Noah, and

that's okay. But you need to know that you have one to fall back on," he replied, squeezing my shoulder. "Always."

I stood beside Logan, unmoving and emotionless for the rest of the service until it was over. Kyle and Lee approached me in the parking lot just as I was climbing back into the cop car.

"Five minutes," Smith, who had accompanied me to the funeral said, nodding at me, giving me permission to go speak to him.

I waited for Smith and Marshall to move away before I turned to face my brother.

"Kyle." I acknowledged, shaking my oldest brother's hand. "It's been a long time."

"It's been too long," he told me in a passionate tone before pulling me into a hug.

"Extended the nest?" I asked dryly, nodding towards where Lee was crouched down and talking to the two little boys. "How many is that – a dozen?"

"Half," Kyle chuckled. "And just you wait until you have a baby in your woman's belly. It's addictive."

"I think I'll pass," I replied in a flat tone, forcing down the image of Teagan, swollen with *my* child inside of her. "I'm not really a family man."

"Shit, that was insensitive," Kyle muttered.

Lee poked her head around her husband's shoulder then, breaking the awkwardness. When her eyes landed on me, her entire face lit up with happiness. "Look at you all grown up," she drawled in that sweet, southern voice of hers. "Cash, Casey, come say hi to your Uncle Noah."

Within seconds two little monsters surrounded me, tugging at the legs of my pants.

"Hi, Uncle Noah," the boys sang out in chorus.

"Uh...hi?" Looking to Lee for help, she smirked and shook her head before taking a few steps back.

"Jesus Christ," I muttered, crouching down to get a better look at them. "Did you go into the cloning business while I was away, Kyle?" I asked when I took in their identical faces.

One of the boys, and I wasn't sure which one, stepped forward and pressed his small hand to my cheek. I almost jumped back from the touch. I wasn't used to feeling anything gentle.

"What's your name, kid?" I asked, not having a clue what else to say.

"Casey," he told me, with blue eyes full of innocence and kindness. "I'm sorry your mommy went to heaven."

"Thanks kid," I croaked out. "Appreciate it."

"My brother Cam said you're the best fighter in the whole wide world," the other boy, Cash, announced excitedly.

"He did?" I replied. "Well, he's right about that."

"Really?" His little face lit up. "Oh man, that's so cool.

"Do you fight all the bad guys?" Casey, clearly the quieter twin, asked. "Are you a superhero?"

"Messina?" Smith called out from the squad car, breaking my train of thought. "Time to go."

"Uh..." I scratched my head and had to dig really fucking deep to find an answer to that question that wouldn't scar the boys for life. "Stay in school, boys," was all I could come up with. I stood and made my way over to Smith and Marshall.

"We'll see you soon, Noah," Lee called out when I was sitting in the back of the car.

"Yeah," I replied, knowing in my heart that it wasn't true.

Uncle Noah.

I wasn't cut out to be anyone's uncle.

Are you a superhero?

Fuck. My. Life.

TEAGAN

I phoned the prison again last night and left a message – my third one this week.

Of course I didn't actually get through to anyone useful, but I had to try, because ever since Hope told me about Noah's mother dying last week, I couldn't get him out of my head. All he had gone through with George Dennis and those criminals had been to keep his mother safe.

And now she was dead.

It made my heart hurt so badly. The unfairness of it all was crippling.

I didn't use my own name when I called and spoke to his correctional officer. Instead, I swiped Hope's phone and pretended to be her, calling to check in on my uncle.

I never expected him to return my call.

But as I sat here in the office of the gym Liam and I had taken over running from his uncle six months ago, with my phone vibrating in my hand, I felt a swell of emotions churning through me.

I didn't want to talk to Noah.

I just needed to know he was okay.

At least I didn't think I wanted to talk to him...

With shaky hands and a nervous disposition, I clicked receive and held my phone to my ear. "Hello?"

"You have a collect call from an inmate at the Colorado State Penitentiary, would you like to accept the charges?" A prerecorded voice asked me.

"Yes, I do," I replied immediately. "I mean I will accept the charges." The line went silent for a moment, and then there was a high-pitched buzzing sound.

"Hope," a deep, gravelly, familiar voice said down the line. "I got your messages. What's wrong?"

"It's me," I replied, hyperventilating at the sound of his voice.

Breathe, I told myself. *Just breathe.*

There was silence; a drawn-out pause before finally he spoke. "And who is *me* exactly?"

"Teagan." I closed my eyes and tipped my head back, stifling a groan.

More silence followed, longer this time, until I couldn't stomach it a second longer.

"Uh...Teagan Connolly," I added, voice high and squeaky. "From Thirteenth Street–"

"I know who you are!" he responded with a bark. "What I want to know is why you're calling me now?" The bitterness in his voice stunned me and I took a moment to steel myself.

"I'm so sorry about your mother, Noah," I blurted out, biting the skin on my knuckles anxiously. "I wanted to call you and... well, I just wanted to tell you that."

I heard his cruel, harsh laugh seconds before his voice was bellowing in my eardrum.

"Let me get this straight," Noah sneered. "You're calling me, after five years of *nothing*, to offer your condolences?" He laughed again, crueler than before if that was even possible, before saying, "You're some piece of work, Thorn – calling me now, with less than three weeks left to serve."

"That is not why I called you and you know it," I snapped, feeling flustered and hurt. "I was worried about you. God, Noah, I know how you felt about your mother."

I opened my mouth to say something else, but he beat me to it, and with his words he buried any hope I ever had for us.

"Don't worry about me," he sneered. "In fact, don't fucking think about me at all. Forget I even exist, Teagan, just like I forgot about you!"

The line went dead, and I sat, frozen to the bone, as his words of malice began to slowly sink in.

All the years I had held myself back from moving on had been pointless, because Noah Messina hated me more than I hated him.

It was really over for us.

And my heart was breaking all over again.

NOAH

"That is not why I called you and you know it," Teagan hissed. "I was worried about you. God, Noah, I know how you felt about your mother."

"Don't worry about me," I interjected, feeling more furious than I had in years. She had some nerve, calling me up after all this time. "In fact, don't fucking think about me at all. Forget I even exist, Teagan, just like I forgot about you!"

And then I hung up on her.

"Goddammit to hell!"

Slamming the receiver down over and over again, I tried to rein in the tsunami of emotions raging through me.

"That fucking woman!"

Anger, pain, and most predominately, lust, hit me straight in the chest like a fucking wrecking ball. Followed swiftly by a huge churn of regret.

Why the fuck did I hang up on her?

Grabbing the receiver, I held it to my ear. "Thorn, you still there, baby?"

Nothing.

Fuck.

Slamming the receiver back down, I stalked back to my cell.

That night, instead of having nightmares about my mother's last moments on this earth, I dreamt of Thorn.

One phone call.

One fucking call after five years and I was a mess.

Christ, I felt like a dog that had been thrown a bone, a scrap of hope.

Somewhere, deep down inside, there was a part of Teagan that still cared about me and I held onto that thought like it was my last lifeline.

Thorn was still out there, thinking about me, worrying... still *waiting*?

All of a sudden, the prospect of my impending freedom was more appealing than ever.

All of a sudden, I had a goal.

I was getting out of here next month, and when I did, I was going to sign any contract or deal the MFA threw in my direction – I knew they were still interested.

When I had all of that done, I would go and get my Thorn, because there was no way in hell I was turning up empty-handed and broke. No, I was going to make something of myself, something good.

And then I was going to make her regret walking away from me – regret leaving me high and dry when I needed her most.

Knowing I could never trust her again wasn't enough to deter me – I was going to make her love me so hard she would *never* contemplate leaving me again.

I was taking back what had always been mine, and Thorn was *mine*.

I just needed to make her remember that.

NOAH

*L*ike Tommy had predicted, I was signed to the MFA exactly two weeks to the day that I was released from prison, with a six-figure salary that within three months had turned into seven figures. One year had passed since I had been released from one cage and thrust into another.

Except this one was different.

This was on my terms and I was the fucking king. The MFA were paying me a shit ton of cash to do the only thing I was good at doing – inflicting pain.

The sweat that dripped from my brow screwed with my vision as I stalked my opponent – my prey. I couldn't see properly, not that poor sight ever affected me.

Fighting for me was primal.

It was gut instinct.

It was in my blood.

My body was primed for this stage. It was all I had ever known. And the pain only encouraged me, turned me on, fueled the beast inside of me. The guy I was fighting, Justin Philippe, was one of those annoying as fuck all-American boys – wholesome and god-fearing. God only knew why the douche was even involved in the MMA circuit. He had a rich daddy and an even richer granddaddy.

Fucker was born with a silver spoon in his mouth. I hated that shit. Seriously, I fucking hated those types of fighters – the ones that were carried.

Every hair on my body stood on end as I pummeled the poor bastard through his attempts to block my left hook. The feeling of adrenalin pumping inside of me was like a drug and I couldn't get enough.

The more blood he shed, the more pumped I became.

I showed no emotion because I didn't fucking feel. I was ruthless, methodical, and composed. To the outside world, I didn't have a weakness, and that made me dangerous.

I wasn't born like this – a heartless bastard. It was something I had turned into as the years passed by and life got cold – something I had been twisted and morphed into.

The crowd roared out my name and it didn't mean a damn thing. These fuckwads didn't have a thing on me and that's exactly how I wanted it.

The women eye fucking me in the crowd didn't faze me either. I didn't raise an eyebrow when panties were tossed in my direction, or when I found naked women skulking around in the backroom after each fight. It was the life I lived now. They were enthralled with an illusion. They didn't know me. None of these women did.

They satisfied my needs – sated an itch that needed to be scratched – but I was only interested in turning the head of one woman.

Smirking to myself, I grappled with my opponent, tackling him to the mat, and executing the final blow.

The bell sounded, and the referee dragged me to my feet, raising my hand in the air in victory.

TEAGAN

I felt shady as hell as I tiptoed down the hallway and into my bedroom with the latest MFA magazine in my purse.

Closing the door behind me, I settled cross-legged on my bed and opened the center page section of the magazine...

MESSINA NEXT IN LINE FOR HEAVYWEIGHT TITLE SHOT

In a rare interview with Noah 'the Machine' Messina, when asked about his commitment towards the MFA, he responded with:

"Many people don't understand the obsession, the fuckin' passion of the sport. But that's 'cause they've never stood in the middle of an arena with seventy thousand people screaming their name.

They've never felt the compulsion of pushing their body to maximum capacity, of working their body until they puke and keep on going.

Fighting is in my veins.

Adrenalin pumping through every pore in my body – fuck there's nothing like it.

You could go to the ends of the earth and nothing

would compare to the feeling of standing in the ring, geared up and ready to inflict pain..."

When asked about his private life, in particular his relationship status, Messina responded by saying:

"I don't have time for a life – for one woman. Been there, done that, and I can safely say it was the biggest mistake of my life. In my experience, women are a dime a dozen – a means to an end – an itch to scratch, a fucking nuisance. No, I'm too busy climbing to the top, being the best and winning. That's my goal, my focus, and my fucking church. I won't quit until I win. I won't quit until I'm carried out of that ring in a fucking body bag."

Ugh.

Tossing the magazine off my bed, I threw myself onto my back and shoved my fist in my mouth. If I didn't, I was going to scream the house down and if I did that, my upstairs neighbor Mrs. Murphy would probably suffer her second heart attack this year.

I wasn't having that on my conscience.

I was such a glutton for punishment.

Seriously, why I tortured myself by watching fight after fight and buying up every magazine and newspaper with his name on it was beyond me.

I needed to get a grip.

I needed to get a bloody life, but I knew exactly where I was going to be on fight night; parked in front of our flat screen with my heart in my mouth, and every other part of my body shaking to the core.

Breakups were hard enough on a woman without having their ex splashed across magazines and television screens, looking hot as hell. Only my ex could land himself in prison for half a decade and come out smelling like roses. The man had signed with the MFA the minute he got out of prison and in the last year had taken the sport by storm.

Noah was a global superstar, and I was an instructor and co-owner of a back-street gym in Cork City. Noah was shagging every woman with a pulse, while I had practically regrown my virginity.

I couldn't explain why I put myself through this, only that I wanted to see him succeed. I wanted to see *him*. Even though I would never admit it to a single soul, I wanted Noah to have a good life.

The door of my bedroom blew inward and in barreled Hope, fresh-faced and mouth agape. "Teegs, did you read what Noah said?"

"Don't say his name in my presence," I snapped, stopping my friend in her tracks. "I mean it Hope; don't utter his name in this room ever again."

Pathetic as it was, I couldn't stand to talk about Noah openly. It hurt too much because at the end of the day, regardless of how much I wanted to, I *couldn't* stop loving him and I couldn't stop *wanting* to hate him. I was a proud woman and talking about it only made me feel weak. I didn't show weakness, therefore when it came to conversations involving Noah Messina, denial was my best friend.

Hope looked momentarily stumped as she stood in the doorway of my room with her iPad clutched between neon painted fingernails. "Can I change he-who-shall-not-be-named's name to asshole and talk trash about him?"

I considered this for a moment before nodding. "Yes, I accept those terms."

Hope grinned and skipped over to where I was laying on my made bed. She could always do this; make me feel like I wasn't completely alone in the world.

My relationship with Hope was one I cherished more than anything. She wrecked my head at times, but the girl was worth her weight in gold.

But no matter how much trash she talked, or how hard she tried to cheer me up, I couldn't shake Noah's words...

"I don't have time for a life – for one woman. Been there, done that, and I can safely say it was the biggest mistake of my life."

"Looks like he's up to his old tricks again," Hope announced. "Whoring and touring." Looking at me with a devious smirk, she added, "At least you made it out with a clean vagina."

"That's true," I laughed, burying my hurt with a smile.

TEAGAN

"*P*ush it harder, Liam. Give me more...I can take it."

"Jesus, you're so damn tight," Liam ground out through clenched teeth, adding more pressure. "Relax your muscles, Teagan, or we're going to be here all day."

"I'm trying...ugh, you're almost... Yes!" Breathless, I let out a moan of contentment as Liam pushed my thigh almost completely parallel to my stomach.

I felt the muscle that had been causing all the trouble snap back into place and I almost cried out hallelujah.

"That'll teach you," Liam grunted, before offering me his much larger hand and pulling me to my feet. "Next time, take on someone your own bloody size. You're not a machine, Teegs."

"Duly noted," I muttered, rubbing my ass cheek.

Stretching gingerly, I caught a glimpse of my reflection in the floor to ceiling mirror and groaned. I looked like shit, I smelled like ass, and I was going to have the mother of all bruises on my behind– courtesy of the huge dick currently signing membership forms in our office upstairs.

"I hate that guy," I told Liam. "I mean it, Liam. If there were any other way around this I would tell Ciarán Crowley and his team of GAA hurlers to take a running jump out of the nearest window." I hated Ciarán. I truly despised the guy. He'd been in our class back in college and had struck up a friendship with Liam that had lasted long after we graduated. I, on the other hand, had only ever received cheap comments and come hither stares from the creep. *Ugh.* "I don't care if he's your friend, Liam. I can't stand the guy."

"Well there is *no* other way around this," Liam hissed quietly, dragging me to the far corner of the gym, out of earshot of the few members that were working out this evening. "We're sinking, Teagan," he growled. "Like fucking stones. This is the first new membership we've had in months."

"We're hardly sinking like stones," I muttered nervously.

"Hardly?" Liam raised his brow in disbelief. "Are you kidding me? Teagan, we're in so much debt I'm seriously debating declaring myself bankrupt at twenty-five."

"I can offer some extra classes," I offered, but Liam cut me off quickly.

"Some more Pilates?" he sneered. "Or pregnancy yoga? Yeah, because that's sure to pay the creditors."

"Excuse me?" I snapped. "Don't be such a snob. I bring in good money with those classes."

"We need this, Teagan," Liam told me in a serious tone. "Thirty men, Teagan. *Thirty.* With a month's payment up front. We are *depending* on these guys and Ciarán is doing me a huge favor." Reaching out, he clamped my lips between his thumb and forefinger. "So keep that shut, and don't ruin this for us," he told me with a smirk. "Or we'll both be standing in the unemployment line by this time next month."

"Well if he touches my ass one more time, *he* will be depending on a life-support machine," I countered, shuddering at the memory.

Liam laughed and that only made me angrier. "Do you think it's funny?" I demanded, feeling wounded. "That those men violate me daily in my own workplace?"

Liam's expression visibly softened. "Come on, Teegs," he said, "You know it's only banter with those guys. I'll have a word with them – tell them to stop."

Checking the time on my watch, I saw that it was going on

six. "Don't bother, Liam. It's not like my personal safety matters to you. Here." Slipping my hand into my bra, I tugged out the lone key and tossed it at him. "You can close up."

Not looking back when Liam repeatedly called out my name, I stalked through the main floor of the gym, through the double doors, down the old metal staircase to the entrance, and out into the Friday night bustle of Cork City.

Rain hammered down on me and I was glad. I needed to cool the hell down and there was no way I could do that when Ciarán Crowley was in my close vicinity.

Pulling the hood of my raincoat over my hair, I popped my ear plugs in and pumped up the volume on my iPod. Gliding my thumb across the screen, I quickly scrolled through songs, settling on Ben Howard's *Oats in the Water* before pounding the pavement.

I needed to run off some steam.

As I padded along, I mentally took stock of my life.

I was twenty-five years old and had my heart broken twice.

The first time had damaged my pride.

The second time had almost killed me.

It had taken me almost a decade to build myself back up from the brink of desolation and I still wasn't over the man that ruined my faith in all men.

It hurt. It was torturous. The pain was beyond fucking brutal and I promised myself to never allow a man to make me feel that way again.

I couldn't talk about him to anyone, not even now, seven years later. It was still too raw, and I swear to god his name sliced skin from my throat whenever I attempted it.

Shame filled me every time I thought about how I had almost thrown my future away for a boy who fucked the school slut the second my back was turned. I had lost my relationship with my uncle because of him. Max didn't want to know me, and on the last occasion I had reached out to him, he had cut me off the line and out of his life.

Permanently.

I had been out on a few casual dates with Liam. They had

never progressed to anything more than dinner and a movie, but at least I had tried. If I was being totally honest with myself, the only reason I had accepted that date with Liam in the first place was because I had read that article where Noah talked about me being the biggest mistake of his life.

Ugh. He made me so damn angry... but as much as I tried, I *couldn't* shake him off.

I just couldn't seem to get over the bastard.

So I kept him a secret in the back of my heart, forced into my nighttime thinking capsule. At night was the only time I allowed myself to think of Noah – because I had needs and he sated them like a fucking porn-star.

My iPod switched onto Maroon 5's *One More Night* and I almost flung the bloody thing in the nearest wheelie bin.

That bloody song...

How pathetic was it that one song had my stomach twisting in knots and my nerves in tatters?

I knew why of course.

It was because of the fight.

He was fighting Horacio Vaughan for number one contender of the heavyweight title this weekend – in approximately one hour and thirty-eight minutes to be exact.

My back was aching so bad I wasn't sure how I was going to scrape up the energy to climb out of the bathtub.

Those extra shifts I was pulling in the gym lately were really kicking my butt. I knew I was overexerting myself, but Liam and I were up to our eyeballs in debt. We were barely making the rent each month and needed to bring in as much money as we could. As it stood, we weren't covering our overheads – hadn't been for eight months. If things didn't start improving fast, the gym would go under.

Twisting the faucet with my toes, I stopped the flow of water and slowly pulled myself out of the tub. As I dried and dressed myself, I let my mind wander.

Tonight was huge for Noah's career.

If he defeated Vaughn, he would be granted a title shot against the current holder, Anthony Cole, in Vegas in December.

Hope was out tonight with some friends she had met at a book seminar last summer, and I was glad. I couldn't watch Noah's fights when anyone was around because my emotions overwhelmed me.

When I was dressed, I grabbed my duvet off the bed, rushed into the lounge, and turned on channel 401 just in time for the main event of the night. Curling up on the couch, I covered myself with my blanket and held my breath, waiting to catch a glimpse of my ex boyfriend.

Horacio Vaughn was introduced first and I rolled my eyes in disgust when I heard him talk trash into the camera.

"Cocky much," I growled in disgust. Vaughn would be lucky if he made it out of the cage walking. Noah was going to annihilate that douchebag.

There was silence for a moment and when Roy Jones' *Can't be Touched* sounded through the speakers of my television, the crowd erupted in cheers and high-pitched screams.

Noah came into view then and my toes curled up in anticipation.

The hairs on the back of my neck stood on end.

The breath in my lungs evaporated in a sharp gasp.

The same as always, I found myself drinking Noah in. Soaking in his beauty. His raw, masculine appeal and the way he captured every single person in the room's attention with his presence alone.

Noah had fuck me hair. He had honest to god, drag your nails through his scalp, mess up the sheets, fuck me now kind of hair. It was black and shiny, with just enough length to grab onto when he was giving you the ride of your life.

His lips were the permanently swollen kind, like someone had just kissed the hell out of them, and the scruff on his jaw only added to the appeal.

His body was ribbed harder than when he was seventeen.

The abdominal muscles on his stomach were ridged, deep and masculine – a stark warning of the dominance and strength inside of him. Like back when we were teenagers, both of Noah's arms were covered in sleeves of intricately designed swivels and loops, and he still had that sexy wolf tattoo on his left calf, but he had added to his collection of body art since then.

Covering his broad back was a huge crucifix with wings sprouting from each side. His hipbone was inked with some Celtic scribe, and he had a red rose tattooed on the side of his ribcage, with a lone, jagged thorn on its stem.

Twisting his neck from side to side, Noah jabbed his fists in front of his face, unfazed by the hoard of screaming fans around him, as he made his way towards the cage.

A wave of supremacy wafted from him.

He stared into the cameras as he made his way out to the ring. His eyes were so intense: dark, hard, and heated. I felt his gaze right down to my toes.

Anger raged through me when a scantily clad woman jumped out from behind the barriers and threw her arms around his neck.

Security removed her immediately but not before she had a good feel of my ex. When Noah reached the base of the cage, a blonde-haired man, covered in tattoos dabbed Vaseline on his eyebrows before giving him a quick hug. Noah smiled warmly at the man before climbing into the cage and envy churned inside of me.

"I expect a clean fight, men," the referee called out, "touch gloves."

And then the bell rang out, signaling the start of the first round.

Noah and Vaughn circled each other like lions, waiting for the other to make the first move.

Vaughn was the first one to attack and I swear to god I felt every blow Noah took as he tried mercilessly to put him away in the first round.

I screamed at the television, cheering Noah on when he

blocked Vaughn's right hook and began a counterattack. Noah's fists were a blur, as he executed blow after deafening blow to Vaughn's face.

"That's it," I hissed, when Noah hit him with a sidekick to the ribs. "Knock his fucking head off, Noah!"

Vaughn narrowly avoided a left hook, deflecting at the last minute and escaping from the corner of the cage he had been beaten into.

"Get up," I screamed, when a nasty uppercut from Vaughn knocked Noah off his feet. Throwing the duvet off, I bobbed around on the couch, jabbing and jolting. "Get off that mat, Noah!"

When I noticed the blood trickling from Noah's eyebrow, a wave of unease rippled through me. "Get your ass back up, Noah," I screeched, frantic. "Come on, baby."

I grinned when Vaughn climbed on top of Noah, clearly thinking he was going to capitalize on him because he was on his back.

What Vaughn obviously didn't seem to understand was that Noah was a grappler – a backstreet fighter. He was brought up street fighting. It had been drip fed into his bloodstream from infancy. Going hand-to-hand on the mat with Noah was suicide.

Proving me right, I watched with pride as Noah overpowered Vaughn, countering his arm bar and gaining the advantage. Tossing Vaughn onto his back, Noah let loose with a ground and pound, finishing him off with hammer fist after hammer fist to the head.

Curled up like a bitch on the mat, Vaughn tried to protect his head with his hands against Noah's unforgiving blows until finally the ref called the fight, declaring Noah the winner.

I watched with a huge swell of pride and an even bigger smile, as Noah climbed to his feet and the official raised his hand in victory. Seconds later, he was surrounded by his background team and a few stragglers as they all attempted to hug and congratulate him on his victory.

"Noah, you just defeated the number one contender for the

heavyweight belt in under four minutes," the official declared as he thrust a microphone into Noah's face. "Tell us, how are you feeling right now at the prospect of fighting Cole in December for the belt?"

Noah, breathless, inhaled a few deep breaths before taking the microphone. "I'm ready," he husked. "I've been ready since March. Cole knows I'm coming for his belt. I'd take it right fucking now if he was man enough to take me on...."

Noah paused mid-sentence when a woman walked straight up to him and stuck her tongue down his throat.

I watched in pure horror as Noah let that woman kiss him, and worse, he dropped the microphone on the mat and kissed her back. It was a good thing I was on my own right now, because tearing up over that big bastard was something I didn't want anyone seeing me do.

"You're my thorn, if you leave me I'll bleed out."

His voice played inside of my head as I watched him on my television mauling the large breasted blonde.

The crowd erupted in wolf whistles and cheers.

Meanwhile, a piece of my heart shriveled up and died inside of my chest.

Why was I torturing myself like this and letting him break my heart over and over again?

Watching that man parade around on my television brought to the surface all the pain, betrayal, and love I had spent so many years trying to block out.

If I were a stronger woman, I wouldn't let him affect me like this. I wouldn't spend every Friday night locked in the apartment with channel 401 on the television and my heart in my mouth. I wished I were a stronger woman – one who didn't get fazed at the mention of her ex boyfriend. But I wasn't a stronger woman. I was just me, Teagan Connolly – a fucking idiot.

Noah was like an echo inside of me; repeating over and over until I felt like I was broken inside, and I couldn't do it anymore. I couldn't let Noah make me *feel* like this.

I *needed* to move on from him.

I *would* move on from him, and I would do it tonight.

Leaping off my couch, I stalked into my bedroom and dressed my ass in the sexiest dress, which just so happened to be a red, sparkly, boob tube little number, before slipping into the highest pair of black stilettos I owned.

Then I smeared on a generous dollop of lip-gloss and proceeded to grab the almost full bottle of Jack Daniels that Hope kept in the cupboard over the fridge for when her dad visited. Unscrewing the cap off the bottle, I swallowed a huge mouthful of whiskey, followed by another and another until I couldn't feel my toes.

When the bottle was drained dry, I staggered out of my apartment and out onto the street in the direction of Reilly's, our local pub, knowing full well who would be there on a Friday night.

DANCING IN THE DARK, WITH NEON LIGHTS STREAMING ABOVE ME, and the alcohol turning to liquid in my veins, I found myself forgetting all about Noah and his big-racked blonde.

Maybe it was the alcohol, or maybe it was the atmosphere, but I was feeling incredibly drawn to the man dancing behind me with his hands clamped on my hips.

Usually I would shove Liam's hands off, but tonight I didn't.

Tonight, I let myself feel for the first time in years.

Tonight, I was moving on from Noah.

Permanently.

Twisting around until we were chest to chest, I stretched up and wrapped my arms around Liam's neck. "Kiss me," I heard myself slur.

"You're drunk," Liam, who was equally as drunk but sobering quickly, told me.

"I don't care." Shaking my head, I tipped my chin up towards him. "Just kiss me."

Closing the gap between our mouths, Liam did as I asked.

Pulling me closer, he pressed his lips to mine, gently at first, as if he was afraid I would break. But then he pulled my bottom lip into his mouth and sucked. A pool of heat settled in my lower belly and I was quickly reminded why I enjoyed his kisses so much when I was a teenager.

He released my lip with a loud pop before thrusting his tongue in my mouth. I fell into it, kissing him back, massaging his tongue with mine. His kiss didn't set me on fire or make my toes curl like Noah always did, but it was sweet and gentle and familiar.

A niggling feeling of guilt fluttered in my chest when Liam gestured for us to leave, but I forced it away and followed him.

I had nothing to feel guilty about.

Sure, Liam wasn't as tall or as physically muscular as Noah; but at six feet, with dirty blonde hair, blue eyes, and a washboard stomach, he was definitely a catch.

And yeah, kissing Liam wasn't the same as kissing Noah, and holding Liam's hand as we walked back to his apartment didn't thrill me like it had when it was Noah's wrapped around mine. But maybe I didn't need to feel that excitement and chemistry with Liam.

Maybe I didn't need to experience that crazy rush of love and lust; hate and passion mixing together that drove me to the brink of madness with want.

Maybe those feelings had never really existed at all.

"I don't want this to be a one-time thing, Teagan," Liam told me in a husky voice when he let us into his apartment and switched on the light. "I was a fool when we were younger," he added, as he pulled me into his embrace and pressed a kiss to my lips. "Don't think I'm letting you go again."

"Don't talk," I mumbled, clawing at his trim waist. I didn't want love and promises. I wanted to move on. I *needed* to. Liam was the safe choice – the wise option. Liam wouldn't hurt me – not like he had.

My fingers found the button on his jeans and I quickly unzipped the fly. "Take me to bed, Liam," I whispered, slipping my hand inside his boxers and squeezing his rock-hard erection. "And bring a condom."

MY DRESS WAS IN A BALL ON HIS BEDROOM FLOOR.

My underwear was cast aside with it.

His thigh was resting on my stomach.

My head was on his pillow, pounding like a drum.

I felt like I'd been run over by a lorry, and all I wanted to do was get out of this apartment, climb into the shower, and scrub my skin raw.

Last night should have been perfect, but it wasn't, because all I had thought about the entire time Liam was inside of me was how it should have been *Noah*.

Even though I had no reason to, I felt dirty. Here I was, in bed with a really decent man, and all I felt was disgust and guilt.

Slowly edging out from underneath him, I rolled off the bed and tiptoed towards the bedroom door, grabbing my trail of clothes in the process.

"Morning, babe."

Liam's voice filled my ears, causing the bile in my stomach to churn and threaten to spill.

"Hi," I managed to squeeze out as I stepped into my dress and pulled it up. Shame. I was feeling it by the bucket load as I searched the floor for my knickers. I hadn't worn a bra last night – because, let's face it, I didn't have much to hold up – so at least I could cross that particular undergarment off the missing list.

"Where are you going?" Liam asked when I had finally found the missing panties and opened the bedroom door.

"Home," I muttered, as I used the doorframe to balance myself so I could step into my underwear. "I'll...uh...talk to you later, kay?"

I didn't wait for his reply. Instead, I dashed out of the room, falling over one of my discarded high heels in the process.

Of course, Liam had the curtains drawn in the lounge, making my escape all the more difficult. Slipping on one heel, I fumbled around on the floor for the other. Did I have a purse with me? I couldn't bloody remember...

"Here." Handing me my other shoe, Liam walked over to the wall and flicked on the light.

"Thanks," I muttered, red-faced.

"Teagan, what's the problem here?" He stood with his hands on his hips and a look of hurt on his face. "I thought you wanted last night as much as I did."

"I did," I blurted out, making my way to the apartment door. "Last night. But now...It's just..."

"You don't?" he offered.

"Look, I'm sorry, Liam," I offered, rubbing my temples. "But I can't do this."

"Do what?" he shot back. "Be with me?"

"Be with anyone," I confirmed quietly before letting myself out.

NOAH

eagan managed to escape her house arrest tonight and I couldn't keep my hands off her. We had only been parked for ten minutes and already; I had her naked and spread open in the back seat of my car.

"Noah, don't leave me on my own..." Teagan whispered, as she clawed at my back. "Please, I know I'm a moody bitch sometimes and drive you crazy, but I'm putting it all on the line for you... don't let me go..."

"Never," I promised, as I pushed inside her. Her pussy sucked me in, pulling on my dick like a vice and I groaned loudly. Jesus Christ, she was so tight; I could hardly control the urge I had to pound into her. But I had to be gentle. She was all mine. Fresh and new and tender. I needed to take care of her.

"Say it," she mewled, rolling her hips upward, meeting me thrust for thrust. "Say you love me."

"I'm in love with you, Thorn," I whispered before claiming her lips with mine...

I WOKE IN THE MIDDLE OF THE NIGHT WITH A THROBBING between my legs that wouldn't fuck off. Her voice continued to haunt me, long after I opened my eyes – a constant reminder of just how good I had it when I was eighteen.

"You can go now," I told the blonde who was lying on my hotel room bed.

Picking her scrap of a dress off the floor, I tossed it to her before heading into the bathroom for a shower.

I needed to wash the dirty feeling off my body.

The blonde had momentarily sated my needs, but now, I was aching again.

No amount of sex from her would satisfy me.

It never did.

I couldn't fucking get any satisfaction no matter how many times I fucked these women or how many different positions I did it.

I was fucking broken.

"WHAT THE FUCK IS UP WITH YOU, MESSINA?" LUCKY DEMANDED when I laid him on his ass for the third time in an hour.

"Nothing," I growled. Reaching out a hand, I helped him to his feet before climbing out of the ring.

"Grateful as I am for the job and all, I didn't expect to be your personal punching bag when I signed up for this," he added, following me over to the bench at the far end of the gym. "Damn man."

Lucky was released from prison a couple of months after me, and I had immediately hired him as a member of my team. I didn't exactly have a position available for the guy, but I wasn't going to let him roam the streets looking for work, find nothing, and fall in with the wrong people. Besides, he was as close to family as I had.

"Sorry," I offered with a grunt before taking a deep swig of water. "I'm not usually this...cranky."

"Did you forget I shared a cell with you for five years?" He laughed. "Who're you trying to fool, man?"

"Noah!"

I turned around at the sound of my name being called. My face broke into a broad grin when Tommy Moyet stalked through the gym. "What's up, T?" Tommy was my go-to guy. He had trained as a physiotherapist, but the minute I had signed for the MFA I had snatched him up. Since then, the guy pretty much organized what time I took a shit when I was working. I was lucky to have him on my team. Hell, I had a team because of him – because he had believed in me.

"What would you think about fighting Davy Bishop in Ireland on St. Patrick's Day?" He asked when he reached us.

"He would think that it's a huge comedown," Lucky interjected with a tone of pure disgust. "Bishop's in the middleweight division. Noah's the number one contender for the heavyweight title."

"Not anymore," Tommy added with a smirk, turning his attention to me. "Bishop's coming up," he told me. "And he's making a big splash about it – saying he deserves a title shot before you. All talk, that guy. Full of bull crap." Tommy grinned. "How about you put that punk in his place on his home turf?"

"I'm in," I replied immediately. "Tell Bishop to name the time and place, and I'll be there."

"Whoa, Noah," Lucky said. "Are you sure about this?" Shaking his head, Lucky let out a string of cuss words. "That's just over ten weeks away, man."

"It's done, Lucky," I told him. Turning to Tommy, I nodded once and said, "Make it happen, T," before resuming my training.

I was sold the minute Tommy revealed the location.

Ireland.

2

PRESENT DAY

TEAGAN

"You've done it again," I announced, as I stood in the doorway of Hope's bedroom with a stack of papers in one hand, and a yellow highlighting pen in the other.

"I have no idea what you're talking about," Hope replied, lying through her teeth, as she continued to tap furiously on the keyboard of her laptop.

She knew exactly what I meant, and she also knew I wasn't leaving this doorway until she answered me.

After a minute of me glaring at the side of her face, Hope let out a loud huff, placed her hands on her lap, and leaned back in her chair, reluctantly giving me her full attention.

"I've read ten chapters, Hope," I explained calmly, shaking the papers in my hand to emphasize the huge favor I was doing her. "And I've had to replace the hero's name in every single one." This morning alone, I had made fifty-eight name changes to the document, and I swear to god, if I had to change the name *Jordan* to *Chad* one more time I was going to lose it.

When she didn't respond, I decided to use tough love to get a reaction.

"Hope," I started. "It has been *seven* years – almost a bloody decade – and you're still moping around the place like a pigeon shat on your head."

"One word, Teegs," Hope shot back coolly, swinging from side to side in her chair. "*Noah.*"

Ouch...

"I'm going to pretend you didn't just say his name in my presence," I replied in a shaky voice before slamming the stack of paper and the pen down on her desk. Hope's comment cut deep, and I had to take a few minutes before I could trust my voice again to sound level and calm. "Your mom called again," I told her. "She wants to know if you got anything unusual in the mail."

"No," Hope muttered, shoving the invitation I knew she was hiding further underneath her keyboard. "Nothing new."

I rolled my eyes at my friend. She was such a little liar. "Hope, I know about your parents' anniversary party tomorrow night," I told her before swinging around and heading back for the hallway. "I got an invite too." There was no way in hell I would step foot on Coloradan soil, but I appreciated Lee's offer all the same.

Hope needed to go though. She needed to start building bridges with her family. She was never going to move on with her life if she didn't face her hometown at some stage. I figured she should do it sooner rather than later.

Stopping at the door, I decided to try a gentler tactic. "Lee knows you're still hurting over him. She wants to help you, Hope. Maybe you should talk to her about how you're feeling. Call the woman back."

"I know you think I shouldn't still think about him," I heard Hope whisper before adding, "I know I shouldn't, but it just won't fade, Teegs. He's in my head constantly and I hate it."

"You're preaching to the converted here, Hope," I replied with a heavy sigh. "Just do what I do and remind yourself that you didn't do anything wrong. Jordan, like he-who-shall-not-be-named, happens to be a man – and therefore a stupid, heinous, inconsiderate bastard." Shrugging, I added, "I'm telling you, Hope, they're all the same..." My voice trailed off when I caught a glimpse of my watch. Ten thirty. *Shit.* "I'm late for work," I muttered. "We'll finish the man-bitching session when I get home, okay?"

I wanted to stay and help my friend through her crisis, but I wanted to *not* go bankrupt that little bit more. Opening on St. Patrick's Day was Liam's latest attempt at saving the gym. Personally, I thought it was pointless. Everyone would be out watching the parade and enjoying themselves, but I didn't bother protesting. I was in the doghouse as it stood.

Grabbing my bag off the couch, I slipped my key into my bra and headed off on my jog to the gym.

"MORNING," I SAID BRIGHTLY WHEN I OPENED THE OFFICE DOOR and walked inside, setting my bag down on the bench behind the door.

"You're late," was all Liam replied, not looking up from the paperwork he had splayed across our old wooden desk.

"Um...there's no one here?" I shot back, gesturing around with my hand. "Relax. I'm here now."

"You know, sometimes I wonder why you went into this partnership with me," he said in a sharp tone, "when you can't even be bothered to come in on time."

Resisting the urge to groan, I walked over to where he was sitting and rested my hip against the desk. "You're one of my best friend's in the world," I told him truthfully as I rested my hand on his forearm. "I want us to get back to the way we used to be." I could feel my face reddening as I spoke, "The way we were before we...you know."

"Had sex?" Leaning back in his chair, Liam lifted his head and stared me straight in the eye. "Before we had sex, Teagan."

"Yeah." Swallowing deeply, I nodded, forcing myself to keep eye contact with him. "Before we had sex." I hated the fact that I had screwed up a lifetime of friendship with Liam. I knew I hurt his feelings when I ran out on him, and I knew I was hurting him now; but guilt ridden or not, it changed nothing, because I couldn't give Liam what he wanted from me – my heart.

It simply wasn't there anymore.

I had left it behind in Thirteenth Street.

Liam was silent as he studied my guilty face. Finally, when I thought he wasn't going to say anything else, he shoved back his chair and stood up quickly. "You fucked with my head that night, Teegs," he told me with a groan as he began to pace our small office. "Made me feel like it was something more than it was." Turning around, he walked right up to me. "You know how I feel about you."

"I do?"

"Yeah," he husked. "You know I have feelings for you, and you used me that night."

"I'm sorry," I muttered, feeling a bucket load of shame. "I didn't mean to."

"I'm not a toy," he continued to say, ignoring my apology. "You can't take me out and play with me for a little while and then toss me back in a box when you're done."

"That's not what I've been doing." I shook my head, rejecting what Liam was saying. "We're friends."

"*Friends* that go out on dates," he argued. "*Friends* that don't see other people." He shook his head and sighed. "I'm the only guy you spend any time with."

"That's not true," I protested. "I hang out with Sean."

"Sean's gay," Liam countered swiftly. "Don't even try and dig your way out of this one –"

"Sorry to interrupt your little domestic, folks," Ciarán Crowley said with a wolfish smile. "But could you turn on the televisions on the treadmills?"

As much as I hated Ciarán and his wandering hands, I could have kissed him for essentially giving me a way out of this horrible conversation.

"Sure," I said brightly, slipping around Liam, and making my getaway. "I'm on it."

"So, gorgeous," Ciarán purred when I had the flat-screen on his treadmill switched on and set up. "Do you have any plans for tonight?" He asked, hitting full speed on the machine before warming up.

"Not a one," I replied, stepping out of his reach. "I'm going to have a nice quiet night with my book." I forced a smile and said, "let me know if I can get you anything else," before walking away.

"A blow job would be great," he chuckled under his breath and I froze.

Swinging around, I marched back to the treadmill and slammed my hand down on the emergency button. It came to a complete stop, causing Ciarán to trip over his own feet and land awkwardly on the belt.

"What the fuck did you do that for?" He snarled, red-faced, as he pulled himself up with the help of the side rails.

"Because you're a member, I'm going to let what you said go this one time," I seethed, pointing my finger in his face. "But if you ever sexually harass me in my own gym again I will cut you."

"Look what you've done, you stupid bitch," he roared, pointing to his ankle. "I have a match on Sunday."

Folding my arms across my chest, I rolled my eyes and smirked. "And that matters to me because?"

"What's going on here?" I heard Liam demand seconds before he arrived at my side. "Teagan?" he asked, looking down at me. "What happened?"

"I'll tell you what happened. That fucking psychopath just cost me the county final." Ciarán snarled. Hobbling off the treadmill, he tested his weight on his ankle and flinched. "I'm out, Liam. Sorry, man, but I'd rather train in a place that actually wants us."

"Good," I shot back.

"Shut up Teagan," Liam hissed, poking me in the side with his elbow.

Holding his hands up, he turned to Ciarán and tried to defuse the situation. "I'm sure this is just a big misunderstanding," he placated. "Teagan didn't mean any harm."

"Yes I did," I piped up, causing Liam to groan. I knew I

needed to shut the hell up, but I couldn't back down. It wasn't in my nature. If Ciarán wanted to take me on, I wasn't holding anything back.

Ciarán's face turned purple. "Honest to god, Liam, I don't know why you waste so much time on her." he roared. Limping towards me, he leaned down in my face and spat, "The guy should go and get himself a real woman. Not a fucking ice-queen with a cardboard pussy."

"*You* would say that," I snapped, losing all tact and grace. "When the only moisture you've ever drawn from a woman's body was when you bored her to tears."

"You're finished," he roared. "No one within a twenty-mile radius will touch this place when I'm through."

"Thanks a lot, Teagan," Liam muttered before chasing after Ciarán who was making his way out of the gym.

I WAS ON MY HANDS AND KNEES, WIPING DOWN THE TREADMILL – more like disinfecting it from that pervert's touch – when Liam eventually returned. The angry expression he wore on his face told me all I needed to know about how it had gone with Ciarán.

Not well.

"Are you proud of yourself?" He demanded when he reached me.

"Yes," I shot back, climbing to my feet. "But I'm thoroughly disgusted with you."

My retort caught Liam off guard and whatever he was about to say fell out of his head as his brows furrowed in confusion.

"That man has been tormenting me for months," I reminded him. "And you did nothing. So don't get all pissy with me for taking matters into my own hands."

"We need his business, Teagan," Liam said, enunciating each word, as if that was supposed to make it all okay. "The gym is going under. What don't you get about that?"

"So I'm supposed to be okay with being touched and

degraded because business is slow?"

When Liam didn't respond I shook my head in complete and utter disgust.

"You wanted to know why I won't consider being with you? It's because if you had any real feelings towards me, you wouldn't allow those men to talk to me – and talk *about* me – the way they do." Tossing my cleaning rag on the floor, I turned my back on him and headed into the office for my stuff.

"It's *banter*," Liam called out, following me into the office.

"It's *sexual harassment*," I corrected, stuffing my phone and the keys of my apartment into my bag. "And if Noah were here..." I cut myself off quickly. "Forget it."

"No. Please go right ahead," Liam, clearly hurt, told me. "Tell me what the infamous ex boyfriend turned jailbird would do. Is he still in prison?" He taunted. "How many years did he get again?"

"Fine," I snapped, furious. "If Noah were here, he would rip that prick's head off." Slipping my arms into the straps of my bag, I pulled it onto my back. "He wouldn't let them get away with it, and he sure as hell wouldn't make me feel like I was wrong for sticking up for myself."

"Finally," Liam sneered, having the good sense to step aside and let me pass. "We're getting down to it. Your *precious* Noah."

"Don't go there, Liam." I warned him in a shaky voice as I marched through the gym, regretting ever confiding in him. "This has nothing to do with him."

Liam knew I had an ex boyfriend called Noah, but what he didn't realize was that he had tickets to go see said ex boyfriend in action later on this evening.

If he did, I think Liam would have a very different outlook.

"It has *everything* to do with him," Liam shot back heatedly. "Go on and deny it, Teagan. Tell me he isn't the reason you're holding back from me."

I left the gym without answering Liam for two reasons.

The first reason being he didn't deserve my answer – he had acted like a complete tool.

And the second reason was I didn't want to lie.

NOAH

Noah

"How are you doing, man?" I heard my trainer ask seconds before he landed in the booth beside me. Tugging a sweet little brunette onto his lap, Quincy pressed a kiss to her neck before raising his beer bottle and clicking it against mine. "How are the knuckles?"

"Still functioning, Q," I told him before taking a swig of my beer. I was sore as shit, but the adrenalin that was still coursing through me numbed the aching.

Quincy was celebrating tonight. So was the brunette on his lap, and the other forty or so people crammed up in the private room of the Krash bar.

I'd done it. Finally. After eighteen months of blood, sweat, and fucking tears I had proved to all the doubters that I deserved to be here. I had fucking *earned* my title shot.

I buried Davy Bishop in the second round tonight, knocked his ass out with a superman. Poor fucker was out cold the second he hit the mat. I could have put him away in the first round, but I allowed him a little more time with it being on his home turf and all.

The venue was a helluva lot smaller than what I was used to, but the victory had the same taste about it as all the others. The taste of *more*. I was hungry for that title. It meant a lot to me. I wanted it to prove a point.

To myself and every motherfucker who ever doubted me.

"Smell that, champ?" Quincy chuckled, bleary-eyed and three sheets to the wind. "That, my man, is the smell of success – of freedom."

Champ, Quincy called me.

Not yet, but I would be...

I was twenty-five years old and had spent the majority of my adult life behind bars, paying for a liar's mistakes. The irony that I was now at the top of the very same game that had gotten me thrown behind bars didn't go unnoticed.

But I wasn't sure if I would ever get used to the feeling of freedom again. It had been eighteen months since I was released and every day since still felt like I was living on borrowed time.

I didn't verbalize my thoughts though. Instead I stood up, tossed another shot down my throat, and headed towards the bar for something stronger.

A dark haired woman caught my attention at the far end of the bar and when I realized who she was my world came crashing down on me...

"Hope?" I called out as I pushed past a drunk couple in my bid to get to my old friend – hell, my *niece*.

My heart was beating erratically in my chest.

"Hope? Is she here – is Teagan with you?"

"Stay away from her, Noah," Hope warned me before rushing from the bar.

Like hell I was staying away from her. The only reason I had accepted Bishop's fucking challenge in the first place was the prospect of seeing her.

Every fucking day since she ran out on me felt like I was hemorrhaging.

She was my Thorn.

And I was getting her back.

TEAGAN

I ended up spending the day in town, watching the parade and window-shopping before picking up a takeaway from the Chinese and heading home. When I eventually got back to our apartment just after seven, Hope was already gone .

Showering and dressing in my pajamas, I settled down on the couch with a large glass of vino and forced myself *not* to turn on the television. I couldn't watch another one of his fights, because when he won – and he *would* win – I couldn't bear seeing him mauling another brainless fan girl. So, stocking up on chocolate and wine, I decided to tuck into Hope's manuscript instead.

"What do I mean to you?" I blurted out, never one to mince words. My cheeks reddened, I could feel them burn, but I kept my eyes on his face.

"Everything," ~~Jordan~~ mumbled, never taking his eyes off the pad he was sketching on. His fingers moved so fast across the paper, so skillfully, as I stared at him, drinking him in.

He looked good, too good for my twin bed he was sitting on – too good not to touch and I was itching to touch him.

His hair was a mess, a sexy mess of curls and his whole body looked entirely too tempting.

God, hormones had officially found me. This was only day three of summer vacation. ~~Jordan~~ and I had at least another month together. How the heck was I going to cope?

"Everything." I tested the word around and decided that was a great answer. "You really mean that?"

"Of course," ~~Jordan~~ added with a chuckle. "You're my little keychain..."

"THIS IS REALLY GOOD," I MUTTERED TO MYSELF AFTER A COUPLE of hours of engrossed reading time had passed. Fetching another bottle of wine from the kitchen, I poured myself another large glass, before snuggling down on the plush cushions on our super-comfy couch and devouring my best friend's latest masterpiece.

"Are you going to tell me what's wrong?" I asked, holding my breath, fearing his answer, hoping he would lie and tell me he was fine because that look in his eyes was petrifying me. He was hurting. I could feel it in the way his hands trembled, I could see it in his eyes. Something was wrong.

"~~Jordan~~," I whispered when he didn't answer.

He didn't look at me.

Instead, he stared downwards. God, I knew this conversation was going to end badly and if I was Ash, I'd know a number of different tricks to take his mind off his problems, but he wouldn't let me touch him.

God knows I'd tried...

"Hope, I don't..." he broke off and rubbed his face with his hand. "Just sit with me," he choked out.

Edging closer to me, he bowed his head, rested his knee against mine and shuddered violently. "This is all I can manage," ~~Jordan~~ admitted. "Please don't ask me why."

"I won't," I told him, forcing myself not to throw my arms around him.

I never asked and I never touched. He would freak out if I did and I needed him close to me. I needed the smell of him in my senses, the weight of his knee against mine. I needed answers.

Dammit...

"I love you, ~~Jordan~~," I whispered, hoping to god and every angel, star, and whatever the hell was up in the sky that he would open up to me. That today would be the day he would tell me his troubles.

"I'm never gonna be the right guy for you, Hope," he husked, twisting his head to look at me. His green eyes penetrated me, burned me. "You'll figure that out soon enough, but it would be a hell of a lot easier if you'd let me go now. Your dad's right about me...."

...As you can tell I've been in love before, but it was the first kind. The sweet, innocent will-never-end kind of love that gently flickers over time but never completely burns out or fades from your heart.

It's a special sort of love really, and sometimes it's the one that lasts the longest – the one you remember when you're old and gray and drawing your final breath into your weary lungs. If I had one wish it would be that I was his...his one love...the one that burned brighter and harder than all the others...the love that lasted the lifetime of the heart it was embedded inside...

It was going on one in the morning when the banging on our apartment door started.

The loud clattering startled me and I leapt off the couch. The manuscript I had been holding in my hand scattered to the floor and I groaned.

I hadn't numbered the pages...

The loud rapping noise continued.

"Hang on," I shouted as I made my way over to the door.

Hope had been doing this a lot lately – going out for the night and forgetting her keys.

Usually I didn't mind because I was either out with her or with the guys, but tonight I hadn't felt up to going out clubbing.

"Hope, I swear to god I am going to tie your key around your bloody..." My voice trailed off the moment I opened the door inward and caught a glance of my roommate's wide-eyed, horrified expression.

"What's wrong?" I whispered, seconds before she barreled into my arms.

"He's here, Teagan," she choked out, squeezing me so tight I could barely breathe. "In Cork...I saw him – at the club," she slurred. "He's here."

"Who?" I demanded, hugging her tightly. "Who's here, Hope?"

"Noah," she hissed, and the ground fell out from underneath my feet.

All the sensations I had felt when I was seventeen came back full force, smothering my heart and sabotaging my ability to breathe easily.

"Oh my god," I managed to choke out.

"You're my thorn, if you leave me I'll bleed out..."

"For what it's worth, my in belongs to you..."

"I'm either fighting with you or I'm fucking with you. There's no middle line, Teagan – not between us..."

My throat closed up.

Every emotion and memory of him that I had spent years forcing into the darkest parts of my mind was resurfacing – fucking flooding me. Noah Messina, the man who stole my heart, the man who shredded it right in front of my eyes...

"He saw me," Hope wailed. "Teagan, he knows you're here."

"What?" My voice was small and frightened. I could feel my eyes bulging in my face. "What did you say?"

Pushing us both into the apartment, Hope swung around and slammed the apartment door before locking the deadbolt. With her back pressed against the wood, she let out a huge sigh of relief. "There," she half-slurred, half-hiccupped. "That'll keep the big douche out."

"A deadbolt?" Shaking my head, I clawed at my hair, as I looked around frantically. "You really think a fucking deadbolt is going to keep him out –"

"Hope!"

I heard my roommate's name being roared out seconds before the sound of banging infiltrated my eardrums.

"Face him, Teegs," Hope slurred. "Just get it over and done with."

"Like you faced Jordan?" I shot back heatedly, before rushing over to help her barricade the door with my body. "Hmm?"

"Hope, I know you're in there. Open the goddamn door, or I'll kick it in."

Oh god, I needed to disappear.

My living-breathing nightmare had arrived on my doorstep and I needed to find the best damn hiding spot that had ever been created in all of time.

Jesus, why couldn't I have been born with magic powers or an invisibility cloak like Harry Potter? Yeah, sure he was up against Voldemort, but I was pretty sure Voldemort didn't hold a flame to Noah Messina.

"Go away, you big ass," Hope screeched, stumbling away from the door.

"Hide," she mouthed to me, and that's exactly what I did.

Running like a headless chicken through our tiny apartment, I dove behind the couch just as the door of our apartment was smashed clean off its hinges.

"Is that any way to speak to your uncle?"

Pain, excitement, and anticipation flooded through me like a shot of heroin injected into the waiting vein of its faithful disciple. He had *that* much of an impact on me.

Steeling myself, I slowly rose to my feet. Inhaling a calming breath, I caught a quick glance of my comatose roommate passed out next to the coffee table before locking my eyes on the cheating bastard in the flesh.

Standing in the doorway of my apartment, with his raven black hair all mussed up and disheveled, Noah knocked the breath clean out of my lungs. His dark brown eyes were focused entirely on my face as he ran a hand through his thick black hair.

Clad in faded denim jeans, a red and black plaid shirt unbuttoned and hanging open to reveal a plain white wife beater, I felt my mouth dry up. Noah was here, back in my life, and just like that I was a wreck. My whole body shook at the sight of him.

Feelings I'd forced beneath the surface flooded me, burning my flesh, pushing me towards him. I *needed* to get closer, the brown of his eyes called to me, and yet I needed to run as fast and as far away as I could. I was powerless – absolutely fucking powerless – just the same as I had been when I was seventeen.

Noah inclined his head in my direction before letting out a heavy sigh.

"Thorn," he acknowledged in his deep, gravelly voice; eyes locked on mine with an intensity I felt right down to my toes. He called me by his old pet name and I felt like I had been sucker punched directly in the stomach.

My heart fluttered around recklessly as the hairs on the back of my neck stood on edge.

Damn him!

"How dare you," I whispered. There were probably half a dozen more productive ways to handle this situation, but as usual, my emotions took over, clouding my common sense and I dealt with Noah the same way I always had.

I went bat shit crazy.

And then I attacked.

Somersaulting over the back of our couch, I launched myself at the big bastard in my doorway. "How dare you come in here!"

"Hear me out," Noah grunted after I'd delivered the first blow to his chest.

"Go to hell," I screamed before swinging my fists and hitting him again and again.

"I've been there, sweetheart," he shot back. Grabbing my wrists to stop me from striking out at him, Noah turned us around. "And it's not fucking pretty."

I continued to struggle, kicking and flailing my arms, claws out and teeth bared in my murderous attempt at hurting the man who had ripped me to pieces so many years ago and in so many ways that I'd been unable to piece my pride or my heart back together.

"Agggghhh." I tried to calm myself down, but it wasn't happening.

Rage, lust, fury, and excitement were thrumming in my veins.

My body was on high alert.

My brain had checked out.

I was running solely on emotion now and I locked onto his shoulder, biting down harder than I'd ever done before.

At that moment, I wanted to rip the man to pieces.

If I had to do that with my teeth then so be it.

"Dammit, stop fucking biting me!"

"Bastard," I snarled, biting down harder.

Shaking me like a rag-doll, Noah pinned me to the wall by my shoulders, before pulling back quickly – out of harm's way, I guessed.

"I see you're still as demented as ever," Noah growled as he pressed me against the wall. "But don't worry. I still find your psychotic tendencies a real turn-on."

"I loved you," I screamed. I was crying hard and ugly, and I was pretty sure my nose was dripping , but I was out of control. I wanted vindication. I wanted revenge. I wanted a fucking explanation, dammit. "I *loved* you, Noah."

"I know," he replied in a gruff tone, dodging my blows. "I know, Thorn."

Furious with myself for admitting such weakness, I lashed out at him. "Get out of my flat," I seethed, chest heaving. "Leave me be!"

"Not until you hear me out," Noah replied calmly, his body

crowding mine, his very presence breaking my heart – ripping me apart. "Talk to me."

The atmosphere between us was clouded with a fucked up mixture of anger and want, and the cold inside my heart that had protected me these last seven years was melting from the inside out at an alarming pace.

"I tried that, remember?" I screamed, holding onto my hurt, before pushing my hair out of my eyes. Noah had broken me and betrayed me, and he had done it in the worst possible way – bedding my enemy. He had taken my virginity, my heart, my trust and my faith in mankind with him. "And *you* hung up on me. Now you want *me* to hear you out? I don't fucking think so!"

Pain like I had never known existed consumed me, tormenting me, and the image of that bitch riding my boyfriend almost drove me insane with a toxic concoction of hurt and anger. "Asshole."

I knew I looked like shit, but I was beyond caring.

I had passed the point of return.

That man had flipped a switch inside of me.

Folding his bulging arms across his chest, Noah glared down at me, his face suddenly serious. "That night," his voice was deep, rough, and his breath was coming short and fast. "You jumped to conclusions. It wasn't what it looked like...you need to hear the truth, Thorn."

"I don't need to hear about what I got a front row view of, Noah." I sneered, feeling less like a twenty-five year old woman and more like a bratty adolescent by the minute.

"There's no talking to you," he growled. "You're right when you're wrong and you never back the fuck down."

"Wow, Noah," I spat, delirious with pain and fury. "It sounds like you're talking to a mirror."

Throwing his hands up in the air, Noah hissed loudly. "You know what, Teagan, I was a fucking idiot to think that you might have actually grown up. But no. You're still the same selfish little brat I used to know."

"Fuck you!" Wrapping my arms around my waist, I tucked my chin downwards and strode forward in the direction of the bathroom, refusing to give him an inch. I needed a moment to breathe and I couldn't do that with him here. "Keep your distance from me," I warned him. "I mean it, Noah. You better not still be here when I get out of that bathroom."

"Don't you dare walk away from me again," I heard Noah warn seconds before heavy footsteps followed after me. "I fucking loved you, Teagan," he called out. "And it was real love." Grabbing the back of my nightdress, he dragged me backwards into his embrace. "It was hard fucking love."

"You lost the right to love me the second you put your lips on her," I said in a flat tone, forcing myself to breathe through my mouth so I didn't inhale his incredible scent. I could feel his heart hammering against his rock-hard chest and it was doing terrible things to my self-control.

"Think about it," he argued in my ear. "I'm a lot of things, but I'm not a fucking cheat."

"Don't bother wasting your words on me because what we had..." I inhaled a shaky breath and spat the words out like I was expelling my body of poison. "What we had, it's dead and gone."

"You're the one who threw it all away," Noah snarled, losing his patience, tightening his hold on me. "Stop being so goddamn stubborn and just hear me out."

"No!" Pulling free, I turned, met his stare head on and narrowed my eyes. "So don't touch me, don't look at me. Don't fucking acknowledge me." I was losing control of myself. "We're done," I hissed. "We never happened." Rage bubbled up inside of me, erupting like a volcano of heat and anger. "We never met. You don't know me."

I needed to get a grip, but every time I tried to grab onto the ledge of something rational, the image of Noah and Reese together – their sweat-soaked naked bodies fused together – impaled my mind and I felt like bursting into flames.

"I wish I never met you." I closed my eyes and inhaled a slow, calming breath before I spoke, "No, scratch that, I wish you never made it out of that car. Because you, Noah Messina, are by far the worst thing that ever happened to me."

There was a long stretch of silence, and when I opened my eyes Noah was gone.

And I was alone with a broken heart and a soul full of regret.

Sinking to the floor, I sat numbly, rocking back and forth, as I tried to piece together what the hell had just happened.

I couldn't explain why I had behaved the way I did, only that Noah seemed to bring out the worst in me – like I did in him.

Why did I have to behave like that? Dammit, I knew I would never forget the pain and betrayal that man had caused me, but I didn't need to carry it around with me for the rest of my life. It was poisoning me and I was tired of being angry.

Even though I knew we were toxic to each other, a relationship made in hell, a small part of me wanted to *be* with him.

An even bigger part wanted to *believe* him.

But the biggest part of me, the part I chose to listen to, was the bitter voice inside. The voice that warned me Noah Messina had all but ripped me to pieces seven years ago, and to get back in the ring with that man would be emotional suicide.

NOAH

"*I wish I never met you...No, scratch that, I wish you never made it out of that car. Because you, Noah Messina, are by far the worst thing that ever happened to me...*"

Goddammit, I had been in Teagan's company for ten damn minutes and already my skin was burning, my heart was fucking hammering in my chest, and I had a hard on that wouldn't lie down.

I walked away from her – I fucking *had* to – because if I had stayed, I would've spurted the same cruel shit she had thrown at me; except mine wouldn't have been a bullshit fabrication of the truth, and Teagan and I tearing strips out of each other wasn't going to fix a damn thing.

Jesus Christ, all I had wanted her to do was shut the hell up for ten seconds and let me speak. All I wanted to do was lay it out there. Have her hear my truth. Make her understand that she had believed a bullshit lie for the best part of a decade.

I knew I'd be better off with a quiet woman; a nice, soft spoken, understanding woman. Hell, even a fucking grown up woman would do. But no, I wanted that little fruitcake. The little nut that never grew up. Thorn had a mouth like a sailor and the heart of a goddamn pit-bull terrier.

Stalking back to the bar, I shoved my way through the

crowd, ignoring every come hither gaze from every barely dressed female that approached me.

I couldn't look at another woman now.

Ordering a whiskey from the bartender, I chucked it back, enjoying the burning sensation in my throat as the alcohol settled in my stomach.

"Don't bother wasting your words on me because what we had, it's dead and gone."

Like hell it was.

Signaling to the bartender for a refill, I dropped a couple of fifty-euro bills on the counter before taking the bottle out of his hand and pouring myself another.

"We're done. We never happened. We never met. You don't know me..."

I got why Teagan was mad – but it didn't change the facts. And the facts were she believed a lie.

I was the betrayed one.

I was the fucking innocent one.

Swallowing the contents of my glass, I grabbed the bottle of whiskey from the counter and pushed my way back through the crowd towards the exit.

No fucking way was I going down like this.

Never in my life had I walked away from a challenge, and I sure as hell wasn't about to start now. Teagan Connolly was a thorn in my fucking side, but I couldn't walk away from her. She had left a permanent mark on me, and no amount of women, booze, or fighting filled the hole she had left inside of me.

I wanted her again and I would have her at *any* cost.

TEAGAN

As I shoved a dresser in front of our doorway, my feeble attempt to safeguard our door-less apartment, I was tormented with a feeling in the pit of my stomach that told me that I had done something terribly wrong.

I didn't have much time to ponder about my feelings though, because seconds after rearranging the dresser, it was shoved out of the way.

"I thought monsters had to be invited in," I exclaimed when Noah stepped through my doorway with a bottle of whiskey in his hand and a look of determination etched on his face.

Stalking into the lounge, Noah slammed a bottle of Jameson on the coffee table with a loud bang before turning around and glaring at me.

"We're not done here," he told me in a low, warning tone, eyes locked on my face, daring me to push him.

"I think we are," I shot back, red-faced, as I backed into the kitchen and far away from the professional fighter in my apartment. Anger was radiating off Noah in waves and suddenly I wasn't feeling as brave as before.

"No, Thorn, we're not."

With eyes dark and full of bad intentions, Noah took a step forward and I automatically took a step back. I felt a shiver of fear run down my spine. If he touched me again I was fucked. If he touched me, I may as well break my own heart. That's how toxic he was to me.

That trickle of fear quickly faded when he crouched down and lifted Hope into his arms. "Which room is hers?" He asked me, standing slowly with my best friend snoring loudly, cradled in his arms.

Ignoring the weird fluttering I had in my chest from the sight of Noah taking care of his niece so tenderly, I muttered, "first door on the right," before busying myself with draining the contents of my wine glass. I quickly refilled it, only to guzzle it down again.

I watched out of the corner of my eye as Noah marched down our small hallway and used his foot to nudge open Hope's bedroom door before slipping inside.

He returned a moment later, looking calmer than he had when he arrived. His presence was still overwhelming me, but he wasn't being hostile. In fact, his mood seemed eerily calm and I found myself easing my finger off the mental defensive trigger inside of my brain – the one I kept cocked and ready to strike when threatened.

"I was going to do that," I garbled, with my lips around my glass. Actually, I had planned to cover her with a blanket because there was no way I could lift Hope by myself. Skinny as she was, Hope had at least four inches on me, and twenty pounds of bone weight – but he didn't need to know that.

His dark eyes traveled past me, looking around briefly, before returning to my face. "It's done now."

"You've changed," I blurted out, taking in his beautiful, hard features. He was crueler now. Prison had turned him darker. Meaner. "You're...different."

"I didn't have much of a choice, Thorn," Noah replied in a flat tone. Wandering over to the coffee table, he retrieved his bottle and put it to his mouth, swallowing deeply. "It was fight or die in there."

Like always...

"I'm not talking about that, Noah." Clasping my hands in

front of my stomach, I studied the beautiful, cold man standing in my apartment. "You're different...with me."

Cocking his brow, Noah seemed to ponder my reply for a moment before nodding his head and taking another deep swig from his bottle. "But you still want me."

It wasn't a question. It was a boldfaced statement and one I venomously rejected.

"I do not," I snapped, red-faced and lying through my teeth. "I stopped wanting you a long time ago, Noah," I added shakily.

"Of course you did," he surprised me by saying as he walked around aimlessly. "This is a good apartment." He stopped at the window and took a slug out of his bottle before looking out. "Nice view."

Oh, so we were doing pleasantries now?
Fine, I could do that too.

"Hope owns the place," I replied, squeezing the stem of my glass so hard I was surprised it didn't crack in my hand. Normally, I wasn't much of a drinker, but with Noah in close proximity, there wasn't a brewery in the country that could have stocked enough alcohol to keep my frazzled nerves at bay.

"I just rent the spare room," I heard myself say before swallowing down another gulp. The wine hit the pit of my stomach and created a pooling, burning sensation. I felt myself growing lightheaded.

"Does she do that often?" He finally asked. Wiping the corner of his mouth with his thumb, Noah gestured to the coffee table – to where Hope had passed out.

"No, she does *not* make a habit out of getting inebriated and passing out." Hope was my best friend and I felt incredibly protective of her. Having Noah question her morals irked me. "She's in a bad place right now," I found myself explaining. "Don't be so quick to judge her, Noah – not when you don't know the facts."

With a hiss of annoyance Noah shot towards me, faster than I anticipated, and I had to force myself not to squirm. The second he slapped the bottle down on the countertop beside me and stepped into my personal space, the atmosphere around us crackled with intensity.

"Like me?" Noah asked me in a heated tone, stepping closer, backing me up against the fridge. His dark brown eyes penetrated me, cracking me clean open, making me feel more exposed than if I were naked and spread open for him.

Suddenly, the air around us became thick and muggy.

"What do you mean like you?" My question was a breathy whisper and my skin flushed with heat; I had to suppress the urge to fan my face.

"You were quick to judge me without knowing the facts." Noah's breath flooded my senses and I could practically taste the mint and alcohol on his tongue.

Leaning forward, Noah placed his hands on either side of my head, surrounding me, caging me in. "You left me in Thirteenth Street to rot," he whispered softly. "Threw in the towel when I needed you most."

"You cheated on me, Noah," I choked out, red faced and eyes watering with temper. All the emotions I felt when I was seventeen came back full force, smothering my heart and sabotaging my ability to rationalize the situation. "I can't get over that." Turning my face away from him, I felt my whole body shudder. "I never will."

Reaching out one hand, Noah trailed his thumb down my cheek before catching my chin and forcing me to look him in the eyes.

"I was a fuck up back then," he told me, his brown eyes searing me. "And I know that I've purposefully hurt you – on more than one occasion – but I *never* cheated on you. Not once."

I wanted to believe him, so damn much, but it didn't make sense.

Nothing made sense when it came to Noah.

"Noah, I *saw* you." I closed my eyes and felt the hot sting as my tears trickled down my cheeks. "Naked on your bed – with her on your lap." Throwing my hands up between us, I placed them on his hard chest and pushed, desperately trying to regain my personal space. "You *betrayed* me."

"Reese fucked me over, Teagan," he snarled. "She took advantage of me when I was too fucking weak to know what I was doing. Goddammit, you were my whole life, Teagan. Why the fuck would I have touched her when I had you – a *future* with you?"

"I don't know why you would do that to me, okay," I screamed as my emotions threatened to overturn my sanity. "I don't know why you ripped me open and humiliated me like that." Fury swished inside of me and I had to steady myself or my pain would spill over and morph into nasty words and cruel remarks. "I've had seven years to torture myself with that question, and I still don't know!"

"You don't know because you were *wrong* about me, Teagan. You made a mistake." Noah breathed harshly against my mouth, eyes still locked on mine. "Admit it."

"No, I didn't." He was lying to me again just like before. Spinning a web of lies and enticing me like a spider would its prey. "I *know* what I saw."

"You're wrong about me, Thorn," Noah countered coolly. "And one of these days you're going to realize that."

Tipping my chin up, I looked Noah straight in the eye and said, "I. Don't. Believe. You," enunciating every word clearly.

"And I don't trust you," he shot back evenly, not missing a beat. "Yet here we are." Smirking, he added, "Why do you think that is, Thorn?"

Shaking my head, I managed to squeeze around Noah and make a break for a quick getaway – or at least it would have been quick if Noah hadn't once again grabbed the back of my nightdress and pulled me to an abrupt stop.

"You had to know this day was coming," he said from behind me. His lips brushed against my ear lobe, one of his hands splayed across my stomach, and every nerve in my body exploded in a frenzy of tingling sensations. "You had to know I would come back for you."

"How come you never moved on?" I whispered, feeling my resolve falter.

"There's no moving on," he countered gruffly. "You should know that better than anyone."

"Don't act so stupid, Teagan. Do you honestly believe he's not going to come looking for you when he gets out? Bringing with him all the danger and trouble that comes hand in hand with gang members..."

Uncle Max's words of warning flittered through my mind, causing me to shiver and my walls of defense to rise up once again.

"You need to leave, Noah," I whispered shakily, not even trying to hide the way he affected me. It was as clear as the nose on my face that I was a mess. "Please. Just. *Go.*"

Noah turned me in his arms so fast that I didn't have a chance to stop him when he hooked me under my thighs with his hands and hoisted me up.

"I'm not going until I get what I came for," he replied in a deep, husky tone, walking us over to the wall, not stopping until my back hit the plaster with a thud. "You."

And then he crushed his lips against mine.

The second our lips touched, a growl tore from the back of Noah's throat and my whole body ignited in fire; an aching of desperation thrummed low in my belly.

The feel of his mouth on mine stunned me into submission.

Wrapping my legs around his waist, I cupped his head in my hands and kissed him with a passion that had been burning for seven years. Everything I felt for him, all my pain, my desire, ignited when his lips touched mine.

Being with Noah was like putting my hand in a fire and enjoying the burn, reveling in the pain, and daring the flames to burn brighter and blind me.

Maybe it was the alcohol running through my veins that was making me so reckless, or maybe it was temporary insanity, but for the life of me, I couldn't think of a good enough reason to stop this. Nothing mattered in this moment except having this man inside my body again.

Shamelessly, I clung to Noah's huge frame, allowing all the passion, pain, and desire that had built up inside to spill out and duel with him as he walked us down the hallway and into my moonlit room.

Setting me down on my feet, Noah broke our kiss to drag my nightdress over my head, and I wasted no time in pushing his shirt down his broad shoulders to join mine on my bedroom floor, before clawing at his belt buckle and quickly undoing his fly.

"I didn't even have a photograph of you," Noah growled against my mouth, kicking off his boots. "All those years... my memories didn't do you justice."

Reaching one arm behind his shoulder, Noah tugged his vest off in one swift move. "But I kept you in here," he told me, tapping his temple before slamming the palm of his hand against his chest. "And in here."

"Noah, I..." I started to say, but my words turned into a gasp when he shrugged off his jeans and boxers and shoved me backwards.

My back hit the mattress followed swiftly by Noah's weight as he landed on top of me.

"Don't say anything." He clutched my neck with his large hand and my pulse quickened, not from fear, but sheer excitement. It was like my body remembered Noah's touch. "Not another word."

Nodding in compliance, I brought my face up to his and poured everything I had into kissing him, letting him know all of the things I was too afraid to say aloud.

Noah kissed me back just as furiously.

Like he couldn't get enough of me.

Like he sensed this was the last night we would ever have.

My fingers trailed over his rock hard stomach. My fingers touched each groove, memorizing the body mine seemed to call out for.

Shoving my legs apart with his knees, Noah knelt between

them. "You're mine, Thorn, and tonight I'm going to remind you of that."

Reaching down, he cupped my pubic bone and stroked my wet folds, growling in approval when I jerked beneath him as bolts of desire rippled through me.

The instant his thumb touched my clit, my eyes rolled back in my head and my body began to rock against his hand. "Yes," I begged, writhing in pleasure, buckling beneath his skilled touch, thrashing in pure unadulterated ecstasy. "Please, Noah."

"You want more?" He purred, upping his pace, grinding his thumb harder against my clit, making the friction almost unbearable.

I wanted to scream.

I wanted to weep, to cry out in joy.

This man, this beast of a man wanted me.

He was here for me, dominating me, taking me over, doing everything I had dreamed of him doing to me for as long as I could remember.

"Tomorrow," Noah grunted, as he leaned over me and replaced his hand with his cock. "When you're aching and throbbing and fucking shivering all over. Remember who made you feel that way," he told me seconds before thrusting inside me. "Me, Thorn," he hissed, filling me to the brim with his erection. "I'm going to fucking ruin you for all other men. You'll only be good for me."

"I will," I cried out, pulling him closer, tightening my legs around his waist. "Wait," I gasped. "Wait..."

He froze inside of me and groaned, "What?"

"Did you win the fight tonight?" I breathed, clawing at his back, pulling him closer.

Noah smirked. "Yeah, baby," he rasped, plunging into me, filling me to the hilt, pounding me with thrust after remorseless thrust. "I won the fight."

I felt so full; he was so big I could hardly breathe.

"That's...uh...wonderful." He felt so right. Inside me, on top of me, his mouth on mine, his tongue on my skin. The taste of him. The feel of his skin. Flesh on flesh. It was everything. I wanted him. I couldn't deny it. I wanted him with a fervor that bordered insanity.

I wanted to do to him more than any other woman could. Take him to new heights. The feel of his muscles flexing beneath his skin was arousing me more than I thought possible and I rocked against him, meeting his every move, pulling him deeper.

"Fuck," Noah hissed after a moment and it was a raw, guttural sound that came from deep inside his chest. Freezing inside of me, I watched as a vein in his neck throbbed. "Condom," he gritted out, jaw clenched tight and strained, as he stared down at me with eyes black with desire.

"Don't you dare stop," I cried out, clawing at his back, rocking against him. The familiar feeling of tightness was teasing my core, causing my thighs to tremble and my pussy to clench uncontrollably. "I'm so close..."

Relief flashed in Noah's eyes and he began to move inside me again. "Thank fuck," he rasped, fucking me harder than before.

Dropping his mouth to my chest, Noah claimed one of my pebbled nipples with his mouth and sucked hard as his hips flexed against me frantically.

"Yes," I screamed, clutching onto the sheets beneath me as my orgasm ripped through me, shattering me, causing me to jerk uncontrollably beneath his beautiful body.

Noah didn't miss a beat, continuing to pump into me as my release rolled through me, sucking him in deeper, pulling him harder, milking him until his big body shuddered and he emptied himself inside of me.

Pulling out, Noah let out a sigh of contentment and collapsed on the mattress beside me.

A hot flush crept over my skin as I clutched the sheets, and desperately tried to scramble through my thoughts and make sense of what the hell had just happened.

Turning onto my side, away from Noah, I curled up in a ball and had a full blown panic attack – internally of course.

I thought I put it all behind me; every memory, the smell of him, the taste of his skin, the undeniable attraction that burned between us, and the danger he represented to my life.

But one hour had changed it all...

Noah Messina had been back in my life *one* hour and I had taken him into my bed – and into my body, and now I was aching in all the places he had told me I would.

"You have a tattoo." His voice broke through the silence that had built up between us and my entire frame tensed up.

"Yes," I whispered, tugging the sheet up so that my back was covered from view. The light coming from the hallway gave him a clear view of my nudity, and I was suddenly very shy around this man.

I felt the mattress shift under his weight and then the cool night air on my bare skin as Noah's hand pressed against my back, gently pushing me onto my stomach.

Smoothing his hand across my skin, he pushed the sheet down further and trailed his fingers over my skin. "Tre...ach," he sounded out ever so slowly, as he gently touched each letter that ran the entire length of my spine. "Treach..." he tried again. "er...ous..."

His attempts broke my heart.

Hearing him stutter over his words showed a side to Noah that few ever saw.

"Treacherous," I filled in quietly, remaining perfectly still with my cheek touching the pillow, not daring to lift my face and allow him to see my vulnerability.

It was too much.

I was too raw around him.

"It's a warning," I finally whispered, forcing down the huge swell of emotions bubbling up inside of me. "A reminder."

"Of me," he said flatly. "Of what I represented to you."

Noah's hand left my skin, leaving me feeling empty, and I twisted around, watching him in all his naked glory, as he slid out of bed and began to dress.

"Treacherous," he repeated, deadpan, as he slipped on his boxers. "That's how you saw me." Running a hand through his messy hair, he hissed with frustration before dropping his arms to his sides, hands balled into fists.

"Yes," I replied honestly. "That's how I saw you."

"And now?" He asked, eyes torn and full of hurt, as he zipped up his jeans and shrugged his vest on over his head. "Is that how you still see me?"

When I didn't reply, Noah nodded stiffly. "I should go."

I wasn't sure what I was surprised at most; the hurt in Noah's brown eyes as he stormed out of my bedroom, or my heart that was screaming at me to *stop* him from leaving.

Rolling out of bed, I tossed my overly long, knotted hair over my shoulder, and grabbed the sheet off my bed to cover my dignity before racing after him. I made it into the kitchen just as he was stepping through the doorway. "Who's the one running now?" I called out in a much shakier voice than I wanted.

Turning in the doorway, Noah stared hard at me. His eyes raked over me, turning darker than they already were, and my cheeks turned bright pink. "Go back to bed, Thorn," he finally said with a heavy, and almost pained, sigh. "It's better this way."

Tightening my hold on the bed sheet wrapped around my chest, I asked, "better for who?" The hurt in my voice was obvious, but I was beyond pretending. Him being here was throwing me. I couldn't think rationally. I was drowning in emotion, losing myself to my feelings for him and I hated it.

"Better for the both of us," he shot back in an irritated tone, gesturing wildly with his hand. "Look, I can't fucking deal with this right now. I've had too much to drink to think clearly."

"So you're just going to walk away?" I asked, appalled. Shaking my head, feeling too exposed and too weak to argue, I walked back towards my bedroom, forcing myself to look impassive, while my heart was hammering against my ribcage. "Go ahead and leave then. At least I'll know where I stand with you this time," I tossed out, stopping in the hallway outside my bedroom door, unable to stop myself from throwing a jibe.

Dropping his hands to his sides, he balled them into fists and stalked after me. "See, this is exactly why I need to leave!"

Rubbing his face with the palm of his hand, Noah took two steps towards me before stopping abruptly and letting out a groan. "I can't think straight when I'm around you," he groaned. "I need to clear my head and think about what the hell just happened tonight–"

"Then you go right ahead and do that," I shot back, not waiting around to watch him leave – I couldn't bear to. Instead, I slipped inside my bedroom and slammed the door shut before locking it. Rushing over to my stereo, I blasted it to the max, desperate to drown out his voice, and the sound of my perfectly concocted world shattering to pieces.

NOAH

"*T*eagan!" I roared, banging on her bedroom door with my fist. "For fuck's sake, don't be like this."

"Go away," I heard her scream seconds before music blared from her bedroom, obviously intending to block me out.

"You know what?" I roared, kicking the door once in frustration. "Fucking suit yourself," I muttered as I turned around and walked away. My brows shot up in surprise when I walked out of her apartment and straight into...

"Colton?" I shook my head and gaped.

What the hell...

"Noah?" Colt exclaimed, clearly puzzled, as he struggled to rebalance himself. "What the hell are you doing here, man?"

"I could ask you the same question," I replied before embracing my nephew in a hug.

"Dad sent me to make sure Hope got her ass on a plane home," he told me with a grin. "It's good to finally see you, man," he added. "It's been too long."

I hadn't seen any of the Carters since my mother's funeral. I knew it was a dick move, but I had needed space, time to come to terms with the direction my life was going in. And time to take on board the fact that I had a family that wanted me. I'd never had that before them, and I had handled it all fucking wrong. "I needed time, Colt," I told him, hoping he would understand my seven-year absence. "I wasn't exactly in the right frame of mind back then," I added in a gruff tone.

"Dude, shut the fuck up," he chuckled, patting me on the back, before staggering through the open doorway of the girls' apartment. "I'm too drunk for this deep and meaningful talk."

Laughing at Colton's easygoing disposition, I followed him back inside, choosing to remain in the doorway. "Hard night?"

"Like you wouldn't believe." I watched as Colton dug around in the fridge for a moment before removing the orange juice and swigging it straight from the carton. "Dude, I'm totally wasted. It'll be a miracle if they let me board the airplane," he told me with a grin.

"When are you guys leaving?" I asked, curious. Checking the time on my phone, I swore loudly when I saw that it was after six in the morning.

Christ, where the hell had the time gone?

"Now," I heard Hope reply as she staggered down the hallway with a pair of sunglasses covering her eyes, and a baseball cap on her head, looking rougher than I'd ever seen her look before. The case she was carrying wasn't closed properly and items of clothing were hanging out.

"Come on, Colt, we're late," she muttered, shoving her case into her brother's arms and pushing him towards me.

Unfolding my arms, I stepped back to let them pass.

"Yes ma'am," Colt replied, saluting me before he stepped through the doorway. "Wait, where the fuck is the door?" I heard him ask himself in a puzzled tone before going out of sight.

"Oh yeah, mister-I-have-no-respect-for-other-people's-property," Hope growled, poking me in the chest with her finger before rushing down the hallway after her brother. "You owe me a door."

"I'll get it sorted," I muttered, forcing myself not to laugh at Hope being all pissy and hung-over.

When she reached the elevator at the end of the hall, Hope swung around and said, "Oh and one more thing, *Uncle* Noah."

"I'm all ears, my favorite niece," I shot back with a smirk.

Hope shook her head and pointed her finger at me. "I heard you two doing the horizontal dance and if you hurt her again, I will personally hunt you down and kill you slowly. And I should warn you, Noah, I'm like a ghost – you'll never see me coming for you." Smiling, she added in a voice as sweet as honey, "It was good to see you. Don't be a stranger," before stepping into the elevator and disappearing from sight.

Scratching my head, I watched Hope leave, feeling confused and a little fearful for my safety. My phone vibrated in my pocket, and I didn't bother checking who it was before putting it to my ear. Besides, I knew full well who was calling.

"I'm on my way," was all I managed to get in before an impressive string of curse words filled my eardrums.

"You can bet your ass you're on your way," was the first coherent sentence my trainer formed, followed quickly by, "If you're not here in twenty minutes you're on your own, Messina. I'm not fucking around this time. I mean it...Hang on a second," Quincy wheezed down the line, "Are you *drunk*?"

"No," I denied before shaking my head and letting out a sigh. "A little bit," I mumbled after a moment. "Sorry."

"You're a pain in my ass, Messina," he roared. "Get your ass out of whatever broad's bed you're lying in and over to the gym *now*!"

WHEN I WAS OUT OF HER APARTMENT BUILDING AND WAS SITTING in the back of a cab on the way to the gym, I found myself brooding over the woman whose bed I had just climbed out of.

Fucking Teagan had been a huge mistake, not because I didn't want her – I did, *badly* – but because it only complicated an already messy situation.

Yeah, the sex had been incredible, and moving inside her was like nothing else I had ever experienced before – it was like fucking ecstasy and coming home rolled into one; her soft, pliant body beneath me, taking what I was giving, pulling me in – but emotionally, nothing had changed. Teagan still blamed me for our relationship ending, and I still resented her for abandoning me. She had her own twisted beliefs on what happened that night and I had the truth. It wasn't like I had thought that one night together would miraculously erase seven years of hurt and pain, but I had hoped it would make some of the anger I had inside of me fade.

It hadn't.

I was still hurting – worse now than ever.

Treacherous.

Throwing my head back, I thrummed my fingers on my knees, forcing myself to believe that I didn't care. Forcing myself to believe that it didn't cut me open. Seeing that tattoo on her spine and knowing it was directed at me hurt like nothing ever had.

She hadn't even denied it.

The woman who hated tattoos more than anyone, had permanently inked her skin with a symbol of warning.

That fucking tattoo had screwed with my head and knocked the hell out of my confidence.

Teagan really thought that about me.

She considered me dangerous to her – treacherous – when the truth was I would do anything to protect her.

Yeah, I was a fuck up in my past, but I turned it around. I was successful now. I'd made something of myself.

Why couldn't she see past the guy I used to be and see the man I was now?

Because the man I was would do anything to keep her out of trouble.

The man I was now would never take those kinds of risks again.

Dammit, why was I letting her get inside my head like this?

I didn't need this shit in my life anymore. I was a grown ass man and I had seen and experienced too much pain to even contemplate getting back in the ring with that little fruitcake. Teagan Connolly was bratty, childish, and incredibly insecure. She was the worst possible thing for me and I needed to forget about her. In a couple of days, I would be back in the States, and too busy with training to think about anything else.

Especially not her.

So why did you follow Hope home, dipshit, a voice inside my head asked.

Because I *had* to find her.

Because even though she hurt me worse than anyone ever had and drove me batshit crazy, there was just something about her that made it impossible for me to permanently walk away.

Because there was a fierce desperation inside of me, a driving urge that kept leading me back to her.

I was lost when it came to that woman.

There was no escaping her.

TEAGAN

"*H*ope?" I croaked out hoarsely, when I woke up Thursday morning, alone on my bedroom floor, naked as the day I was born, and nursing the headache of all hangovers. "I really need a cuddle right now," I called out weakly. "And some painkillers."

When she didn't answer, I gingerly dragged myself to my feet, and tossed on my nightdress before padding across the hall. Pushing her bedroom door inward, I saw her empty, unmade bed and frowned.

Stumbling back into the bathroom, I showered in a semi-conscious state of awareness. It wasn't until I was out and had dried myself off and had gotten dressed for work that I noticed the lipstick scrawled note on the bathroom mirror.

Gone back to The Hill with Colt.
Call you later.
H. X

"WHAT THE HELL?"

When had Colton been here?

Shaking my head in confusion, I headed into the kitchen on a mission to find some painkillers – and a time machine.

"Whoa," I exclaimed when my eyes landed on the man standing in my kitchen. "Who the hell are you and what are you doing in my flat?"

"Your boyfriend called about getting a door fitted," he informed me, and it was only then that I noticed the freshly painted door hanging where our old one had been.

"Wow, that's impressive," I muttered before stumbling back to his previous statement. "Wait, he's not my boyfriend."

The man shrugged, clearly not bothered about my romantic status.

"I'm not paying you," I added, folding my arms across my chest. I couldn't if I wanted to – my bank account was in the red.

"It's already been taken care of," the man replied before picking up his toolbox and heading over to the door. "The keys are on the counter. You have a good day now," he told me before leaving.

When he was gone, I grabbed the new set of keys off the counter before heading out. Even though the last place I wanted to be right now was at work, especially since Liam and I were in a fight, I knew I couldn't let him pick up my slack.

How I planned to walk into the gym and pretend I was fine and be professional when my whole world had been turned upside down was beyond me, but I would damn well try.

On my walk to the gym, I found myself pouring over last night's events. My behavior toward Noah had been disgraceful. I wasn't so stubborn that I couldn't admit that.

I wondered if I could ever stop being such a manic bitch and just sit down and talk it all out with him like a grownup. I never seemed able to because I could never get past the red-hot flames of rage and desire that took me over whenever I was in his presence.

When I was with Noah, I lost myself in the moment. My brain checked out. I reacted on instinct, on my feelings.

Last night everything had gone from bad to worse, then hot and full of passion, to downright awful, in the space of a few short hours. And in the cool light of day, without any alcohol in my bloodstream, I was embarrassed because of my behavior. I was ashamed of how I had let myself down in front of him.

"Reese fucked me over, Teagan..."

The sincerity in Noah's voice when he spoke those words was so pungent that I would have believed him if I hadn't seen it with my own two eyes.

"...Goddammit, you were my whole life, Teagan. Why the fuck would I have touched her when I had you – a future with you?"

I *didn't* know. That's why it *still* hurt so badly. All those years had passed and I was still stuck in that moment – absorbing all that pain.

"You don't know because you were wrong about me, Teagan. You made a mistake."

God, I think I wanted to be wrong about him more than I wanted my next breath. Noah was rude, and bold, and rough around the edges, and he infuriated me more than any other human being on this planet; but I *wanted* to believe him.

"You're wrong about me, Thorn, and one of these days you're going to realize that."

Those words continued to torment me long after I arrived at the gym and received a frosty reception from Liam. They stayed throughout the rest of the morning, and with them, came the creeping feeling of doubt.

"Tomorrow... When you're aching and throbbing and fucking shivering all over. Remember who made you feel that way..."

Noah's words trickled through my mind, causing me to flush deeply.

He had made good on that promise.

I was aching...everywhere.

NOAH

I was sore as shit and in a sour mood. No amount of exercise or strenuous activity seemed to ebb the antsy feeling inside of my body. I had been off kilter since I arrived here this morning. I was hung-over and thrumming with barely contained anger.

By lunchtime, I had knocked out the three sparring partners Quincy had lined up for me. Lucky was the unfortunate bastard currently dodging my blows.

"Are you still brooding over your girl, Messina?" His voice broke through my concentration, causing me to falter and drop my guard, giving him the perfect opportunity to sock me in the jaw.

"Drop it, Lucky," I growled, shaking off the blow as the sweat trickled between my shoulder blades. I was regretting mentioning to him that I had run into Teagan last night. I was still reeling over what had happened and I didn't need his two cents.

Resuming my rhythm, I danced around on the mat, twisting and jabbing, throwing uppercuts and upsets before landing a sweet left hook to his jaw.

"You guys talking about the smoking hot brunette Noah chased out of the bar last night?" Quincy piped up from outside the ring. "Don't blame you one bit for chasing down a woman like that, Messina. *Hmm...*"

Faking a left hook, I fell back on my left foot before hitting Lucky in the jaw with a straight jab from my right. Fucker went down like a deflated balloon.

"What the hell, Noah," he groaned, sprawled out on the flat of his back.

"What the hell is right, dipshit," I growled, standing over my ex-cellmate. "That's my niece you're talking about."

"I didn't fucking say it," he groaned, taking my outstretched hand and climbing unsteadily to his feet.

"You were thinking it," I barked.

He grinned. "I was so fucking thinking it."

I knocked him on his ass again.

Chuckling, Lucky climbed to his feet and said, "And another thing, I can't believe you fucked her bareback."

"Dammit to hell, man. I told you that in confidence," I snarled. Waiting until he was steady on his feet, I socked him again in the mouth.

"Look around dipshit," Lucky, never one to mince words, pointed out without a second's hesitation, as he rubbed his chin.

I did and realized Quincy had moved to the far end of the room and was on the phone.

"I told you what happened," I hissed in a low tone. "I had too much to drink and got caught up in the fucking moment." *You did it because you want to keep her and you'll do whatever it takes to make that happen,* a niggling voice inside my mind taunted me.

Shaking my head, I forced the thought down quickly, refusing to acknowledge to my brain what my sub-conscience knew was true. "Just drop it."

"And if she ends up pregnant?" He stated without any qualms. "Getting caught up in the 'moment' just might have cost you eighteen years to life, Noah. What do you think about that?"

"Do I look like the kind of man who walks away from his

responsibilities?" I shot back heatedly, glaring at my friend. "Just do yourself a favor, Lucky," I growled, spotting Quincy returning out of the corner of my eye. "And mind your own damn business."

"Alright you two pussies, get back to work," Quincy ordered. "Noah; I wanna see you work more on your right hook. You may be a southpaw, but I want you to fight with both."

"I thought this was supposed to be a winding down period," Lucky groaned, falling into stance once more. "You did win last night, right? Or was I watching a different fight?"

"That's enough out of you, Lippy," Quincy shot back, red-faced. "Dedication is the breakfast of champions." He turned his attention to me and barked, "I don't give a fuck if you're more comfortable with your left, Messina. That right hook of yours is a weakness."

"Come on in here and I'll show you how weak it is," I muttered under my breath before getting back to work.

TEAGAN

The rest of the day passed without a word from Noah, and by five o clock that evening, I couldn't take another second of silence. My nerves were frazzled and I was all out of patience. I had questions, a bazillion of them, and I knew I wouldn't be able to function properly until I got the answers.

"I'm finishing up," I told Liam when I stalked into the office and grabbed my bag and hoodie that evening.

"Are you heading to Krash Saturday night for Steph's thirty-fifth birthday?" he asked me nervously, following me out of the office and through the gym. "You're invited too."

"I don't know," I told him, not really paying attention. I didn't care whose birthday it was and Stephanie Murphy was Liam's cougar friend, not mine. I had only met the woman a half dozen times on nights out. I barely classed her as an acquaintance and Liam was on my shit list.

My only focus was seeing Noah again, and well, the rest I would figure out when I saw him. I rushed out of the office and through the gym; the urgency I had inside me to see Noah was like a driving force, pushing me out of my comfort zone, compelling me to go to him.

I was halfway down the metal staircase when I heard Liam

calling out my name. Reluctantly, I stopped and inhaled a calming breath before turning around.

Liam was delaying me and it was pissing me off.

"Come out Saturday night," he repeated. "I need to talk to you about something."

I narrowed my eyes in suspicion. "About what?"

He sighed heavily. "I was a dick yesterday. I want to make it up to you."

Shaking my head, confused and uninterested, I mumbled, "yeah, fine. Text me the details," before turning on my heel and rushing off.

There was only one gym on this side of the city that was decked out with the caliber of equipment and security that a prized MFA fighter like Noah would require. And I would've bet my last fiver that was where I would find him.

TEAGAN

*M*arching through the entrance of Frankie's Gym several pairs of eyes landed on my face, but I didn't care. I walked straight past the reception desk that was crowded by women dressed like freaking hookers and numerous photographers and reporters skulking around. Obviously, they had come to the same conclusion I had and were looking for Noah.

The man on the desk stood up when he watched me stalk past but quickly sat down again when he noticed my attire. I hadn't bothered changing out of my work clothes that consisted of skintight, three quarter length black gym pants and a yellow t-shirt and I was really grateful that I blended in.

There was an elevator, but I chose to take the back staircase instead. I had a bad omen when it came to elevators in gyms. Besides, I knew where I was going. I had been here several times in the last six months trying to poach their members. The gym was on the first floor. The pool was on the ground floor. Noah wouldn't be in any of those places. No, he would be in the underground boxing ring.

White painted walls and cold concrete floors greeted me the minute I stepped out of the stairwell and into the room, and my eyes immediately honed in on Noah. It wasn't hard to point him out. A six feet four inches, tattooed-covered, sexy as hell fighter kind of stood out against the backdrop of middle-aged paunchy dudes. He was standing in the center of the ring sparring with that blond man I was used to seeing with him on the television every fight night.

"Whoa, little lady, mind stepping back?" The tall, broad, bald-headed man standing outside of the ring with a stopwatch in his hand told me when I approached. I recognized him from the magazines I'd read. His name was Quinn Jones and the man was MFA royalty. "This is no place for a little thing like you."

"Yes," I shot back heatedly. "As a matter of fact, I do mind." Turning my attention to the ring, I cleared my throat and called out, "what did you mean when you said she took advantage of you?"

"Not here, Thorn," Noah growled, as he continued to spar with the blond guy, not breaking his stride to look in my direction.

Refusing to be ignored, I walked over to the half-opened cupboard, removed a pair of gloves and pulled them on before marching back to the ring and climbing in.

Tapping Noah on the shoulder when I reached him, I stood up as tall as I could and said, "now you can spar with me, or you can talk to me," I told him, "but you *cannot* ignore me."

"Teagan," Noah growled in annoyance, spitting out his mouth guard. "Get the hell out of here."

"Teagan?" The gorgeous blond guy announced, taking a step back from us. His face broke out in a wide grin and he shook his head in amusement. "Now I get it."

"*No*, you don't," Noah warned him as he ripped off his gloves and tossed them on the mat before turning his attention back to me. "Leave. Now."

"Not until you tell me what you meant when you said that?" I repeated. I trailed my tongue over my bottom lip, panicked and flustered by this magnificent male in front of me. I itched to run my fingers all over his abs and feel those ridges and grooves, his tattooed covered skin, the dust of hair beneath his navel that was cut off from sight by the waistband of his sweatpants.

Shaking my head to clear my thoughts, I raised my glove-covered fists in front of my face, fell into stance, and jabbed.

He blocked immediately, catching my fist in the process. "I'm not having this conversation here," he hissed, pulling me closer. The smell of man and soap and sweat flooded my senses and I almost groaned in approval.

"Seven years, Noah," I whispered, letting my vulnerability spill out. "I've spent seven years in hell because of *you.*" Breaking out of his grasp, I bounced back on my heels before attacking once more, striking him in the midsection. "You do that with me and you walk out? And now you won't even talk to me – you won't explain." I hit him with all my strength but I was the one who grunted from the impact. "Have you any idea how that makes me feel?" How could he do this; walk back into my world and automatically become the most important person in it?

"I've already explained, Thorn, and you won't fucking hear it!" Stalking towards me, he leaned over me, forcing me up against the ropes. "And I walked out because I didn't want to *fight* with you." He pressed his forehead against mine, and glared down at me, causing the atmosphere in the room to intensify. "Not because I didn't want *you,*" he told me heatedly, eyes flashing with anger.

The air around us thickened and I could feel my body come to life.

Adrenalin spiked through me.

He was so close to me, there was barely an inch between our mouths, and it took every ounce of self-control I had inside of my body not to lean forward and press my lips to his.

"God, I hate you," I hissed through clenched teeth, not meaning it one bit. I hated the way Noah made me feel, and the way he made me doubt everything about myself, but I didn't hate *him.*

That was the problem.

"Of course you do," he sneered. "Now are you done?" He

asked before taking a step back. "Because I need to train and you're in my way. I'll call you later – when you're *stable*."

He turned around, dismissing me, and it infuriated me even further. "You don't get to do this to me, Noah," I called out shakily, moving around him so that we were chest to chest once more. Slapping my fists against his chest, I shoved him hard. "You don't get to walk back into my life, screw everything up and walk back out again."

When he didn't respond, I shoved him again and then again until I was full out hitting his chest. As for Noah, well he didn't even flinch at my touch. He just stood there, his face void of emotion, letting me hit him over and over.

"Don't you dare turn your back on me," I demanded. "I'm not one of your fan girls." Noah was blowing up my world and I was losing control. He was back in my life less than a day and I was a total wreck. "You don't get to treat me like I'm a cheap fuck." I knew I looked demented. Hell, I knew I was *acting* demented, but I couldn't get a grip on myself. I was completely taken over by emotions – by him.

"What do you want from me, Teagan?" Noah demanded, livid. "Jesus fucking Christ." Grabbing my arms, he shook me like a rag doll. "What. Do. You. Want?"

"I want you to apologize to me and mean it," I admitted brokenly. "I want you to tell me that you're sorry for ruining everything we had." Sniffling, I forced myself to look him in the eye, even though I knew I looked and sounded insane. "But most of all, I want you to tell me what *she* gave you that I *couldn't*."

I felt him tense up and for a brief moment I feared he was about to explode, but then he turned to the blond man who was standing uncomfortably in the far corner of the ring.

"Keep her away from me, Lucky," he told him in a flat tone before climbing out of the ring.

"I *loved* you," I called out, voice breaking, as I watched him walk away from me, knocking over every piece of equipment he passed.

"You didn't love me enough!" He roared, slamming both his hands against the door before he walked out.

"You should go home, Teagan." I felt a warm hand clamp down on my shoulder and squeeze gently. "Noah's hurting right now. He needs to deal and he can't do that with you here."

"Don't," I warned the man Noah had called Lucky as I roughly shoved his hand away. "Don't you dare."

"Keep pushing him and he'll crack," he warned me in a calm tone of voice, holding his hands up in front of his chest. "Trust me."

"Not a chance," I hissed before climbing out of the ring and chasing after Noah.

NOAH

I couldn't do this anymore.

I *couldn't.*

I was done this time and I meant it.

No one was worth this fucking agony.

Not even her.

Stalking into the empty changing room, I shed my clothes and stepped into a shower stall. Slamming the palm of my hand against the round chrome nozzle, I flinched when the frigid water hit my skin. Good. I needed to cool down because I was two seconds away from losing it.

"Get your hands off me!"

Teagan's voice echoed through the room and my whole frame tensed up. Goddammit, why couldn't she just go away and let me calm down? It was obvious I wasn't in a clear frame of mind to talk to her, and contrary to Teagan's beliefs, I *didn't* want to hurt her.

Turning around slowly, I watched through hooded eyes as she stalked into the shower area and headed straight for me. My mouth ran dry at the sight of her, my pulse skyrocketed, and my fucking dick was hard in an instant.

"Walk away, Thorn," I warned her as I knocked the water off and tried to step around her. "Before I do something I regret."

"I didn't love you enough?" She screamed, ignoring my

warning, blocking me from leaving. She drew her hand back and hissed, "I loved you too much!" before lashing out at me.

The sound of the slap as her hand connected with my cheek reverberated through the room, taking with it what little self-control I had left.

And in that momentary loss of control, I picked Thorn up and dumped her on the floor of the shower before turning the cold water on her.

Wiping the blood off my cheek from where her nail had caught my skin, I glared down at her as she sat on the cubicle floor. "You're a bad fucking woman for me," I snarled, shutting off the water before backing away from her. Grabbing a towel out of my locker, I tossed one at her, before taking out another and drying myself down. "You mess with my head, you fuck with my performance, and you drive me batshit crazy."

"I d-don't know why I d-did that," she said, teeth chattering, as she crawled out of the stall to retrieve the towel I'd thrown for her. Shivering and with her drenched hair plastered to her face, she whispered, "I d-didn't m-mean to m-make you b-bleed."

Guilt churned inside of me at the sight of her on the floor. Smothering a groan, I moved towards her, a fucking glutton for punishment. Crouching down in front of her, I reached for the towel and wrapped it around her small shoulders. "You've been making me bleed for years," I told her hoarsely, angry with myself for the amount of emotion in my voice. "What's another scratch to the list?"

"You said she took advantage of you," Teagan said. "How?"

Rolling my eyes, I suppressed the urge to roar. "You're like a broken record." Straightening up, I turned around and walked over to my locker. "Just go home, Teagan."

"What did you mean, Noah?" She repeated, not letting it go. "I need to know what you meant."

"You really wanna do this?" I demanded, slipping on my boxers and then a pair of black sweats. "Here?" I gestured at her soaking frame. "Like this?"

"I need you to tell me," she replied stubbornly.

So we were doing this.

Thorn was finally ready to hear my version of events.

Fine.

"That night at the quarry, after I freed you from the car and told you to run, the cops picked me up and took me to the station before charging me." Shrugging on a clean shirt, I slipped my feet into my Nikes before turning around to face her. Keeping my face void of emotion, I folded my arms across my chest as I spoke. "Kyle bailed me out and brought me back to Thirteenth Street on house arrest... he ended up giving Reese a ride back from the station too."

"I hid in the back seat of Kyle's car." Guilt consumed her features when she whispered; "I shouldn't have left you there." She walked over to the bench opposite me and sank down – fucking collapsed.

"I told you to go," I said in a gruff tone, feeling a hole piercing through the defensive armor around my heart. I watched as a lone tear trickled down her cheek and I itched to wipe it away. "I needed you to be safe from them." The thought of JD getting his hands on Thorn had been the driving force behind my decision to get her out of there. I had no regrets about it. JD drove us off the road that night and I was under no illusion of what would have happened if he had gotten his hands on her. He would have made me pay for my defection with *her* blood.

Teagan roughly wiped her eyes with the back of her hand and inhaled shakily. "But I should have *stayed*, Noah."

"Doesn't matter now," I shot back, dismissing her regret and the burning pain in my chest. "I was in a bad fucking way after the crash, Thorn," I said, continuing quickly. "My ribs were all fucked up and I had a concussion, so when Reese handed me a shitload of painkillers I didn't think twice about taking them – before telling her to *go*."

Teagan's face contorted in actual pain, but I didn't let that stop me. I was getting this off my chest once and for all, regardless of the painful memories it was resurfacing.

"And then, when I was out of it and too fucking drowsy to

know who was there," I snarled, chest heaving with anger and pain. "Reese Tanner climbed on top of me and *raped* me."

"No." Teagan's voice was laced with desperation and anger as she shook her head, fervently denying what I had told her – like I knew she would.

"*Yes*," I shot back, just as passionately. "You wanted the truth, Thorn, well there it is."

"She didn't... She couldn't have. I saw you with her," she rambled, voice rising hysterically. "You were *enjoying* it, Noah."

"Because I thought it was *you*," I roared back hoarsely.

"This makes no sense," she muttered, arguing with herself. "I know what I saw." Throwing off the towel she had around her shoulders, she leapt up and paced the floor. "Why didn't you report it?"

"I did, Teagan, and they didn't believe me either – laughed in my goddamn face," I added, running a hand through my hair and laughing harshly. My body was trembling, but I forced myself to continue and lay everything out there. "When I came to and saw you leaving, I lost my goddamn mind and went after you – "

"You followed me?" she whispered, covering her mouth with her hand. She took a step towards me before taking two steps back.

"Damn fuckin straight I followed you," I shot back, chest heaving. "You were my whole life. I wasn't about to sit back and watch you leave me."

"But you said you were on house arrest." Her brows furrowed. "And you totaled your car at the quarry the night before, so how did you even follow me..." Her voice trailed off and her eyes widened as the pieces of the jigsaw fell into place in her mind. "Oh Noah," she croaked out. "What did you do?"

"I broke into your uncle's house, swiped your car keys, and stole your car," I tossed out without shame or remorse. "I wrecked that too, in case you were wondering." I laughed harshly. "Your uncle loved that. Fucker threw me under the bus for it."

"He pressed *charges* on you?" She demanded, appalled, as she closed the gap between us.

"Of course he did," I hissed, throwing my head back in a fucked up mix of pain and agitation. "He wouldn't pass up the opportunity to keep you away from me for an extra year or two."

"I can't get my head around this," she whispered, pressing her fingers against her temples. "I can't..."

"Can't or don't want to?" I shot back in disgust.

She blanched. "What do you mean?"

"You wanted an explanation, and I gave you one. You needed an outlet for your anger and I let you use my body as a punching bag." Reaching out, I caught her chin and lifted her face, forcing her to look me in the eyes and fucking hear me. "But if you're waiting on me to apologize for something I didn't do, then you'll be waiting until hell freezes over."

"You're not perfect in this either, Noah," she screamed, pressing her small hands against my chest, putting space between our bodies. "You lied to me too," she rambled, clutching at straws. "You were supposed to get on that plane with me, but you didn't. You *left* me."

"That was different," I replied flatly, leaning against the lockers behind me.

"How?" She demanded, getting up in my face once again. "How is you leaving me any different?"

"Because I left you to save your goddamn life," I roared, cupping the back of her neck and dragging her closer to me. "They knew you were my weakness and if I didn't fight that night they would have gone after you. They would have used you against me – hurt you to hurt me. I was *always* coming back for you, but I couldn't put your life in danger."

Pressing my forehead against hers, I inhaled short, fast breaths as I struggled to remain in control of myself. "Admit you were wrong, Thorn," I hissed, eyes locked on hers. "Just *say it* and we can move on."

She shook her head as tears trickled down her cheeks. "I can't."

"What the hell is wrong with you?" I demanded, releasing her roughly. "Why can't you just swallow that damn pride of yours?"

"How can I believe you?" She whispered almost frantically as she clawed at her hair. "How can I be sure you're not making this up? You walk back into my life after all these years and expect me to believe this...crap?"

"Because I've *never* lied to you," I roared, furious and hurt. "Not fucking once. And somewhere deep down in that frozen fucking heart of yours, you know it."

"This is too much." Dropping her head, she let out a harsh sob. "It hurts too much."

"It doesn't matter anyway," I said wearily, feeling the last glimmer of hope inside of me shrivel up and die. Shaking my head, I turned around and grabbed my bag out of my locker before throwing it over my shoulder. "Believe what you want, Thorn. I'm done."

She swung around and gaped at me. "What do you mean?"

"I mean it's over, Teagan," I told her. "I'm done."

"Why?"

"Why?" One word that caused the rage inside of me to explode violently. "*Why*?" I repeated again, unable to believe my fucking ears. "Are you actually asking me that?"

"Yes why," she choked out, rushing around me to block the doorway. "Why did you come back for me? Why did you sleep with me and tell me all this if you're done?"

"Because I wanted to prove a point," I roared in her face. "I wanted to see if I could still get you on your back with your legs spread open, and it turns out I can." I was an asshole – being unnecessarily cruel to her, and I knew I should stop, but I was fucking wounded. She didn't believe me. She doubted me like every other motherfucker and I couldn't get past it. "You were an itch I needed to scratch Teagan. That's all."

"Fine," she screamed. "Walk away. Leave me."

I didn't respond. Instead, I turned my back on her and stormed out of the changing room.

"Wanna talk about it?"

Those were the first words Lucky said to me when I walked through the doors of the gym.

I shook my head.

"Just get me the hell out of here, man."

"I'm on it." He fell into step with me as I stalked up the back stairwell of the gym and out into the street.

Cameras flashed in my face the second I stepped out the front entrance and into the heavy shower of rain.

People called out my name, looking for a picture and an autograph but I couldn't do it.

Not today.

Not with the fucking blonde fruitcake from my past and that look of disbelief in her eyes. Goddammit, fighting was my sanctuary and in the ring I was king. I couldn't afford to lose focus. I had to stay in control. Teagan was blowing everything I had spent the last eighteen months working for to pieces.

"Noah, wait!" Teagan called out when I reached the rental car, and I threw my head back and cursed loudly.

Ignoring every ounce of common sense I had inside of me that was demanding I ignore her and walk the fuck away for once and for all, I turned around.

TEAGAN

Fear of losing him permanently propelled me as I scrambled through the crowd that had formed outside the entrance of the gym, calling out his name at the top of my lungs. "So that's what this was all about for you – to prove a point?" I asked, breathless when I reached his side. "Why would you do that to me?"

My eyes landed on the cut on his cheekbone and I cringed. I shouldn't have put my hands on him. Violence was never the answer. I knew this, but when I was around him, my brain checked out and my heart did the thinking. And right now, my heart was hurt, angry, and confused. I was losing it.

Everything I had worked for was crumbling down around me. I was falling in love with him all over again and it was overwhelming me.

"Careful, Thorn." Noah's words were laced with sarcasm as he glared down at me. "Keep chasing after me like this and I'm gonna start to think you care."

"I *do* care!" I shot back, teeth chattering, as my whole body trembled. "You think I walked away and didn't think about you?" I knew that's what he thought. "Well you're wrong. I did think about you. Every day. Dammit, Noah, I left because I *loved* you," I admitted, voice breaking. "And the pain of your betrayal hurt me more than anything in my entire life."

"I'm not doing this with you again," he warned me.

Rain poured down on us, soaking our clothes, exposing my vulnerability and his. And when Noah turned to get into the car, I lost it.

"Don't go!" I strangled out, grabbing his forearm to stop him from climbing into his car – to stop him from leaving me.

"Give me one good reason to stay," he roared, his big body trembling, as he gripped the car door with more force than needed.

Stay because I can't bear the thought of losing you again.

Stay because I'm a fucking mess without you.

Stay because I'm never as alive as I am when I'm with you.

Stay because I need you in my life...

All of the reasons I had inside of me and I couldn't speak a word. I couldn't make my lips form them because I knew that If I admitted it out loud – if I verbalized the fact that I had been wrong about Noah, that I was to blame for my own broken heart and seven years of misery – then I would be to blame for him being left in a prison cell alone to rot, and I was fairly certain that guilt would consume me.

I was in love with him before I knew the truth, and now, I felt like I was drowning in emotions.

But instead I just stood there like the stubborn coward I was, begging him with my eyes to not leave, feeling the ground disintegrate beneath my feet as he retreated from me.

"I thought so," he growled, pulling his hand roughly away.

I stood motionless, with my hands wrapped around myself, as I watched Noah turn away from me and climb into the passenger seat. He slammed the door shut and stared straight ahead as the car pulled off.

NOAH

"*D*amn, that was painful to watch," Lucky said when we were back in my hotel suite. Grabbing an armful of beers and a bottle of tequila from the minibar, he dropped them down on the coffee table in the sitting room before going back for a couple of shot glasses. "What a fucking train wreck." He let out a heavy sigh as he flipped the cap off with this lighter. "And her face when we drove away?" He shook his head. "I've never seen a woman wear devastation like that."

"Let it go," I warned him. Walking over to the couch, I sank down, bone tired and demoralized. Leaning forward, I rested my elbows on my knees and dropped my head in my hands.

The image of Teagan's tearstained face and her voice when she asked me to stay was haunting me. I didn't need Lucky's running fucking commentary. I'd experienced the devastation firsthand.

"It's over," I added in a gruff tone. "Case closed."

"You've got a serious case of denial, man. The worst I've seen." Shrugging, Lucky took a slug of his beer from his bottle before settling down on the couch next to me. "Do you love her?"

Letting out a groan, I rubbed my face with the palm of my hand before grabbing my beer off the table and swigging it back. "You've met her – you've seen her in action. I'm not a masochist, dude. I don't take pleasure in having strips torn off me. Of course I fucking love her." Whether I still loved her or not didn't change the facts. And the facts were Teagan and I couldn't be in each other's company without arguing.

Slamming the bottle back down on the table, I picked up the shot glass of tequila Lucky had poured out for me and tossed it back.

"I can't *not* love her," I hissed, feeling the alcohol burn through me. "But I can't trust her either," I admitted gruffly. There was so much hurt still there, so much fucking water had gone under the bridge that I wasn't sure if we would ever get past it.

"Why?" He straight-out asked me.

"Because –"

"Because she walked away?" He filled in for me. "And you're afraid that if you let her back in she'll do it again?"

"All right, Dr. Phil," I grumbled sarcastically, feeling a little unnerved that Lucky had hit the nail on the head. "Give the psychoanalysis a break."

"Messina, there's a reason you took the fight against Bishop – and it's the same reason you didn't use protection. You know it and so do I," he told me. "It's because of her."

Of course it was because of her.

Everything I had done since the age of seventeen was because of *her* – because to me, she was *everything*.

That's why it hurt so fucking much when I looked her in the eyes today, told her the truth, and was met with disbelief.

"Doesn't matter anyway," I tossed out. "By this time next week, I'll be back on home soil and won't have time to think about her."

I had a nationwide tour of North America with the MFA coming up. I was flying home in a couple of days and should be concentrating on that. I didn't need the distraction and fucking upheaval in my life that came with loving that woman.

I needed to put her in the past.

"You sure about that?" Lucky asked, unconvinced.

"Abso-fucking-lutely." Slugging back the remainder of my

beer, I nodded firmly, forcing myself to believe my own words even though deep down I knew it was my pride talking; the absolute fucking hurt and horror of having Teagan look me in the eyes and *not* believe me. "Once I'm back on the road she won't even be on my radar."

"What a fucking horrifying feeling that must be," Lucky mused sadly. Shaking his head, he stood up and stretched his arms out. "To push the one person you've worked so hard to prove you are worthy of away."

"What?" I asked, deadpan, with my bottle resting against my bottom lip.

"You *love* her, Noah," Lucky shouted. "And the girl I met today loves you right back, man." He threw his hand up in the air, clearly agitated. "Every move you've made since I've known you has been to get *her* back. To prove to her that you are *worthy*. Because in your mind she is *it*. And that fucking terrifies you. Be honest with yourself, man," he said earnestly. "You are scared shitless that it's not enough – that *you* aren't enough –"

"Of course I'm scared!" I roared. "She drives me crazy." Flinging my beer bottle across the room, I jerked to my feet, agitated and fuming. *"She* is fucking crazy. I never know where I stand with her," I snarled, chest heaving. "There isn't a damn thing I wouldn't do for that woman and the thought alone terrifies me." I ran a hand roughly through my hair and hissed in frustration. "Thorn has the ability to bring me to my knees, Lucky. She is fucking *lethal* to me."

"So fucking what," he countered, not missing a beat. "Love is crazy. It's insane, and that burning intensity you two share?" He shook his head. "That's rare, man. That's a once in a lifetime kind of deal."

"Why do you even care?" I asked, furious. "What's it to you?"

"Because you're my brother, dipshit," Lucky shot back just as furious. "You're my fucking family, man, and there's no way in hell I'm gonna sit back and watch you walk away from your future."

"What do I do, man?" I choked out. "How do I fix this?"

"You do what you do best," Lucky replied, patting my shoulder. "Fight."

Lucky was right.

Teagan had been the focal point of my life since I was seventeen years old. I could lie and pretend to myself all I wanted but the truth was still there. And the truth was, Teagan Connolly was all I had ever wanted and I was fairly certain she was all I would ever want.

I needed to fight for this.

I needed to fight for *us*.

TEAGAN

Teagan

"*D*id you get dressed without drying again, Teegs? You look like a drowned cat."

Those were the first words that came out of Sean's mouth when he opened his apartment door and noticed my appearance.

In the heat of the moment and in the middle of my mental breakdown, Sean was the one person I could think of to go to. Hope was in America. I didn't have any family. And Liam...well, Liam wasn't an option anymore. "I can't...breathe," I gasped, as I barreled into his arms and held onto him for dear life, crying hard and ugly. "I can't...oh god, Sean..."

Raped.

Noah said he was raped.

Reese had raped him.

I believed him.

And I left him there to deal with it alone.

"Babe, come on. Calm down," Sean coaxed as he walked us both into his apartment and set me on the couch.

Dragging the throw off the back of the couch, Sean

wrapped it around my shoulders before heading into the kitchen only to return with a massive bar of chocolate in his hands.

"You know, I don't think I've ever seen you cry," Sean mused, when my cries had turned to sniffling. Sinking down on the couch beside me, he pulled me onto his lap. "What happened?"

"Noah happened," I whispered, clenching my eyes shut and burying my head in his chest. My mind flashed back to the scene I'd caused at the gym and a wailing noise tore through me. I was so ashamed. "I've screwed everything up, Sean."

"Noah?" Sean asked, confused, waiting for me to fill in the blanks.

"Messina," I muttered, forgetting that Sean didn't know the ins and outs of my tempestuous relationship with my ex.

His brows rose in surprise and he leaned back to look at my face. "As in the fighter?"

"As in my ex," I admitted sheepishly.

His lips curled into a perfect O as he gaped at me, unblinking. "Well I wasn't expecting that," he breathed, eyes burning with curiosity. "You mentioned you had an ex from America, but I didn't realize you were talking about *The Machine*."

"He wasn't *the machine* when I knew him," I whispered sadly. "He was just...Noah."

Resting my head on his chest, I found myself confiding in Sean; filling him in on every dirty detail of my life starting from the night I watched my mother take her final breath in that car, to Liam breaking up with me when Uncle Max relocated us to Colorado.

I laid everything out there about my time at Thirteenth Street; the good, the bad, and the downright awful parts that made me look like a lunatic.

I told him about how I wrecked Noah's car with the paint, the night that had sparked this crazed obsession, and every other moment that had followed.

The nights I spent at the Ring of Fire, watching Noah take on men twice his age.

I told him about Noah saving me from Gonzalez, and the

numerous occasions he had protected me from George and JD Dennis, taking beatings to be with me.

My face heated when I told him about the night in the elevator.

I broke down when I explained about the night Max disowned me.

I disclosed every slither of crucial information that had led me to this moment, every single event in my life that had brought me to this point, grateful to get it off my chest, and Sean listened intently, never judging, never interrupting.

"And then he broke my door down so I slept with him before throwing him out," I heard myself say and cringed. "But then I got mad because he left, so I went to Frankie's and caused a huge scene." Groaning, I added, "I slapped him and he tried to drown me...and now I'm here."

Sean let out a whistle. "And all of this happened in the space of twenty-four hours?"

"What can I say," I mumbled, cheeks burning. "We had a lot to catch up on."

Jumping to his feet, Sean went into the kitchen, returning a few minutes later with a pair of glasses in one hand and two bottles, one with vodka and the other with coke, stuffed under his arm.

"When I first saw you at my door, I thought chocolate and a *Friends* marathon would be enough to cheer you up." Setting the glasses and bottles down on the coffee table in front of us, he leaned over and pressed a kiss to the top of my head before pouring our drinks. "But now I'm thinking we need vodka to deal with this shit storm."

"Why do you have to be gay, Sean?" I asked with a sigh, taking the glass he was holding out for me. "It's not fair," I grumbled, taking a sip of my vodka and coke. "You're the perfect man."

Sean chuckled. "You have no idea how many women at the salon ask me that question." Settling down beside me, he clunked his glass against mine and sighed.

"Do you think I'm crazy?" Sitting cross-legged on the couch,

I plucked a loose thread off the cushion on my lap and said, "to be this...*devastated* over a man I dated for two months in high-school?"

"Officially two months," he corrected, pointing his finger in the air. "Unofficially, a hell of a lot longer and deeper than that."

"What if he can't get past it?" I squeezed out. "I've been going over and over it, and if I were in his shoes, I don't think I could." Covering my face with my hands, I stifled a groan. "And just say that he *can* forgive me. What if it's different now?" I whispered. "What if that fucked up, bloodlust chemistry between us fizzles out?"

"If you don't try, you're going to spend the rest of your life wondering and regretting," he told me.

I knew he was right, but I was terrified.

I never wanted to feel the pain of having my heart broken by Noah Messina again, intentionally or not. I wasn't sure I would survive that kind of aching twice in my lifetime.

"I'm nothing out of the ordinary, Sean," I admitted. "And Noah? He lives in different world to us. *Supermodels* drop their knickers for him like they're giving him his five fruits a day. There's no way I can compete with that."

"You don't have to compete with anyone, Teagan. That's what you don't seem to get," he said. "That man flew halfway across the world and landed on your doorstep." Shaking his head, he sighed impatiently. "That doesn't say the end of the line to me."

"It doesn't?"

"No, Teagan, it doesn't," he shot back with an irritated tone. "It says the man is driven by desperation, devotion and *love*." Slapping his hand down on my thigh, Sean squeezed and said, "he's here, he's hot and he's fucking yours. So what are you going to do about it?"

TEAGAN

I spent all day Friday curled up in a ball on my bed ignoring phone calls from Liam and avoiding contact with the outside world, basically too ashamed to lift my head off my tear-soaked pillow. I didn't eat breakfast or lunch. I didn't have the appetite. Noah's voice remained in my mind; his face the fore point of my every waking thought all day long and I couldn't stop tormenting myself with the ugly truth.

Noah had done serious time in prison.

Because of me.

He broke his fucking bail.

Because of me.

Max had pressed charges on him.

Because of me.

He was at the quarry that night.

Because of me.

He gave up his own freedom to keep me safe.

Kyle Carter had been right all along. I hated the way that man was *always* freaking right. It was so infuriating. I should have listened to him. I should have listened to my heart and not my stupid pride. Look where pride had gotten me. Seven years of bitterness and regrets.

"I wanted to prove a point. I wanted to see if I could still get you

on your back with your legs spread open, and it turns out I can. You were an itch I needed to scratch Teagan. That's all."

Pride and stubbornness kept me from running back to him – from throwing myself at his feet and begging for forgiveness. The hurt in his eyes haunted me. I saw it in those brown depths. I saw the pain I had caused when I questioned him. I also saw the truth.

To be honest I couldn't understand why he had given me the time of day, let alone taken all my crap when I had let him down in the worst possible way. I was emotionally drained and feeling sorry for myself, and no amount of chocolate and alcohol stemmed the pain.

By Saturday afternoon, the depression had well and truly set in and so had the hunger. I made a pot noodle in the microwave and I ate it half raw, not bothering to cook it any longer. I didn't deserve fully cooked meals anyway. When I finished my crunchy pot noodle I did something I hadn't done in years.

Taking my guitar out of its case, I settled the strap on my shoulder and grabbed a pick. I hadn't played since I was eighteen, I couldn't bear to; but the moment my fingers touched the strings, I realized it was like riding a bike.

Allowing my fingers to glide over the strings, I closed my eyes and sang my own acoustic version of Johnny Cash's *Ring of Fire*, finger picking my way through the instrumentals, falling into the sweet melody.

Feeling every note right down in my core, meaning every lyric that spilled from my lips, I belted out the chorus at the top of my lungs, releasing with it all the unspoken words festering inside of me.

My front door flew inward and I fell off the couch, mid song, taking the hit to my body in my bid to protect my guitar.

"Jesus Christ," I hissed as I lay on the flat of my back gaping up at Sean who was standing in the doorway of my apartment. "How'd you get in?"

"It was unlocked, babe," Sean announced cheerfully as he sauntered into my apartment with a bunch of beauty products in his arms. Dropping what he was carrying on the kitchen countertop, he made his way over to me. "Nice voice by the way," he added, taking my guitar from me and setting it back in its case. "I didn't know you played."

Climbing to my feet, I rubbed my hip that was stinging from breaking my fall. "I used to play," I muttered, confused. "I was sure I locked that door." In fact I was certain. Hope and I had many arguments over the years because I was so, and I quote, 'anal' about keeping the apartment secured.

In my defense, Hope had never been kidnapped out of her sleep by a tattooed muscle head or chased down by the mob. I reckoned my habits were well justified, which was why I was so surprised at myself for leaving the door unlocked last night.

"Stop delaying," Sean said, shoving me down the hallway and into the bathroom. "Get your ass in that shower," he ordered, flicking it on. "I'll find something for you to wear."

"What...Hey – stop," I hissed, slapping his hands away when he tried to forcibly remove my t-shirt. "What are you doing, you Perv?"

"Teagan," Sean shot back, rolling his eyes. "Trust me when I say that you have *nothing* I want to see. No offense."

"None taken," I grumbled, slapping his hand away when he moved for my shirt again. Forcing Sean to turn around, I stripped quickly and climbed into the tub before pulling the curtain around me. "So tell me why you've barged into my apartment and manhandled me into the shower?"

"I'm staging an intervention," I heard him call out, and then the sound of drawers clanging open and shut filled the air. "No way in hell am I allowing you to wallow in your own self-pity for another night."

"Sean?" I asked nervously, when the sound of a hairdryer roared to life. "What are you doing out there?"

"*We* are going to Stephanie's birthday bash with our friends," he informed me. "And *you* are going to be the best dressed female there."

"No, I'm not," I groaned, leaning my head back, letting the water wash over me. "I can't –"

"You're coming out with me, Teagan," Sean said in a warning tone. "If I have to drag you there kicking and screaming." Seconds later, a razor was thrust around the shower curtain and into my hand. "Shave," he ordered. "Everything."

———

LESS THAN TWO HOURS LATER, I WAS HAIRLESS AND HAD BEEN poked and prodded in more places than I cared to remember. Thanks to my flamboyant friend, I was feeling tipsy from our pre-pub drinks and coated in a fresh layer of fake tan and dolled up more than I'd ever been in my life.

Sean had insisted on curling my hair so that it was flowing loosely down my back, with little sprigs of glitter and tiny clear colored jewels in it. He had completed my look with smoky eyes and clear glossy lips.

"Well, you are a miracle worker," I conceded as I admired myself in the full-length mirror in the bathroom. Dressed in a short white dress with sky-high beige wedges and a matching beige blazer, I had to admit Sean had mad skills in the style department. "Jesus," I breathed in amazement, cupping my tiny breasts that looked amazing with the bold plunging neckline of the dress. "I actually look like I have more than fried eggs."

Sean threw his head back and laughed. "Your breasts aren't small," he assured me, as he clamped his hands down on my shoulders and led me back into the kitchen. "They're perky," he offered, smothering his laugh with his glass of vodka and coke. "Men like perky."

"They do?" I cocked one finely shaped brow and grabbed my glass off the counter before taking a sip. "Name one man who'd take small and perky over big and bouncy?"

"Oh, I don't know," Sean teased. "Perhaps a particularly fine-assed fighter kind of man?"

"Don't," I whispered, cringing at the thought. Dropping my head, I felt what small semblance of excitement I had built up disintegrated. "I fucked everything up," I whispered, feeling more disappointed in myself than I had felt before. "He hates me."

"Babe, I am nowhere near close to being drunk enough for round two of *that* conversation," Sean announced, draining the last drop of his vodka and coke and setting the empty glass down. "So just put him on the back burner for tonight," he added before grabbing his jacket and shrugging it on and heading for the door. "Tomorrow you can go right back to moping around in your pajamas."

As I trailed after Sean, a long, thinly shaped box on top of the counter caught my eye.

"Hang on," I called out, making a beeline for the box. "What's this?" I hadn't noticed the box being there earlier, but then again, Sean had dumped so much on the counter it made it sort of impossible.

"Oh yeah, I found that outside your door when I got here," Sean replied, walking back to me. "I forgot to mention it." Shrugging, he added, "Well hurry up and open it."

Lifting the lid of the box, my eyes widened when I saw the lone red rose inside, with a single thorn on its stem. Resting beside it was a small white card.

"It's from Noah," I whispered, biting down on my lip, cheeks burning. Only Noah would send me a rose that resembled the tattoo he bore on his side. Excitement fluttered inside of me as I picked up the card and read the inscription.

Tick Tock.

"TICK TOCK?" SEAN, WHO WAS LOOKING OVER MY SHOULDER, asked. "Wow, that's...romantic?"

"What do you think he means?" I asked quietly as I lifted the rose out of the box and cradled it to my chest.

I knew I looked like an idiot, standing in my kitchen

clutching a jagged edged rose like it was my lifeline, but to me it *was* a lifeline. This stupid flower was giving me hope and I couldn't stop grinning like an idiot.

"It's beautiful, Teegs," Sean placated as he took my rose and placed it back in its box. "But I didn't spend the last two hours slaving away so that we could analyze a fucking flower." Grabbing my keys and purse, Sean thrust them into my hands before shoving us both out the door of the apartment.

"What do you think he meant by that?" I asked, struggling to maintain balance in my skyscraper wedges as Sean half dragged me down the stairwell. "Tick tock?"

"Maybe it's a sign," Sean replied when we got outside. Waggling his eyebrows, he wrapped his arm around my shoulder and chuckled. "His way of telling you it's only a matter of time before he rocks your world again."

I wasn't sure, but I had a definite bounce in my step for the rest of the evening.

NOAH

$\mathcal{J}$ spent the next two days training like a goddamn animal and punching my way through my problems, fighting my frustrations away.

By the time Saturday evening rolled in, all I wanted to do was find Teagan and try and work through this shit bomb of a relationship we had created. Enough time had passed by for us both to cool down, and now it was time to work this shit out. But apparently, I didn't have a say in my plans for the night because Nick Leversteen, the CEO of the MFA had flown in to Cork and was on his way to speak with me in person.

He was due to arrive any minute and I was dressed like a fucking idiot to welcome him. Honest to god, I felt like I was being pimped out here.

"Why am I dressed like this?" I growled, glaring at my coach who was responsible for my attire. Pulling roughly at the tie I had on, I loosened it before rolling up the sleeves of my black shirt. I wasn't a suit man. I was too big and they were always too fucking tight. My arms were constricted in the fabric of my shirt, and my thighs were bulging against the material of my black suit pants as I paced the floor of my suite. I was an ex-con, illegal fighter turned professional fighter – not a fucking businessman.

"Do you know what this means for your career?" Quincy

declared for the fourth fucking time in the space of an hour and I had to resist the urge to strangle him. "Having the big man himself meet you in person?"

No, I didn't fucking know what it meant because the stupid old fool hadn't explained to me what the hell was going on.

Lucky, who was sitting calmly on the couch sipping on a beer and smoking a cigarette, winked at me. Oddly enough, his calm disposition was having a soothing effect on me and I sank down next to him. Patting my thigh, he passed me his cigarette and I took it gratefully, inhaling a deep drag.

"None of that shit now, ya hear?" Quincy warned me, swiping the cigarette from my hand and stubbing it out with his thumb and forefinger. "Keep those toxins away from my boy, Lippy," he growled, glaring at my ex cellmate. "He's conditioning right now so keep your degenerate antics to yourself."

Lucky threw his head back and laughed. "Hear that, Messina?" He asked, highly amused. "General Dickhead thinks I'm a bad influence on you."

A knock sounded on the door of the suite and I smothered my laugh as Quincy's expression changed from murderous to enchanted.

"Be on your best damn behavior," he told me, leaning down to rearrange my tie. "And let me do the talking. And *you*," he hissed, pointing at Lucky. "Keep your trap shut."

Lucky shook his head when Quincy rushed off to answer the door. "What fucking ever, man," he muttered, nudging my shoulder before taking another sip of his beer. "Just be yourself, man."

"Nick," Quincy welcomed. "Long time no see, old friend. Come on in."

Standing up, I walked over and greeted the three men standing with Quincy – each one kitted out in finely tailored suits.

"Noah Messina," Nick Leversteen announced, eyes alight.

Ignoring Quincy, he stepped towards me and extended his hand.

"Nick," I acknowledged, shaking his hand firmly. I'd only

met the boss man once before – back when I first signed with the company.

"Did you watch my boy's last fight?" Quincy interrupted, obviously not trusting me to speak for myself. Wrapping his arm around all our bosses shoulder, Quincy led the men over to the couch area. "Impressive, huh? Noah's got one hell of a left hook."

"How's it going, man?" Lucky acknowledged when Nick took a seat beside him. He tipped his bottle in Nick's direction before taking a swig.

Quincy's face turned purple and I shook my head in amusement as I followed after them.

No one was changing Lucky.

Sitting down on the coffee table, I listened to the pleasantries and boring as fuck small talk between the three men and my coach, nodding every once in a while when Quincy gave me the eye.

To be perfectly honest, I didn't have a clue what was happening and I cared even less.

All I wanted to know was that I wasn't getting fired, and once I learned the answer to that question – when Nick mentioned a pay rise – I pretty much zoned out, letting my thoughts trail to Thorn.

Always Thorn...

Her heartbroken expression, when I left her at the gym, was still in the fore point of my mind – not by memory – because the fucking paparazzi had snapped it.

I wondered if she had seen the front page of this morning's papers. I seriously doubted it because knowing Teagan, she would have thrown a colossal tantrum at the sight of having our private life splashed all over the papers. I was used to it – this was my life now. I'd signed up to being in the public eye, but she, on the other hand, had not...

My cell phone buzzed in my pocket, distracting me from my thoughts, and I pulled it out quickly. Checking the screen, I swiped my finger across it and put it to my ear before getting up and walking into the bedroom.

"Tommy. How's it going, man?" I asked, sinking down on the edge of my bed. He had stayed in the states, organizing and preparing everything for the tour next week and to be honest, I hadn't realized I was missing the fucker until he called me.

"Not good, man."

"What's wrong?" I asked, tensing up.

"Don't freak out okay," Tommy placated. "I have everything under control..."

"Tell me," I gritted out.

"Your rental house was broken into last night," he said with a heavy sigh. "Nothing was taken," he added quickly. "And the cops already have three teens in custody. They're convinced it was just some overzealous fans."

"Is that it?" Shaking my head, I sagged in relief. "Shit, man, I thought something was wrong."

He was silent for a long time and a trickle of unease crept up my spine. "What *aren't* you telling me?"

"It's weird, Noah," he confessed. "Nothing was taken, but there was...there was something weird about it."

"Weird how?"

"Newspaper cuttings," I heard him say. "Scattered all over your room."

"Cuttings of what?" I asked him, confused.

"Of you, man," he told me. "From yesterday's papers right back to your arrest seven years ago."

"Well shit," I muttered. "Cole?" I asked, thinking it might be an intimidation tactic on my competition's behalf.

"Not his style," Tommy replied without hesitation. "I'm just... look, I could be completely wrong when I say this, but I think you need to watch your back."

"You think it's someone from before?" I asked, frowning.

"I can't say for sure, but there were pictures of you and Teagan," Tommy whispered. "Pre-jail pictures, man. Why would anyone from your present have those?"

"What kind of pictures?"

"Stills of you and *her* in the elevator that night."

"Fuck." I knew that fucking CCTV footage would come back to haunt me someday. "The press?"

"They're already on it, man. It's everywhere here," he told me. "Should be reaching your side of the world by the a.m. And another thing," he added in a low tone. "There's been some... talk around this neck of the woods."

"About?"

"The Ring of Fire being back up and running."

"God fucking dammit, Tommy!" Jerking to my feet, I paced the floor as my skin heated with anger. "He's back in business?"

"Should I call the cops?"

"And sign your own death certificate?" I shook my head and snarled. "Don't you fucking dare," I warned him. "Involve the police, Tommy, and you won't make it through the night, man. That prick has eyes and ears everywhere." I knew that better than anyone. There was a reason the Ring of Fire had gone undetected for so many years; brown envelopes and dirty cops.

"What do you want me to do?" He asked nervously.

"Go about business as usual," I instructed him. "Keep your head down and your goddamn mouth shut."

"Noah, I'm..." his voice broke off and guilt churned inside of me.

"I know, man," I whispered. "I don't blame you."

"Messina!"

Growling in agitation when I heard my name being called, I spoke in a low tone, "Look, I know you're scared, man, and you should be. But whatever you do, Tommy, do *not* go to the cops –" I paused mid-sentence when Quincy poked his head around the door.

"Come on, kid," he told me, eyes twinkling with excitement. "Nick wants to hit the town to seal your brand new deal."

"I'm coming," I told him, waiting for him to leave before putting the phone back to my ear. "Tommy, I have to go," I muttered. "I'll be back in a few days and I'll sort it out. But just... just hang low until then."

"Be careful, Noah," Tommy whispered down the line.

"You too, man," I replied before knocking off the call and

sinking down on the bed. Leaning forward, I rested my elbows on my thighs and covered my face with my hands.

One phone call and I was reminded of exactly why I didn't get close to anyone. There was no getting away from my past. There was only one way this was ending.

Either he died or I did.

There was no other way around it.

The bedroom door creaked open again but this time it was Lucky. I watched as he closed the door behind him before walking over to the bed and sitting down beside me. He didn't speak a word or ask me any questions. He just waited.

"JD's back." I choked out when I was ready to talk.

"What's the plan?" He asked in a quiet tone, looking me straight in the eye. "Can't sit back on this, man," he added, knowing all about my past. Hell, he'd had five long years in a jail cell to learn all about it. "We need to deal with this – get him before he gets you."

"It's too dangerous," I whispered, "I'll sort this on my own."

"*We* will sort this together," Lucky corrected me, eyes flashing with anger.

"I can't ask you to get involved in this, Lucky. It could cost you your life, man," I growled, jaw clenched. "You don't know the kinds of people JD's mixed up with. He has people *everywhere*." I knew first hand about JD's pull. Money talked and power pulled. JD Dennis had both. "Dirty lawyers. Bent cops. Indebted inmates. There's a reason he wasn't caught all those years ago." Exhaling heavily, I whispered, "You don't know him like I do, man. He gets in your head." I tapped my temple in frustration. "Takes away everything fucking good until all that's left is the bad."

Memories of my mother locked away in that institution flooded me and I jerked to my feet. "You don't want any part of this," I told him as I paced the floor. "Trust me."

"You seem to have confused me with a man who has something left to *lose*," Lucky snapped, standing up and shoving me hard in the chest. "All I got in this whole damn world is you, Noah. And I'll be fucked if I sit back and let you handle this on your own. So it's like I said earlier, *what's the plan?*"

If this was anyone else I wouldn't think twice about refusing their help, but Lucky could handle himself.

He'd seen the ugly side to life.

He had this carefree attitude that hid truth that lurked just beneath the surface.

And that truth was Lucky was darker, and seen darker shit during his time in prison, than I could comprehend.

He knew what it felt like to drain a man of his life, and he would do it again without a second's hesitation if I asked him to, and he knew that I would do the same for him.

That was a fucking bond like I'd never experienced before.

It was like he said; he was my brother.

"It's gonna be close to impossible to find him," I told him. "He has a remarkable talent for going to ground and disappearing."

"Fair enough, but you've got one thing going for you that you didn't have before," Lucky replied, strategizing. "You're Noah fucking Messina. You're a celebrity man, in the public eye. JD can't get to you directly and he knows it, which means..." He paused mid sentence and shook his head.

"Which means?" I demanded, heart hammering in my chest.

"Which means he'll have to use another method to flush you out," he replied in a flat tone. "He's gonna bait you, man. Spider web tactics. Have you come to him."

"Bait me with what?" I hissed, furious. "Those fuckers took everything from me seven years ago."

"I can think of one exception," Lucky shot back. "A sassy, little blonde with a mouth like a sailor."

"No!" I shook my head, rejecting the thought that I had once again put her in danger. "No goddamn way. It's been seven years. She's off their radar."

"You sure about that?" He countered. "It's like you said, Noah, no one is ever truly off their radar, not men like JD, so why would he forget about the girl you walked away from his father for?" Shaking his head, he sighed heavily. "I hate to tell you, man, but whether you want to admit it or not, that woman is your kryptonite and your enemies know it. That makes her the *only* target."

"Fuck," I hissed, pulling at the ends of my hair in frustration. He was right. Lucky was *always* fucking right about this kind of thing. He had killer instincts, and an adept ability to think like the bad guy. "I need to get her out of here. Someplace safe."

"Look around, Noah. We're in the back ass of nowhere in Ireland, man. There's nowhere safer for her to be," he interjected confidently, appeasing me just a little. "JD obviously hasn't traced her down here," he added, "so let's concentrate on keeping it that way.–"

Lucky paused when the door flew inward, slapping against the opposite wall.

"Come on, you pussies," Quincy snarled, glaring at us. "You don't keep Nick Leversteen waiting."

"Jesus fucking Christ, Q," I roared. "Give me a damn minute."

"We're coming," Lucky interjected, patting my shoulder. "Calm down, man," he whispered in my ear before pushing me out the door. "We've got this."

TEAGAN

Teagan

*O*n the walk to the pub, I made a silent vow to *not* cause any scenes, but the dynamics of the night changed drastically when I walked into Reilly's bar and locked eyes on none other than Ciarán fucking Crowley, perched at our usual table with Eoin, another hurler but less touchy feely than his captain, Stephanie the cougar, Imogen, a girl I was only vaguely familiar with, and Liam.

Three rounds in and I was quickly learning that coming out tonight had been a massive mistake. Aside from the evil glares and snide comments Ciarán was throwing my way, Liam was in a horrible mood. He dutifully ignored me and froze me out of every conversation, purposefully keeping his back turned to me, which was quite a feat considering we were sitting at a round table. Besides Sean who was his loving self, Imogen was the only other person who made a conscious effort to include me, but it was clear that I wasn't welcome.

When my phone rang just as I was draining my fifth Cosmo, I felt like weeping in joy. Slipping out of my seat, I shoved through the throngs of people inside the bar and out the front.

"Hi, Teegs."

"Hope!" I sagged in relief at the sound of my roommate's voice on the other line. "Are you okay?"

"I'm okay," I heard her say quietly.

"Are you crying?" I asked, appalled, sticking my finger in my other ear to drown out the bustle around me.

"Oh, Teagan," she sobbed down the line. "He's engaged."

"Who's engaged?" I asked, confused.

"Jordan."

"What? No he isn't." I shook my head, rejecting this mind fuckery. "Hope, he can't be."

"He is," she sniffled. "Oh god."

"Where are you?" I asked, worried.

"I just landed at Shannon," she told me. "I should be home in a few hours –"

"Dammit," I muttered when the line went dead. I slapped my piece of crap phone with my hand in frustration before trying to switch it back on, but it was lifeless.

"Having a good night?" Stephanie's husky voice came from behind me and I jumped before swinging around and receiving a mouthful of second hand smoke.

"I've had better," I spluttered, waving my hand in front of my face to blow the smoke away from me. "Happy birthday, by the way," I offered as an afterthought. "You look great." She did look great and it sucked. Stephanie was wearing a red bodice style dress that emphasized her large bosom and killer curves, complimenting her flaming red hair.

"Can I give you some advice, sweetie?" she asked, before sucking on her cigarette. "Woman to woman?"

"No, but I get the feeling you're going to give me some anyway," I muttered under my breath as she closed the gap between us, dwarfing me by a good four inches.

"Stop stringing Liam along," she said cattily. "He's one of the good ones and you made him look like an idiot."

"Excuse me?" I blanched, not sure I was hearing this right.

"You've led him on for years." Stepping closer, she brushed a tendril of my hair back off my shoulder and smiled sweetly. "Sleeping with him only to break his heart."

"Whoa," I interrupted her, having heard quite enough. "Just back up a minute." I held my hands up, backing away from her, determined not to make a scene.

Liam and I weren't together, and with the exception of that one drunken night months ago, *nothing* had ever happened between us. But I'd be a liar if I said I wasn't fuming that Liam had discussed it with *her*. This outing was really starting to show the wolves from the lambs and I was left with a bitter taste in my mouth.

"I have no idea why you're bringing up my personal history with Liam into this conversation, Stephanie," I told her, forcing myself to remain calm. "But if it's because you want to get with him then by all means be my guest. He's a free agent."

"It would have been nice of you to let him know that before your dirty laundry was splashed all over today's papers," she hissed.

"What?" I shook my head and gaped at her. "Seriously...what?"

"Oh come on, Teagan," she sneered, rolling her eyes. "Don't pretend like you don't know what I'm talking about."

"I'm not pretending," I shot back, feeling the heat creep into my cheeks. This woman was on some special sort of drugs. What a freak. "I genuinely have *no* idea what you're talking about."

"There you are!" Sean's voice filled my ears seconds before his arm came swooping around my shoulder. "Are you ready to hit the club?" He asked as the others filed out of the bar.

"That woman is such a bitch," I muttered as I watched her walk arm in arm down the street with both Ciarán and Liam.

"Now, now, Babe," Sean chuckled, tucking me into his side and protecting me from the cold. "Jealousy is an ugly trait."

"I'm not jealous of her, Sean," I shot back, disgusted he would even think that. "She's welcome to Liam, since he apparently likes to talk about his bedtime antics." Knowing

Liam had told her about us made me sick to my stomach. Memories of how he had treated me when we were teenagers flooded me. He was the same rat bastard who had dumped me during my very first blowjob, then jumped into a relationship with another girl from school before the bed was cold. I was far from pristine but Liam was no knight in shining armor either.

"Then what's the problem?" Sean asked when our friends were well out of earshot.

"I'm mad because she had the cheek to corner me outside the bar," I grumbled. "And start spurting all this crap about how I should have thought about Liam's feelings before my dirty laundry was splashed on the papers." Shaking my head, I leaned closer into him. "That woman is warped."

"Ahh...about that," Sean chuckled nervously when we reached the entrance of Krash Bar. "You kind of made the front page of today's papers with Noah."

"What?" I shrieked, twisting around to gape at him. "And you didn't think to tell *me*?"

"I thought you already knew," he replied, grinning shamelessly as he paid us into the club. "And that's why you were holed up in the apartment."

I removed my jacket and took Sean's one out of his hands before handing them into the cloakroom attendant, along with my bag.

"No," I hissed following after him as he stepped into the club and made a beeline for the bar. "I didn't fucking *know*. If I knew I wouldn't be *here*." I gestured around and then back to myself. "And especially not dressed like this!"

"Well we're here now," he said cheerfully. "And you look fierce. So let's just enjoy the night."

"Fine," I muttered, ordering a round of tequila and paying for it with the emergency twenty I had stuffed into the cup of my dress. "But I'm getting drunk," I told him as I sprinkled a dash of salt on the back of my hand and then his before quickly licking it off and tossing my shot back. Grabbing a slice of lemon, I shoved it in my mouth and sucked, cringing when the salty tang was overpowered by the bitterness of the lemon juice.

"Guys, are you coming?" Imogen called out, waving us over to a security guarded door. "Stephanie just talked us into the VIP section upstairs."

"We're coming," I called out before snatching Sean's shot and tossing it back. "Consider it compensation for your omission of the truth," I slurred, patting his chest with my hand.

Sean raised his brow and smiled. "Come on you little firecracker," he chuckled, taking my hand and helping me over to the door. "Let's get you away from the bar for a while."

Surprisingly, security did let us up the staircase to the VIP section and I snickered when we reached the top of the stairs. "I wonder which one Steph the Cougar slept with to get a free pass in here."

"Never mind which one of them she slept with," Sean muttered, pointing towards the far corner of the room.

My gaze trailed over to where Sean was pointing and my heart sank into my ass. "Oh crap," I whispered, coming to an abrupt stop the second my eyes landed on Noah. He was in one of the leather booths on the other side of the dance floor, surrounded by staff, fans, and *our* fucking friends.

Disgust and envy flooded me as I watched Stephanie squeeze past the other men who were sitting in the booth. When she reached Noah, I watched like a hawk as she leaned into his ear. I couldn't hear what she was saying to him, the music was drowning everything out, but when Noah nodded once and Stephanie pulled out her phone, gesturing for the others to follow her, I quickly figured it out.

I was fairly certain that my mouth was hanging open as I watched our friends all squeeze into the booth to get their picture taken with Noah. "Did she just..."

"Sit on his lap? Yep." Sean filled in for me, watching the same spectacle unfold, as Stephanie sank down on Noah's lap and wrapped her arms around his neck, flaunting her big breasts in his face like a weapon of male destruction.

"Come on, Babe," Sean said in a determined tone of voice, reaching for my hand. "Let's squash this."

I shook my head when he took my hand to lead me over. "I'm not going over there," I told him as panic clawed its way out of my stomach and into my throat. Tonight, I was determined to be on my best behavior. No outbursts and no slapping, but Stephanie was pushing me. Seriously, that woman was number one on my throat punch list. I watched Noah as he smiled and placated his admirers. Envy swirled inside of me. It was a natural emotion for me and when it came to Noah Messina, jealousy was my middle name. Tugging on his hand, I dug my heels into the plush carpet. "I mean it, Sean. I...I need to go."

"No," he countered, dragging me across the dance floor to the booth where our friends were fan-girling all over my ex. Shoving me forward, Sean kept a death grip on my hand. "You need to step up," he argued. "That is your man, Teagan Connolly. So get off your high horse and go claim him."

"What if he doesn't want to be claimed?" I asked, admitting my deepest fears. "What if we go over there and he ignores me?" *Or worse, walks away again...*

"Well, it looks to me like you have two choices," Sean grumbled. "You can either go over there and face him like a woman, or be a coward and let Stephanie sink her claws into him. Pick your poison, Teagan."

"Okay," I whispered, steeling myself for rejection and giving up the fight of trying to break away from Sean. I was going to have to face Noah sometime. I knew I didn't deserve him, but I wanted him badly enough to make a fool of myself trying. Noah was worth swallowing my pride, and as Sean had so sweetly pointed out, getting off my high horse for. I wanted to be the woman who went home with him tonight. Pathetic or not, there it was. I wanted Noah Messina more now than when I was seventeen and I was, once again, willing to bend my morals in order to be with him.

I was in serious shit.

NOAH

*N*ick and his men didn't stay long, just long enough to sign and raise a toast to my extended contract, before leaving to catch his flight.

He'd put a tab on the bar for us for the rest of the night, with strict instructions for me to let loose and enjoy myself before the grueling training started up next week.

Letting loose and enjoying myself was a fucking impossible thing for me to do after the information I had received tonight, but I was trying.

It was like Lucky had said; if they knew where she was, they would have got to her by now. Teagan was safer here than anywhere else, and I needed to calm my ass down.

Quincy was celebrating the good news by drinking himself into a stupor and mauling every woman that looked sideways at him. For a man in his forties, Q had the stamina of a horned up teenager.

Lucky was being his normal self; cool, calm, collected and completely unfazed by the multi-million dollar contract I had just signed – or the women who were throwing themselves at us.

I watched in amusement as he continued to drink it up, all the while fending off overly friendly female admirers, grinning and politely declining every offer, like I knew he would.

I had met the kind of women he messed around with and I knew full well that none of the women that had approached us tonight would work out for him.

He was a fuck and chuck kind of man.

One night only.

The guy had two rules he lived and fucked by – never bring them home, and never go back for seconds – and none of these women fit that bill.

The women here tonight were good women, horny and up for a good time, but no way in hell would they be up for the kinds of things he was.

To be fair to Lucky, it was a good fucking rule, guaranteed to keep feelings and emotions out of it, but sometimes it bothered me that nothing seemed to faze him. It was like that part of Lucky had checked out years ago when his girl was killed and he was just...blank inside.

Sitting back with a beer in my hand, I felt on edge as I studied everything that was going on around us. As much as I tried, I couldn't fucking relax. I was coiled tight with tension, waiting for that prick to make his next move...

"You're Noah Messina, right?" A smoking hot redhead asked, stepping into my line of vision and distracting me from my thoughts.

"The last time I checked," I replied dryly. Never mind the fighting; I deserved that huge ass pay rise for putting up with this constant fucking interruption into my life.

Stifling back a growl, I put on my professional face and asked, "what can I do for you, Red?" even though I already knew what she wanted.

They only ever wanted two things; my dick and a photograph.

Well, one of those was out of bounds, so I gave her the nod for the picture.

Squealing, she flagged down her gang of friends and waved them over before squeezing past Quincy and Lucky and landing her ass down on my lap.

"I watch all your fights," she purred as she wrapped her

arms around my neck and posed while her friend snapped away with her phone. "You are so much *bigger* in real life."

"I bet," I grumbled, resisting the urge to toss her on the floor. "Are you done?"

"Just one more," she promised before calling out, "Guys, come here. I want a photo of all of us with The Machine."

"Jesus Christ," I muttered under my breath. "Fine."

"Excuse me," the brunette who was taking the photos said to Lucky. "Would you mind taking a photo of all of us with Noah?"

"Sure thing," Lucky chuckled, standing up and taking her phone, highly amused at my discomfort. "That's what I'm here for."

I glared at Lucky who was laughing his ass off at my expense. He knew I hated this shit.

Within seconds of calling her friends over, I was surrounded by three guys and the brunette, who had settled down beside Red.

I tolerated the photographs, I even did the small talk and pretended I was interested, but when Red dropped her hand, I'd had more than enough.

"No chance, sweetheart," I growled in her ear. I wasn't putting out. She needed to discover some boundaries and learn not to put her pussy on a taken man's lap. "Up. Now."

"What's the problem?" Red purred, clearly not taking the hint, continuing to massage my dick with her hand. "I'm not looking for anything serious," she added, "just one night with no strings."

I wasn't fucking buying, but from the hungry gaze Quincy was giving her, he was, so I stood up and dumped her on his lap before sitting back down.

"Not interested?" Lucky chuckled, bumping my shoulder with his when he sat down beside me.

"If I'm getting my dick wet, I can guaran-fucking-tee it won't be her pussy around it," I growled, feeling pissed off and flustered.

Swiping a bottle of Bud off the table in front of me, I

chugged it back, draining it dry. "I need to go see her, man," I hissed, slamming the empty bottle back down on the table. "I can't fucking sit here and pretend nothing's wrong."

"Your luck just rolled, Messina," Lucky replied in a low tone, inclining his head towards the dance floor. "Looks like the bait has come to you."

My eyes scanned the room and locked on Thorn. She was huddled next to a lanky, blond – clearly gay – guy who was trying to force her over to our table.

All of my anger over the way she had treated me the other day evaporated the second I laid eyes on her, which was what always happened; I couldn't stay mad at her and I couldn't stay away from her.

I wished she would hurry the fuck up and make her decision. I needed to know whether I was chasing after her ass tonight or not.

A burning ache settled in my chest and I found myself rubbing the skin over my heart as I watched her. Jesus Christ, she looked like an angel, dressed in white with that blonde hair of hers flowing down her body. All she was missing was the halo.

"An angel with a devil tongue," Lucky piped up, reading my thoughts, and I smirked.

Teagan had a tongue like a cobra; venomous and posed to strike when threatened. She was constantly on guard and I loved the fact that I had always been able to penetrate those walls she built around herself.

From day one I had gotten underneath those walls she put up to keep people out. Problem was, it was the same for me.

At some point between wrecking my car and breaking my heart, she had gotten under my skin and had become my greatest weakness.

Slapping my shoulder, Lucky added in a serious tone, "see man, she's perfectly fine," before getting up and making his way through the crowd to the bar.

"Hey there," Teagan's companion said cheerfully when they reached our table. "Mind if we join you guys?"

"It's actually pretty full here, Sean," Red replied in a sickly-sweet tone, lifting her head from Quincy's mouth long enough to speak. "Maybe you guys should find somewhere else to sit."

Teagan's face turned bright pink and that protective streak inside of me roared to life. "Then move," I told the redhead without hesitation.

Red gaped. "Excuse me?"

"Sit down, Thorn," I said gruffly, ignoring the annoying fucking viper, eyes locked on Teagan as I shoved up and made room for them to sit.

The friend I now knew as Sean took the spot furthest away from me, giving Teagan no option but to sit next to me. I made a mental note to buy the man a drink later.

Teagan looked like a skittish foal as she maneuvered her way around the table before sitting down beside me, using her hair as a curtain between us.

"My name's Sean," the friend gushed with a smile, leaning over Teagan to shake my hand. "I'm a huge fan of yours, Mr. Messina."

"It's just Noah," I replied, accepting his hand. I could feel Thorn's body trembling as she kept her head down and spent an uncharacteristic amount of time studying her neatly trimmed fingernails. "And thanks for the support," I added, and oddly enough meant. "Appreciate it."

"Could I...bother you for a photo?" Sean's cheeks reddened as he looked from Thorn's face to mine. He smiled almost guiltily. "Please?"

"Yeah," I agreed, smirking when Teagan's head snapped up and she mouthed the word *traitor* to him.

"Great," Sean chuckled, pulling his phone out of his pocket, visibly sagging in relief. Clambering awkwardly over Teagan, he knelt in front of me with his phone held out for a selfie.

When he was finished taking his picture, I tossed him my phone and drew Teagan into my side, holding her possessively, letting all the fuckers here know *don't touch*. Sean's eyes lit up as he took several pictures with my phone.

"Now," I whispered into her ear when her friend returned my phone to me. "I'll have a photograph of you."

She nodded once before dropping her head to stare at her hands again.

"You're not gonna talk to me?" I asked after a moment, highly amused at this coy version of Teagan. She was usually all piss and smoke. It was why I loved her. Reaching for my beer, my hand grazed her bare thigh and she jumped. "Easy baby," I chuckled, before leaning back and snaking an arm around her. "I've touched you in far more intimate places."

"I don't really know what to say to you," Teagan said in such a quiet voice that I had to lean closer to hear her properly. "Well, obviously I do know what I *should* say," she added, eyes cast downward. "But I really don't see how it can change things now." Sighing heavily, she whispered, "Never mind. I'm rambling."

"You look real fucking good tonight," I told her, wanting to put her at ease. It was obvious she was on edge and I didn't want her to feel that way around me. Clamping my hand down on her smooth, bare thigh, I shifted closer, aligning my body with hers as I leaned into her ear. "Stop hiding your face from me," I whispered, tucking a curl behind her ear. "Look at me."

She shivered and looked me up and down slowly before flushing the color of the sun. "You look...dapper," she choked out. Throwing her hands up, she covered her face and sighed heavily. "The clothes." She gestured at my attire. "That's what I...meant."

"I'm just out of a meeting," I replied, smirking, enjoying her eyes on me. Fucking loving the way she looked at me with that hungry glint in her eyes. "You know me, Thorn," I added huskily. "They can put a suit on me, but they can't change me."

"I don't want to change you," she blurted out of nowhere. "I want to own you."

Her words caught me unaware and I blanched.

"You already do," I said slowly, eyes locked on her face as I tried to gauge her reaction.

She looked so unsure as she searched my face, desperate to see if I was joking.

I wasn't joking.

I meant every word.

I felt it right down in my bones when she reached over and took my hand in hers, entwining our fingers. The feel of her flesh on mine fucked with every fiber of my being and set me on fire.

Jesus, I was burning for her.

I could smell her – she was all coconut scented shampoo and woman – and I leaned closer, breathing her in, reveling in her. Loving her more than she would ever know.

A large group of women approached us then, shoving their way into the booth and asking for a picture.

Teagan's face fell when I got up and stood for a photo with the women and I felt weirdly guilty. Like I'd done something wrong by just doing my job.

After I politely declined their offers of buying me a drink, I sat back down next to Teagan, and growled in frustration when she slid further away from me.

"What?" I asked. "You're pissed at me for taking a damn picture now?"

"I'm jealous," she shot back without an ounce of hesitation. "I don't like girls throwing themselves at you, Noah." Looking me in the eye, she tucked a stray curl behind her ear and scrunched her nose up in distaste. "Especially ones with plastic tits and peroxide hairstyles."

"Yeah." I grinned. "Those ones are the worst."

"It makes me sick to my stomach," she grumbled huffily. "Seeing them touch you and paw you and...ugh!" she threw her head back and sighed, clearly flustered. "We're supposed to be in a fight and here I am bitching and moaning like some jealous girlfriend when I have no right."

"Do you know how many nights you've kept me up?" I asked in a soft tone, tipping her chin up towards me. "Every. Single. Night."

Leaning in, I pressed a hard kiss to her lips. I couldn't

fucking stop myself. She was so adorable when she was being all pissy and cute.

"You have no reason to be jealous," I told her, stroking her pouty bottom lip with my thumb. "They can look, they can talk, they can invent all the imaginary stories they want, but at the end of the day, it doesn't change a damn thing for me," I assured her. "Because I only want you."

"Really?" She was shaking so bad the vibrations were running up my leg and wreaking fucking havoc on my self-restraint.

Looking in her eyes, I wanted so much to give her my all. I wasn't going to lose her again. "Come back to the hotel with me," I whispered. Fuck tact. I needed her. Right fucking now. No fucking way was JD getting his hands on Thorn. I didn't care what I had to do to keep her safe. I would do it and I would do it gladly. She was my goddamn life. I wasn't letting a hair on her head go astray.

"I can't," she moaned weakly, shifting closer to me.

"Why not?" I purred, clenching her hip tightly.

"What about...Sean," she breathed, eyes dark with lust. "I came here with him."

"He'll survive without you," I told her in a gruff tone, "I won't," I finished before crushing my lips to hers.

Snaking my tongue out, I licked her bottom lip and immediately she opened up, giving me access. Her fingers dove into my hair, tugging and yanking, as she kissed me back with a desperation that mirrored mine.

"Say it," I dared her, breaking the kiss, eyes locked on her pretty face. When she shook her head, I caught her chin between my thumb and forefinger and forced her to look at me. "Say it, Thorn," I repeated in a gruff tone.

One word.

That was all I needed.

One fucking word.

"Say it and we can move on."

My heart was hammering in my chest.

This was it.

The moment I had waited seven years for.

She believed me.

I could see it in her eyes, all the guilt and regret.

People were watching us, obviously noticing she was the woman from the papers, and a few were even going as far as taking pictures with their phones.

Fucking let them.

I was too immersed in the conversation unfolding to care.

My focus was entirely on *her.*

"Noah, I'm...I'm..." Teagan opened her mouth and then shut it quickly. "I need to cool down," she blurted out before slipping out of her seat. "I need to... Sean," she hissed, grabbing her friend's hand and dragging him out of his seat.

"Stubborn as ever," I muttered to myself as I watched Thorn escape to the dance floor. Oh yeah, she was sorry. But I needed the words.

"I'll see you in the a.m., boys," Quincy piped up with a shit eating grin on his face as he slipped out of the booth, arm in arm with the redhead.

Stopping in front of me, Red leaned into my ear and whispered, "Last chance, big boy."

"I'll pass," I replied flatly, taking a swig of my beer.

"Your loss," she spat before shimmying out of the booth and attaching herself to my coach.

"Christ, Quincy better not take a leaf out of your book with that one," Lucky, who had arrived back with two beers, chuckled as he sat down beside me. Passing me one bottle, he took a deep drink from the other before saying, "Women like that are a dime a dozen with an eighteen to life commitment fee."

TEAGAN

"You're not gonna talk to me?" Noah asked, leaning closer. Stretching his hand out to grab his beer, he accidentally grazed my bare thigh and that was all it took to make me squirm. Heat crept through my body, starting in my toes and settling on my cheeks. "Easy baby," he chuckled. Leaning back with his beer in one hand, he placed his other around the back of my seat. "I've touched you in far more intimate places."

"I don't really know what to say to you," I admitted quietly, knowing I needed to lay it all out there, but *really* not wanting to. "Well, obviously I do know what I *should* say," I rambled, feeling like a tool. "But I really don't see how it can change things now." I was far too tipsy for this conversation and Noah looked entirely too good to argue with. If I didn't get the words out right this would end in disaster and that *terrified* me.

"You look real fucking good tonight," he told me. Dropping his hand to my thigh, Noah shifted closer to me and leaned into my ear. "Stop hiding your face from me," he ordered in a soft tone, tucking a curl behind my ear. "Look at me."

I did look at him and it caused my body to ignite in a raw spasm of lust. He was too much. Too beautiful. Too everything. "You look...dapper," I blurted out before mentally kicking myself. Throwing my hands up, I covered my face and stifled a groan. "The clothes." I pointed to the black shirt, tie and suit pants he had on. "That's what I...meant."

"I'm just out of a meeting," he replied, enjoying every minute of my discomfort. "You know me, Thorn," he teased, gesturing to his clothes. "They can put a suit on me, but they can't change me."

"I don't want to change you," I heard myself say. "I want to own you."

My declaration caught us both by surprise and I watched in horror as his brows shot up. "You already do," he replied slowly, frowning at me like I was a puzzle he couldn't quite figure out.

Well, he was my puzzle; all six feet four inches of his tattooed, ripped and perfectly molded body. And he was a puzzle I desperately wanted to solve. I searched his face for truth, and when I found it in his eyes, I reached out and took his hand in mine, wanting nothing more than to fall into this man and never resurface.

He only had to look at me and my heart went crazy in my chest, hammering against my ribcage, demanding to get to him. It was like I had no control over it. I felt myself being physically drawn to Noah, edging closer and closer...

"Oh my god, Oh my god!"

"Noah, we love you!"

The chorus of women's screams as they lunged for Noah enraged me. I watched horrified, as Noah smiled and nodded at the women, and when he stood up to take a group picture with them I thought my head would explode. The women threw themselves at him – they literally fucking threw themselves at *him*. I was burning with jealousy. I couldn't hide it. It was obvious, etched all over my sour expression, even when he returned to my side. "What?" Noah asked, more like growled in frustration, as he studied my face. "You pissed with me for taking a damn picture now?"

"I'm jealous," I admitted without an ounce of shame. He knew that about me anyway. I wasn't revealing a new ugly trait.

It was on him if he was surprised. "I don't like girls throwing themselves at you, Noah. Especially ones with plastic tits and peroxide hairstyles."

Noah grinned in amusement, which only pissed me off more. He was loving this. I knew he was. It was clear from the smug expression on his face that my discomfort was amusing him. "Yeah," he purred. "Those ones are the worst."

"It makes me sick to my stomach," I hissed cattily. "Seeing them touch you and paw you and...ugh!" I threw my head back and groaned, feeling so damn worked up. "We're supposed to be in a fight and here I am bitching and moaning like some jealous girlfriend when I have no right." I was pathetic. Completely and utterly pathetic...

"Do you know how many nights you've kept me up?" he asked in a soft tone, interrupting my thoughts, as he tipped my chin up towards him. His brown eyes speared me when he whispered, "Every. Single. Night." Leaning forward, he pressed a rough, hard kiss to my lips before pulling back to stare into my eyes. "You have no reason to be jealous," he assured me, stroking my lip with his thumb. "They can look, they can talk, they can invent all the imaginary stories they want, but at the end of the day, it doesn't change a damn thing for me. Because I only want *you.*"

"Really?" I panted, unable to stop the tremors that were racking through my body.

"Come back to the hotel with me," he asked – no, he ordered.

"I can't," I whispered, though everything inside of me was screaming, *yes!*

"Why not?"

"What about...Sean," I breathed. "I came here with him."

"He'll survive without you," Noah growled, cupping my neck, dragging me closer. "I won't."

The minute his lips touched mine a fierce throbbing ignited low in my belly, my pussy clenched, and my body welcomed him home. Plunging my hands into his sexy, disheveled hair, I dragged his face closer to me, and clung to him, kissing him back with everything I had.

"Say it..." Noah growled, ripping his mouth from mine. Tipping my chin upward, he leaned forward, looked into my eyes and whispered, "Say it, Thorn. Say it and we can move on."

"Noah, I'm...I'm..." I opened my mouth to speak, but the stupid words wouldn't come out. Dammit, why was it so hard for me to admit that I had been wrong? "I need to cool down," I finally blurted out before scrambling out of the seat.

"I need to cool down...Sean," I hissed. Needing to get out of the environment that was overwhelming me, I grabbed Sean's hand and dragged him out of the booth.

Smirking, Sean nodded and followed me onto the dance floor. "Babe, he is out of this world," he called out over the music, wrapping his arms around my waist and drawing me closer to him as N-Trance's *Set You Free* blasted through the speakers.

"Less talking, more dancing," I shouted back as I worked my ass off, grinding, thrusting and jiggling, and basically pulling out my best sexy moves. Wrapping my arm around Sean's neck I shook my hair out, and swayed against him, all the while looking over his shoulder at Noah's table.

When I noticed his empty seat, my heart accelerated in my chest and my step faltered.

Stepping back from me, Sean grinned and pointed towards the bar before slipping away.

"Where are you going?" I called out moments before two hands clamped down hard on my hips and dragged me backwards into a wall of rock hard muscle.

"Does it make you feel good?" Noah growled in my ear. "Knowing you're affecting me."

"Am I?" I breathed, resting my head against his chest, swaying my hips to the music.

"What do you think?" He growled, thrusting his crotch into me. I could feel his arousal digging into my back and it was turning me on like nothing had before. I felt drunk and dazed, and erotically horny, as I moved against him. Noah's strong hands on my skin were all I could feel – all I ever wanted to feel for the rest of my days on this earth.

Noah Messina had me.

The fucker had all of me and he knew it.

The hypnotic sound of the dance music hummed around us, cocooning us in our slick soaked bubble of lust.

He held me close, with his large, bruised hand splayed across my stomach, like he was claiming me, like he was marking his territory.

The song ended and quickly rolled into Jason Derulo's *Want To Want Me.*

Not missing a beat, Noah took my hand and twirled me away before pulling me back towards him again, dropping one large hand to press against the bare skin just over my ass.

He moved incredibly. He was all ripples and rock hard groves as his muscles bunched and strained underneath the fabric of his black shirt.

I was breathless with lust and panting as I tried to keep up with him. He led me, and even more surprisingly, I let him. He was fucking me with his eyes and claiming me with his expression.

His predatory smile told me it was going to be rough, hard and all night long.

I couldn't freaking wait.

He was just so big and huge and handsome and full of life.

Every woman in the club was drawn to him and it had absolutely nothing to do with his celebrity status and every-thing to do with his raw animal magnetism. He was alpha male perfection.

Dipping his face, he pressed a fast kiss to my lips, pulling back quickly and then turning me around so that my back was against his chest.

Sprawling his hand across my lower belly, he thrust against my ass, pulling me closer with every grind, hitting every fucking spot.

Noah moved to the beat, grinding, pressing, touching,

moving in perfect sync with the sound playing from the speakers. I was lost to him.

"Hmm." Raising my hand above my head, I cupped his neck and rested against his strong chest, letting him have me. His hands on my body, owning me, taking control of me was undeniably welcome. I wanted to give myself up to him again. All my power. All my trust.

"We're going to bring it right back, now folks," the DJ called out over the microphone as the song came to an end. "Here's a little number from a few years back."

The lights darkened and everything slowed down.

Pulling me closer, Noah rested his cheek against my head as he moved us slowly.

My hand looked so little, felt so incredibly fragile against his as the lyrics of Wyclef Jean's *911* rang through my ears, setting alight a fire in my heart I knew I could never douse.

With one hand wrapped around mine, and the other pressed firmly against my lower back. Noah looked down at me, immersing me in the brown hue of his eyes as the music drowned out my racing heart that hammered against my ribcage.

"I got your gift," I told him. "I have to say, I wouldn't have put you down as a flowers man, but I loved it."

Noah looked down at my face and frowned. "What gift?"

"The red rose with the thorn?" I smiled like an idiot. "It was sweet."

"I don't know anything about it, Thorn," he replied, shaking his head. "I didn't send you any flowers."

"Oh, and I suppose you don't know anything about the card either?" I teased. "What the hell was up with that anyway?"

"What card?"

I rolled my eyes. "Oh Noah, come on. Stop pretending –"

"What card?" he asked, his voice rising.

"The one in the box," I heard myself whisper.

"What did it say, Teagan?" He demanded, stopping mid-dance. His gaze darkened, actually, he looked kind of murderous. "Tell me."

"Tick tock," I told him, feeling uncertain and afraid.

Noah's body tensed and he let out a string of curse words, but I didn't have a chance to dwell on it because the sound of glass smashing nearby startled me.

I swung around to see what the hell was going on. My heart sank when my eyes landed on Liam who was having a full-blown meltdown, kicking over tables as he stalked towards me with a face like thunder.

"Just keep walking, Liam," I told him when he reached us. "*Please.*"

"It's bad enough you're all over the papers with him," he slurred, glaring at me. "But you have to rub it in my face now too?"

"Am I missing something here?" Noah asked in a heated tone.

"No," I replied, eyes locked on Liam, willing him to fuck off. "Absolutely nothing. So just leave me alone, Liam."

"Oh, I'm nothing now?" Shaking his head, Liam pointed his finger in my face and roared, "you're a heartless bitch. A fucking *whore*!"

Oh god, now you've done it, I thought to myself seconds before Noah shoved his hand away.

"Say that again, asshole," Noah snarled, as he stood chest to chest with Liam. "I fucking dare you."

"Noah, don't," I screamed, diving between them. Placing my hands on his face, I forced him to look at me. "Hey," I coaxed, desperate to calm him and stop him from doing something he could get into trouble for. "Don't do this." Even with the skyscraper heels I had on, Noah still towered over me by a good five inches.

"He doesn't get to talk to you like that," Noah snarled, clearly livid, as he inhaled short, fast breaths. "No goddamn way, Thorn."

"I know," I coaxed, stroking his face. I kept my body between both men as I turned around. "You need to go, Liam," I warned him. "You need to walk away right *now*!"

"So you don't want a relationship with me, but you're

prepared to be this guy's next fuck?" he demanded, furious. "What the hell, Teagan?"

"You have no idea what you're talking about," I shot back, trembling. I never wanted to hurt Liam, but this needed to stop. He was acting like I had been unfaithful to him, when in fact, the only person my heart felt like I had been unfaithful to was Noah. "So drop it."

"Have you fucked her?" Liam demanded, goading an already worked up Noah.

"Liam," I hissed, mortified. "Shut up."

Clamping his hands on my hips, Noah dragged me backwards and into his embrace. "I've had her in ways you couldn't begin to imagine," Noah shot back, furious.

"Oh, this is perfect." Shaking his head in disgust, Liam let out a harsh laugh. "You don't even know him, Teagan!"

"He's Noah, you asshole," I screamed, losing all tact and what was left of my patience. "He's *Noah*," I repeated, voice breaking with emotion. "*My* Noah!"

"Yeah, the great Noah Messina," Liam sneered, and then his eyes widened in realization. "Wait a fucking minute," he hissed, looking at Noah and then shaking his head. "Noah as in your ex?" Liam gaped at me. "The ex?"

"The ex, the current, and the fucking future, asshole," Noah snarled, pushing against my back.

Sniffling, I nodded my head. "And I love him," I added, throwing it out there. Everything had gone to hell anyway. I couldn't see the point in denying my feelings anymore. With drunk, pointless tears streaming down my cheeks, I let out a quivering sigh. "I'm in love with *him*."

Noah's hands tightened on my waist. "You do?" He whispered.

Nodding, I wiped my cheeks with the back of my hand and exhaled a sharp breath. "I never stopped."

Turning me in his arms, Noah's attention was focused solely on me. "Say it, Thorn," he said in a tone thick with emotion as he pulled me flush against him. "I need to hear you say it, baby."

"I know you do," I whispered, clutching his arms. "And I'm sorry for making you wait seven years to hear it –"

"Don't worry, Messina. I took real good care of her while you were gone," Liam interrupted from behind me, taunting Noah and destroying the moment. "I had a real good time keeping your bed warm!"

The snarl that tore from Noah's throat was truly terrifying. Shoving me aside, Noah lunged for Liam.

"Steady up, buddy," Lucky, who had arrived back just in the nick of time, warned him. Blocking his path to Liam, Lucky put his hands on Noah's shoulders and shoved him back. "He's not worth ruining your career over."

I stood, paralyzed with shock and fear, as Lucky wrestled Noah back to the booth.

Swinging around, I searched the club for the rat bastard himself who had aptly skulked off.

Spotting him at the bar, I made a beeline for him. When I noticed who Liam was standing next to at the bar my heart sank.

"Ciarán," I squeezed out through clenched teeth. "I need to talk with Liam in private."

"Give us a minute," Liam told Ciarán, and surprisingly, he listened.

"Catch you later man," he told Liam before smirking at me. "I'll see you real soon, Ice Queen."

"Fuck you," I spat before turning my attention back to Liam. "Why did you do that to me?" I demanded when Ciarán had disappeared out of sight. "We're supposed to be friends, Liam."

"I'm not your friend, Teagan," he sneered. "I'm your stand in." The smell of alcohol from his breath was so strong it was making me dizzy. "Why did you sleep with me, Teagan?" He demanded. "When you were always planning on going back to *him*?"

"I didn't plan *any* of this," I shot back, shaking. "I never meant to hurt you, Liam, but I love *Noah*." Exhaling heavily, I added, "And I can't change my feelings no matter how bad it hurts you."

"What about when he retires?" Liam demanded. "He's a fighter, Teagan, they tend to burn out fast. And they're not exactly known for fidelity," he added cruelly. "I've worked my ass off to win you back. To bring you home. I can give you more than him," he choked out. "I can give you stability."

"I want *Noah*," I repeated, flustered.

"The ex con?" He hissed in disgust.

"That's right," I spat back. "The *ex con*. You need to stop thinking there's a future for us."

"So what, you're just going to leave me for him?" Liam sounded appalled.

"I was never yours to leave," I reminded him tersely.

"That's bullshit, Teagan, and you know it," he hissed. "We've been together for seven damn years."

"No," I corrected him, steeling my resolve. "We've been *friends* for seven years." Letting out a sigh of barely contained impatience, I growled, "Look Liam, we had sex. Once. And it was fair to middling, but there was *never* any passion between us and you know that."

He shook his head. "You are making the biggest mistake of your life," he warned me. "This is wrong, Teagan. There's no future for you in his world."

"I love him," I shot back, lip quivering. "Do you get that? I want to be with him."

"And you think he feels the same?"

"Yes."

"He doesn't *love* you," Liam shot back. "He wants to possess you – because you walked away from him. That's not reality, Teagan, that's control. He only wants you because you're the one that got away. When he's had his fill, he will walk away from you, and you will be alone."

"Stop saying that!"

"What are you going to do when he gets bored of you and tosses you to the curb, huh? Come back to me with your tail hanging between your legs?" I heard Liam roar, but I didn't respond.

I was past the point of burning anger and I needed to remove myself from this environment and fast.

Rushing blindly down the stairwell, I squeezed through the throngs of people in the bar downstairs, pushing and shoving them out of my way in my bid to get to the exit. Breaking through a gap in the crowd, I slipped through the side door of the bar and into the back alley.

NOAH

*S*canning the bar for Teagan, I saw red when I spotted her arguing with *Liam*. Fuck, even thinking his name made me want to break something. I would break something – his fucking jaw.

"Calm down," Lucky ordered, blocking my way. "Noah, I mean it," he added, pushing me back down on the seat when I stood up and tried to move around him. "You're losing it and you need to get a fucking grip, man."

I couldn't focus on a word Lucky was saying to me, not when every fiber inside of my body demanded I go back there and pummel that bastard, firstly for touching her and then for bell ragging about it.

"Noah, you're drunk," Lucky told me. "And he's a walking ticket back to prison." Crouching down in front of me, he forced me to look at him. "Do you want that to happen?" He added. "Do you want to get slung back in a cell and leave her unprotected?"

"No," I grumbled, feeling the fight fade out of me. "Shit man, he knows she's here," I repeated for what had to be the fifth time in five minutes as I pulled at my hair and thrashed around like a deranged lunatic. "He sent her that goddamn rose, Lucky." I knew what it meant. One single red rose in a box. That note. "He's been following me, man," I snarled. "Every fucking move I've made. Waiting for his chance. And coming here?" I shook my hand and hissed. "I sealed her fucking fate coming here." Exhaling a pained groan, I added, "He knows where she lives, man. She's not safe here."

"Okay. I hear you," he coaxed. "So just shut the fuck up and let me figure this out." Moving over to sit beside me, he kept one hand firmly clamped down on my shoulder as he spoke. "We are going to walk out of here without causing a scene or getting arrested," he instructed calmly, the wheels in his brain working at a far quicker pace than mine. "You are going to get your girl and take her back to the hotel with you. And in the morning, when you've slept off what will undoubtedly be the hangover from hell, you're going to convince her to come back to the states with us while I make arrangements."

"What arrangements?" I asked, as I searched the crowd for Thorn.

"It's like you said," Lucky growled. "JD knows where she lives so she can't go back to her apartment. Now that he knows where she –"

"She's gone," I hissed. Stumbling to my feet, I scanned the room again. "She's not fucking here, Lucky."

"Okay," Lucky said with a weary sigh. "Now we can panic."

TEAGAN

"Thank you, Jesus," I muttered when the sharp night air hit my face, cooling me down, and stomping out the claustrophobic feeling that had been building up inside of me.

Footsteps behind me startled me. I swung around and groaned loudly when I saw who was there.

"Oh, for the love of god," I muttered. "Go away, Ciarán."

"Look at the Ice Queen," he purred, prowling towards me. "All alone."

Turning my back on him, I headed for the main street and as far away from Ciarán as I could. He was bad news, and I knew enough to not be in dark alleys with bad men.

"Don't walk away from me, you little bitch," he snarled as he grabbed the back of my dress and tried to pull me backward, further into alleyway.

I felt the fabric tear, the strap holding my dress giving away in his hand and he fisted my hair, pulling me roughly to a halt.

"You and I have some unfinished business."

"Get your hands off me," I screeched, reaching up to claw his hands out of my hair. "I mean it," I growled, digging my fingernails into the flesh of his hands.

"Did you think I wouldn't get you back for that little stunt at the gym?" He hissed, releasing my hair roughly before shoving me forward. Staggering forward, I couldn't maintain my balance and landed hard on my knees. "The look suits you, Teagan," he taunted as he towered over me. "On your knees at my feet."

"You're going to pay for that," I warned him as I scrambled onto my feet and charged forward.

Screw not causing a scene.

No man was going to put his hands on me.

Over my dead fucking body.

Fury drove me on as I threw my hand back and slapped him in the face.

Ciarán's head twisted sideways and he covered his cheek with his hand, momentarily stunned, but then he raised his arm back and punched me in the face.

He hit me so hard and with such force that I was propelled backward.

My back hit the wall of the bar with a hard thud before I collapsed on the ground in a heap.

"Here's a friendly warning," Ciarán snarled as he stood over me, taunting me. "Don't give it if you can't take it."

My back was aching. Every muscle in the upper half of my body was burning in protest. Every fiber inside of me was screaming *don't get up*. Stay down. Let it go.

But that fire inside of me, the one that had protected me my entire life, was burning a hole through me.

That fire was niggling and tormenting me and ordering me to get back up.

That fire was saying don't you dare go down like this.

"You think you're a big, tough man, don't you?" I cried as I forced myself to get back up. "Hitting women?" Climbing unsteadily to my feet, I hacked up as much salvia as I could and spat in his face. "You're a piece of crap, Ciarán."

Clamping his hands on my shoulders, he slammed me against the wall. "You're going to pay for that," he hissed, eyes flaring with anger. "You're gonna get it now, bitch."

"Teagan!" I heard Noah's voice calling out and relief flooded me. *"Teagan!"*

"Noah," I screamed as I tried to make a break for it, but Ciarán grabbed my arm and dragged me back. "Noah, help me!"

NOAH

arreling through the crowd, I shoved everyone out of my way as I took the staircase three steps at a time.

"Teagan!" I roared, as I pushed my way through the bar, searching every face for hers and coming up empty. Fear was choking me, propelling me forward, commanding that I find her as I burst out of the front entrance of the bar roaring her name at the top of my lungs. "Teagan!"

"*Noah*!" I heard her scream out and I ran full speed in the direction of her voice. "*Noah, help me*!"

The minute I turned the corner of the back alley my blood ran cold.

One of the prick's from earlier had Teagan shoved up against the wall, with his fists curled around her arms.

He had his hands on her arms.

His hands were on *my* Thorn.

"Noah!" Teagan cried out in relief as she scrambled away from the prick who was manhandling her.

Her dress was ripped.

That was all I could see.

Her ripped dress and her bloodstained knees.

Moving purely on instinct, I lunged forward, spearing the son of a bitch in the stomach.

Taking him to the ground, I pummeled his face with my fists.

Fuck the MFA.

Fuck everything.

I didn't work as hard as I did for as long as I had to watch this piece of shit put his hands on my Thorn.

"Noah," Teagan cried out, pulling on my shoulder. "Please stop," she begged. "I'm okay, baby. I'm fine –"

"You're not okay," I roared. "He put his hands on you. He put his hands on what's mine!"

"I didn't touch her," he spluttered, covering his face with his hands in his pathetic attempt at protecting himself from my fists. "Not the way you're thinking... Teagan, tell him."

"Don't speak to her," I roared, trembling with rage. "Don't fucking look in her direction, you pathetic sack of shit." Shoving off him, I dragged him to his feet. "Hit me," I ordered as pure fucking elicited rage rushed through my body. "Come on you piece of shit. You wanna hit someone, then hit me."

The sound of police sirens filled the air, but I didn't stop.

I fucking couldn't.

I was going to kill him and I was going to enjoy every damn moment.

TEAGAN

Teagan

The moment Noah stepped into my vision I felt my body sag in relief.

He looked like an avenging angel, dressed in black- dark, dangerous, and poised to inflict pain.

I watched as his eyes drifted from my torn dress to Ciarán's hand on my arm.

His eyes clouded over with pure unadulterated rage.

His expression turned murderous.

And then he attacked.

Noah moved so quickly I barely had a chance to jump out of the way when he charged Ciarán, knocking him to the ground.

Straddling him, Noah let loose, unleashing his fury, as he pummeled him.

"Noah," I choked out, pulling on his shoulder, trying to stop him from doing something he couldn't come back from. "It's okay," I coaxed, trying and failing to pull him off Ciarán. "I'm okay –"

"You're not okay," Noah seethed. "He put his hands on you. He put his hands on what's *mine*!"

"I didn't touch her," Ciarán spluttered, covering his face with his hands, protecting himself from Noah. "Not the way you're thinking... Teagan, tell him."

"Don't speak to her," Noah roared. "Don't fucking look in her direction, you pathetic sack of shit."

The sound of police sirens filled the air, but Noah didn't stop. I didn't think he could stop.

Climbing off him, Noah stood up and dragged Ciarán to his feet. "Hit me," he ordered, holding his hands up in the air. "Come on, you piece of shit. You wanna hit someone, then hit me."

"Get the hell away from him!" Liam's familiar voice trickled through my ears seconds before he barged past me with Eoin hot on his heels. I watched in horror as Eoin grabbed Noah from behind and held him up as Liam and Ciarán attacked him.

"Get off him, you bastards," I screamed as I rushed over to where they were triple teaming Noah and pulled at the back of Eoin's shirt, grunting in pain when his elbow connected with my stomach.

Noah broke out of Eoin's hold but not before Liam's fist connected with his jaw.

Spitting a mouthful of blood, he smiled, his white teeth stained red. "Savor that," he told him before lunging forward and head butting him. Noah's forehead connected with Liam's nose and when his blood sprayed I felt a little lightheaded. "It's the only free shot you'll get from me!"

Out of the corner of my eye I could see a crowd forming in the alley and panic clawed through me.

"Noah, we need to go," I called out shakily. "We need to go now."

He couldn't fight outside the cage.

It was against the rules and we were causing a scene.

He could lose everything he worked for because of this.

Because of me.

Wrapping my arms around his waist, I tried to force him away but it was like trying to move a mountain. "Please Noah," I begged. "They're not worth the shit on your shoes."

"She wasn't saying that when I had my cock buried inside her," Liam called out.

Noah snarled and charged forward, taking me with him because there was no way I was letting him go.

When I noticed Lucky rushing down the alley towards us, I almost wept with relief.

"What the hell happened to the plan?" Lucky hissed as he wrapped his arm around Noah and helped me drag him backwards in the direction of the street.

"I changed it," Noah growled, chest heaving, as he pushed against us, eyes locked on Liam and the guys.

"I gathered that," he replied dryly, dragging Noah away from the carnage.

When we reached the street, Lucky steered us over to a waiting taxi before shoving Noah into the back seat.

Turning around, Lucky looked me straight in the eye and said, "get in there and do whatever you need to do to calm him down. The driver's taking both of you back to the hotel. Do *not* leave him on his own tonight." Looking back toward the alley and the crowd that was watching us, he sighed heavily. "I'll go do some damage control."

I didn't wait to ask questions.

Instead I nodded and scrambled into the backseat.

Wrapping my arms around Noah's neck, I straddled him, clinging onto him for dear life as the driver pulled away.

Noah didn't say a word to me the entire drive to the hotel.

He didn't touch me either.

He just sat in the backseat with me on his lap and stared out the window as his chest rose and fell quickly.

And I got the distinct impression that trouble was brewing.

NOAH

*T*he minute we stepped foot in the hotel suite the adrenalin and pure fucking rage that had been bubbling up inside of me came to a head.

Pulling at my shirt, I ripped it off my chest and slung it over the back of the couch in the sitting room area before stalking off in the direction of the bedroom.

Slamming my hands against the double doors, I stalked inside and away from Teagan.

I couldn't be around her right now.

I was out of control and every time I looked at the bruise forming under her left eye and that fucking ripped dress, a little more of my sanity disappeared.

Images of the prick touching her were all I could think of.

How long had it been going on?

Did she love him?

"Fuck!" Grabbing the lamp on the nightstand next to my bed, I flung it against the wall, watching as it shattered to pieces. It wasn't enough to dispel the anger inside of me. Not enough by half.

Ripping the nightstand out of its slot, I tossed that too, and then the television, the laptop, and everything that wasn't nailed down.

I should have come back for her sooner.

I should have boarded a plane the day I was released and dragged her home kicking and screaming.

Goddammit, I was so jealous I could taste it.

The thought of him touching her, being inside her, fucking putting his mouth on her drove me batshit crazy.

The door opened inward and I tensed.

"Are you going to talk to me?" Teagan asked in a quiet tone. "Or do you want me to leave?"

Like hell she was leaving me again.

We were having this out.

Right fucking now.

TEAGAN

*T*he minute we stepped foot in the Presidential Suite at the hotel, the shit hit the proverbial fan.

Pulling at his black shirt, Noah ripped it off his chest and slung it over the back of the couch in the sitting room area before stalking off in the direction of the double doors at the far side of the room. Slamming both doors open, he disappeared from view.

Slipping out of my shoes, I crept over to where Noah had disappeared, and listened to the carnage occurring on the other side of the wall. The sound of glass shattering and furniture overturning filled my ears and I cringed.

Steeling my resolve, I stepped inside. The bedroom looked like a tornado had passed through it. There was furniture overturned and glass on the floor. In the middle of the wreckage stood Noah, looking more furious than I'd ever seen.

"Are you going to talk to me?" I straight out asked him, watching him tense when I spoke. "Or do you want me to leave?"

"When?" He finally asked, jaw clenched.

"A few months back," I whispered, knowing full well what he was asking me. He wanted to know about Liam. "I was drunk and lonely and trying to move on from you," I added quietly, thinking back to the worst mistake of my life. "It only happened one time."

"How long?" He managed to grind out as a vein throbbed in his neck.

"How long what?" I whispered, feeling nervous and unsure.

"How long did you wait before you let him put his dick in what's mine?" Noah snarled, chest heaving. "How long have you been messing around with him? How. Fucking. Long, Teagan?"

"And what about you?" I screeched, defending myself. "Did you think of me when you were fucking all those women on tour?"

Noah's face turned a dangerous shade of purple. "You want to go there?" he asked, tone menacing.

"You're going there," I countered, angry and guilty and broken inside. "I was with *one* man, Noah. One man. One time. Can you say the same?"

"I don't know what the fuck I was doing with those women," he roared in my face. "But I can tell you what I was thinking," he added, chest heaving. "I was thinking that the only girl I've ever loved left me to rot in a jail cell. And that girl is living her life with god knows who. I was thinking a few hours of affection might stem the god-awful fucking feeling of rejection. That someone out there could heal the loneliness inside of me. The pain you left in me splintered me apart, Teagan. The fucking hole in my heart is gaping. And yeah, I tried to fill it with other women, but I never could. Because when I came to, looked at their faces, and realized it wasn't you lying next to me, I wanted to die–" His words broke off and he shuddered. "You broke me and you abandoned me." His eyes turned hard again. "And now I know. All those sleepless nights worrying myself sick about you! I know he was the one keeping your bed warm while I was sleeping on a fucking slab in prison."

"I promise it wasn't like that," I shot back, feeling both embarrassed and rejected. Noah was losing control, he was barely holding onto his temper by a thread, and I wasn't going to push him over the edge.

"Then how was it?" I watched as a vein ticked in Noah's

neck. His words were laced with sarcasm and pain as he shook his head and laughed humorlessly. "Don't tell me; you fucked him and thought of me?"

"Yes, as a matter of fact I did. I thought about you! One time! One fucking time, Noah," I hissed back. "Because I thought you betrayed me."

"How many goddamn times do I have to tell you," he growled as he stalked toward me. Backing me up against the door, Noah leaned down and hissed, "I *didn't* fucking betray you."

"Don't you think I know that by now?" I demanded, pressing my hand to his chest, feeling all his heat and hardness. "God, Noah, don't you think I've realized that I'm to blame for all of this?"

Knowing Noah was innocent only made this conversation ten times harder.

I had abandoned him.

I had left him to rot in a prison cell for five years and I had slept with Liam.

I had forced him to the back of my mind and I had carried on with life.

I had left him behind.

It made me want to scratch my own eyes out. I was royally sickened with myself.

And still, when I was in trouble, he was the first one to defend me. To jump in and save me over and over again. I could live a thousand lifetimes and never deserve him.

"I know I've screwed everything up. I get it, but you need to understand that your life terrifies me, Noah," I cried out. "Your choices, your history, your mood swings, and how you make me feel all scare me to death. You *terrify* me, Noah!" I choked out, panting, as adrenalin rushed through my veins. "But when I'm with you, I feel safe, and alive, and like I belong. You do that to me," I told him. "You bring those emotions out of me. No one else."

"You think it's any different for me?" He shot back, chest heaving. "You are the only thing I am afraid of on this planet," he roared. "You have the ability to destroy me. I *never* put myself in the position to be hurt before you and you rip me open daily. You're the one who's treacherous."

Shaking my head, I let out a harsh cry. "What's the fucking point anyway?" I choked out. "Nothing I can say can fix this or rewind the last seven years."

Leaning against the door, I threw my hands in the air in weary defeat.

I was in the wrong.

I knew it.

He knew it.

But now I accepted it, and that made it hard to breathe.

For the first time in our fucked up relationship, I was owning my faults and it hurt like a bitch.

I felt like a knife was piercing through my heart, tearing strips off my soul. "There's no way you can still want me –"

"I will *always* want you, Teagan," he shot back, his voice thick with emotion. "There will *always* be a way back for us." I watched as Noah clenched and unclenched his fists as he struggled to stay still. "Just keep talking," he ordered in a tight tone of voice as a vein in his neck throbbed. "Get it all fucking out, I *need* to hear it."

So I did.

"I've spent the best part of a decade believing I wasn't good enough for you. Believing that I wasn't good enough to *keep* you," I admitted, voice broken, with tears streaming down my cheeks as my emotions boiled over. "I know I was wrong, but back then all I knew was that the one person who I trusted more than my own family, who I loved more than anyone on this planet, had betrayed me. And even then, I *still* wanted you and that made me hate myself more than I've ever hated you." Shaking my head, I exhaled a broken sigh. "And then you were released and I never heard from you. Months later, you're everywhere; the television, the Internet, the papers. And I had to watch you with those girls, rubbing it in my face on the TV. I couldn't cope with the rejection or the pain, so I ran to the one person who I knew wanted me. Liam was safe; he couldn't hurt me because I didn't have any room left inside of me to store the pain. You say you want me, Noah, but I didn't know that back then...so I tried to move on from you. I tried to force myself into believing Liam was what was right for me –"

"He's not what's right for you, Teagan," Noah hissed. His eyes never left mine as he took a step back and said, "he's what's *safe* for you. I'm what's *right* for you. Me." He beat his fist against his chest and that small, passionate display of male dominance caused me to clench tight in anticipation. "That fucker wants you," Noah snarled. "He wants inside what's *mine*."

Regaining the space he had put between us in two short strides, Noah placed his hands on either side of my face and stared into my eyes for a long moment.

"I'm going to fuck him right out of you," he growled before slamming his body against mine and claiming my mouth with his in a kiss so rough, my heartbeat soared and my core pulsed with need. I could taste his blood on my tongue as it dueled with mine, plunging into my mouth, owning me, taking me over.

Pulling back, Noah took my bottom lip between his teeth and tugged hard. "This is mine," he hissed, dropping his hand to cup my pussy. "From here on out, this belongs to *me*. You got it?"

There were no words in my vocabulary at that moment that I could squeeze out.

I wasn't a submissive woman, but this man...he broke all my rules.

Nodding my head, I sagged against him, wanting him to claim me, needing to forget that I had let another man touch me where only Noah had before.

"He doesn't love you. He wants to possess you — because you walked away from him...when he's had his fill, he will walk away from you and you will be alone."

. . .

LIAM'S WORDS IMPALED MY BRAIN AND I TORE MY MOUTH AWAY from Noah's. "Tell me you're with me for more than revenge," I asked, breathless and panting.

"What?" Noah grumbled, breathing hard, his eyes never leaving my face. "Are you for real?"

"Tell me all of this is not just to prove a point, Noah," I repeated. "Tell me you're not going to walk away from me when you get bored."

Dropping his hands from my face, he turned around and strode over to the opposite side of the room and opened the bathroom door.

"I don't fucking believe this," he said, laughing humorlessly before disappearing inside only to reappear in the doorway a few moments later with a black t-shirt in his hands.

Tossing it towards me, he said, "Put this on," before gesturing at my ripped dress. "I can't look at you like that."

"Tell me, Noah," I growled as I caught the shirt mid-air and flung it down on the bed.

"Tell you what?" He demanded. "That everything I've done – every fight, every training session, every drop of blood I've spilled, and every ounce of blood I've shed – has been for you? For this moment? To be standing in front of you, looking into your eyes, and showing you how much you mean to me?"

I opened my mouth to speak but Noah got there before me.

"I memorized every inch of you. I fucking loved you even when I hated you most," he roared hoarsely. "You broke my trust, Thorn, you ripped my goddamn heart out of my chest, but you're *still* the only one I want by my side. At my lowest point all I wanted was you. At my highest point all I want is you. I must be a masochistic bastard because after all these years and all this pain I still want to halve my soul with you. Split myself down the center and give you ownership of me."

Exhaling heavily, he added, "Is that enough honesty for you, Teagan, or would you rather just go on doubting my intentions?"

Noah didn't give me a chance to answer before disappearing into the bathroom again and this time he closed the door behind him.

Seconds later the sound of a running shower filled my ears.

Letting it sink in, all his words of love and promise, I felt shame.

Shame for denying this man for so long.

Knowing I had to do something to fix this, I stripped off my clothes, crept over to the door, and slipped inside.

My eyes honed in on Noah and I moaned in appreciation.

He was standing in the shower with his back to me, head bent, as the water cascaded over his huge muscular frame.

My eyes drifted over every inch of his skin, soaking in his raw masculine beauty, studying the huge, black tattoo that covered the whole of his back. I lowered my gaze and my core clenched. He had an ass that I swear to god, you could crack walnuts with. Everything was just so... tight and firm.

I wanted to taste every inch of his skin to see if it still tasted the same, felt the same. He was more of a man than I had ever seen.

Padding over the cold marble tiles, I drew back the glass door of the shower and stepped inside.

His body tensed when I wrapped my arms around his stomach.

The atmosphere changed almost instantly, thickening, and I honestly didn't know which way this was going to go.

But then he exhaled heavily, covered my hands with his, and my body sagged in relief.

"I'm so sorry, baby," I whispered, pressing a kiss to his back. He needed to hear this, and in this moment, I would say and do whatever it took to ease his pain. "For everything."

"Thorn..." he groaned, squeezing my hand.

"I never stopped loving you," I choked out, kissing his back again and again. "You're still my *in*."

His big body shuddered, his head bowed, and it humbled me to know that I affected him like this.

"Don't play with me," he whispered in such a tender and

uncertain voice that I wanted to cry. "Don't tell me this if you're gonna take it away again."

"I won't," I vowed. My heart was hammering so hard I thought it would burst through my chest. "Let me back in, Noah, and I won't let you down again. I *promise*."

Reaching around, Noah caught my arm and drew me up against his chest. "You better be damn sure about this, Thorn," he croaked out, holding me flush against him as the water poured down on us. "Because I'm not letting you go again." Dropping his face, he said, "if you're with me, you're with me for life. No more chasing after you. No more games."

Nodding my head, I whispered, "I'm in," before raising my face to his and claiming his mouth, kissing him deep and slow.

His tongue snaked out and dueled with mine, as we held onto each other.

It was slow and sensual and everything I had been missing all these years.

Wrapping my arms around his neck, he hoisted me up and took a step forward, pressing me against the wall of the shower, caging me in with his beautiful body.

I knew I was playing a dangerous game, I wasn't on birth control, but I couldn't deny this man entry to my body.

So I opened my legs willingly, giving myself up completely, wanting nothing more than to be with him.

"I was always coming back for you, Teagan," he said hoarsely as he pressed against me. "I just needed to get my life in order first. I needed to have something to offer you...a better life than the one you had. I wanted to make you love me so hard you would forget where *you* started and *I* ended."

"Mission accomplished," I whispered, barely breathing.

Smiling, Noah slipped inside me in one fluent movement, filling me up.

The wetness of our bodies caused the friction inside me to ignite as we slipped and slid against each other.

His hands never left my face and his lips never left my lips as he slowly rocked into me.

We barely moved.

We just swayed in and out, reveling in being together again as one.

Each claiming the other.

Showing each other how much this night meant, how pivotal this moment in time was for us.

No foreplay.

No fooling around.

Tonight was about becoming one again.

TEAGAN

*H*e stood naked in the middle of the bedroom, the epitome of male virility. With a towel wrapped around his shoulders, he showed no shame, no shyness; he was just completely at ease with who he was and what he looked like. The muscles. The sheer masculine dominance set me on fire. I was excited, tingling, and drooling just watching him do something as mundane as dry himself off.

"You're staring."

"Can you blame me?"

Noah snorted and continued to towel dry his hair.

I waited for him to climb into bed before asking, "What happened here?" His skin was dusted in scars.

Some I remembered and some I didn't.

I trailed my fingers over the rigid silver line on his ribcage and then to the one just below it.

"Knife wound," he drawled lazily as he laid on his back, allowing me to explore him. "That one too."

"And this?" I whispered, moving lower, resting my palm on the largest welt marking his beautiful body. I felt him shudder beneath my touch. "How did you get this?"

"That's a burn mark, Thorn," he croaked out, covering my hand with his. "From the car crash."

"You were burned that night?" I managed to squeeze out.

Memories of the flames around the car Noah and I had been trapped in flooded me and I flinched.

"I'm so sorry," I choked out.

"I know you are," he replied and I hoped he was hearing my apology – the depth of my remorse.

The sadness I felt for where his life had taken him overwhelmed me. He'd been in prison, his mom had died and he'd been all alone for the majority of his life.

"My turn to investigate," he interrupted, obviously not wanting to talk about it.

Rolling me onto my back, Noah rested on his side above me and trailed his fingers over my naked skin.

"So soft," he whispered, nudging my belly with his nose. His breath against my skin caused the tingling between my legs to intensify. His eyes darkened when he moved his hand to rest between the apex of my thighs. "What about here?" He whispered, trailing his thumb between my wet folds, circling my clit slowly, watching me like a hawk to gage my reaction. "Do you still like it when I touch you here, Thorn?"

"Yes," I whispered, my breath hitching in my throat as I writhed under his touch. I wasn't blessed in the breast department, but when Noah's mouth closed over one, taking my pebbled nipple into his mouth and grunting in appreciation, I forgot all about my insecurities.

The feelings he provoked in me were like nothing I'd ever experienced before. It was as if his body had been created for the sole purpose of pleasuring mine. We fit together perfectly. I wanted to lick him. I knew that sounded crazy and fucked up but it was the truth. I wanted to hold his head to my chest and cradle him there, care for him. Nurture him. And then lay on my back and let him do everything I had never allowed another man to do to me.

I wanted to be the one to nurse his wounds and rub him down after each fight. I wanted to be the woman he had on his arm. I wanted him to want me like I wanted him. It was a deep, carnal want.

He was a real man.

Unlike anyone else I'd ever met and I wanted him to possess me, body and soul. I wanted to tie him up in so many knots he would never leave. I loved him that much.

"See the way your body responds to mine," he whispered, kissing each of my breasts. "It's because you're my mate," he added in an almost desperate tone. Shifting so that he was resting above me, Noah pushed my thighs apart and nestled between them. "Your body wants my body, and my heart wants yours," he rasped before filling me in one deep thrust. "We fit together."

Stroking his cheek with my hand, I forced him to look at me as I pressed myself against him, letting him have me, exposing my soul to the man who owned it.

"What are your plans?" He groaned, burying his face in my neck as he plunged inside of me.

"For when?" I gasped, tightening my legs around his hips, as my back arched upward. "Tomorrow?"

He shook his head. "No, Thorn." I felt him smile against my skin. "For the rest of your life."

I didn't answer him.

I couldn't.

The sensations rushing through me made it impossible to form a coherent sentence.

So I answered him with kisses, I told him I loved him with my touch, and I promised to never leave him with my tears.

Afterwards, neither of us spoke a word – there was nothing left to say.

We just lay together in the dark room, unmoving, still joined.

I was lost to Noah and I knew I was never going to find my way out. Consuming love and infallible obsession. There was no way out of this for me. I was bound to him. I always had been. I always would be. I didn't believe in soul mates but if I did, I just knew he was mine. We were a broken mess. We fought. We argued. We all but killed each other. But we couldn't live without one another and that was what mattered. Noah Messina consumed my every waking thought. He made me feel like I was born for the sole purpose of being his mate. His woman. The other half of his wounded soul.

Both of us were screwed up beyond repair. But it didn't matter. I would follow him, and I would earn his trust back if it was the last thing I did.

Three days was all it took.

Three days to have my world turned upside down.

Three days to find out everything I had ever believed was a lie.

Three days to make me lose my inhibitions and fall.

Finally, as the seconds turned into minutes and his breathing turned deep and even, exhaustion claimed me, and I fell asleep tangled up in Noah Messina.

NOAH

When I woke up it was still dark outside and Teagan was still in my bed, wrapped around me like ivy. I stretched out my stiff limbs and she grumbled in her sleep, protesting at being disturbed, before snuggling back into my side.

Contemplating leaving this bed in the morning was a fucking painful thought. Here in this bed, our own personal bubble protected us. I was naked, she was naked, and there were no barriers between us. No walls of insecurity and hurt and no fucking danger.

When I left this bed that would all change.

Reality would seep in and fuck with my happiness.

Craning my neck so I could look at her, my heart accelerated in my chest at the sight of her head resting on my chest. The moonlight shining in from the window cast light upon us, illuminating her face in a soft glow.

"I love you, you little fruitcake," I whispered, stroking her cheek with my thumb. "But you don't make it easy."

"I heard that," she grumbled, peeking out at me with one hazel eye.

Rolling her onto her back, I held myself above her, resting my full weight on my elbows. "You were supposed to," I teased, unable to resist pressing a kiss to her cute little button nose.

Nudging her legs with my knee, I growled in approval when she let her thighs fall open, looking like a disheveled angel.

"I want you to be my biggest fan," I told her, pinning her arms above her head. Lowering my face to hers, I pulled her swollen bottom lip into my mouth and sucked. "I want to hear you screaming my goddamn name when you watch me fight, and I want to see pride on your face when I win. Because I *will* win, Thorn. Every single time. I'll win for you." I wanted her to stay with me *for me*. Not the fame or the money or the fucking power. But for me. Just me. Broken and screwed up as I was. I wanted to be enough for just once in my life.

"I've always been your biggest fan." Shoving against my chest, I let Thorn push me onto my back and watched through hooded eyes as she climbed on top of me. "And that has nothing to do with your career."

Fisting my dick in her small hand, Thorn raised herself above me and rubbed herself against me. "But why does it matter so much to you?" She whispered, staring down at me.

"Because I want your admiration," I hissed. Grabbing her hips, I rammed her down on my dick. "I want your devoted acceptance." She was so wet that I slid all the way into her tight little pussy. "And I want your fucking love."

"You have it," she cried out as she bounced up and down on my dick. Her pussy around me was fucking heaven. She slammed down hard, and I growled in approval.

Fuck me, I didn't remember this version of Teagan. I wasn't complaining though. She could play with me all damn night.

"Oh god, Noah, you have all of me," she screamed.

"Are you sure about that?" I hissed, thrusting upward when she came down hard. "Fucking own me, Thorn."

She upped her pace, riding me harder and faster, pinning me to the mattress with her hips.

Reaching up, I took her perky breasts in my hands, twisting and pinching her nipples until she pulsed around my dick, squeezing me so tight that I shot off like a cannon inside her, filling her with my seed, and fucking loving her when she snuggled down on my chest, leaving our bodies joined.

NOAH

*T*he next time I woke it was to the sun streaming in the window and a loud hammering noise coming from the other room.

Wanting to stay here with Thorn, but knowing I had to face the music, I slid out from underneath her and covered her naked body with the sheet that was rumpled up at the foot of the bed.

Reaching down, I grabbed my pants off the floor before creeping out of the room, stepping over the broken glass and furniture that was evidence of my loss of control last night.

Closing the door behind me, I slipped on my pants before walking over to the door and pulling it inward.

"You stupid son of a bitch." Those were the first words Quincy said when he stormed into the suite looking like death warmed up, followed quickly by, "Do you have any idea of how much trouble your stunt at the bar last night has cost you?"

Lucky strolled in after him with his Ray Ban's on, a paper tray balancing four disposable cups in one hand, and a plastic bag swinging from the other.

"Hello to you too," I muttered, swinging the door shut behind them. "And if you don't mind, keep your goddamn voices down," I added, folding my arms across my chest. "Thorn's still sleeping."

"Thorn?" Quincy's face turned a darker shade of purple. "You smoke a special sort of cigarette, Messina?"

Strolling over to the couch, Lucky sank down on the couch. "It's what he calls his woman," he chuckled, removing goodies from his plastic bag and tucking into a sugar glazed donut. "As in, *thorn in his side*," he added, licking the icing off his fingers. "I think it's cute."

"So that explains the tramp stamp," Quincy grumbled thoughtfully, scratching his bald head as his gaze drifted to the tattoo on my side. "Huh."

Walking over to the couch, I sank down beside Lucky, shaking my head when he offered me a donut. I didn't eat that processed sugar-filled crap and Lucky knew it. "How much did it cost me?"

"Thirty grand," Lucky piped up. "Ten a man." He bit into another donut before adding, "Silence is expensive."

"That fuck deserves a lot worse than he got – and I barely touched the other two," I shot back, irritated that those bastards were walking around with my goddamn money. Teagan's bruised face flashed through my mind and the only regret I had was not putting them out of commission – permanently.

"Do you have any idea how long it took me to convince those bastards not to press charges on you?" Quincy demanded, furious, as he began to pace the floor. "You're all over the internet, dumbass. You were filmed at the bar last night and it's already gone viral."

"Two things," Lucky chimed in. "First, don't call him a dumbass. And second, if I recall correctly, *I* was the one who spent the night talking them down. *You* were the one getting your dick sucked by that viper redhead."

"Well I was the one that caught an earful of it from Nick," Quincy huffed, turning his attention to me. "He's raging and seriously considering pulling your contract. Wondering if he needs a loose cannon on his payroll."

"Shut the fuck up, Q," Lucky grumbled. "Nick won't do shit. The MFA ratings have gone through the roof since Noah signed. He can't afford to fire him."

"Well the disciplinary board has called an emergency meeting first thing tomorrow morning," Quincy hissed. "So pack your shit because we fly out in a couple of hours."

"That soon?" I blanched. "I thought we weren't due to fly out until Thursday."

"Yeah, well plans change, Messina," Quincy shot back angrily. "After last night's stunt, it's out of my control."

"Did you manage to *convince* her?" Lucky asked, taking a sip from his cup of coffee, hinting at the conversation we had last night at the bar.

"No," I snapped, eyes flaring. And I didn't want to bring it up around Quincy. The less people that knew about JD the safer. "I haven't had a chance."

"I bet," Lucky snickered. "Busy night and all."

"Convince her of what?" Quincy demanded. "You need to keep your head clear, Messina," he ordered when neither of us explained. "Forget the fucking woman. This is your career on the line."

"Watch your mouth," I warned him. "If Thorn's not on board with this, then you're gonna have to work your magic and get that meeting pushed back." Shaking my head, I added, "I don't give a fuck what you say, Q. I'm not leaving unless she's sitting on that plane beside me."

"Hold up, Noah. Think about this, man. Q has a point here," Lucky piped up, offering his two cents worth. "This is your career you're talking about. You need to go home and appease the suits. I can stay here and *handle* things until you get back."

"I. Am. Not. Leaving. Her," I snarled. "So back the fuck off."

Throwing his hands up, Quincy shook his head and stalked over to the door. "Be on that fucking plane tonight," he warned me. Pulling the door open, he turned and hissed, "I don't give two shits about your flower woman. Your ass better be in that seat come one o clock."

Quincy slammed the door shut and I leapt up off the coach. "Thanks for the support, asshole," I hissed. "I thought you of all people would understand considering what happened to Hayley."

I cringed the minute the words were out of my mouth. It was a dick move and I knew it.

I didn't even try and defend myself when Lucky sprang off the couch and punched me in the face.

I deserved it.

"Do not," he snarled, chest heaving, as he paced the floor, struggling to rein in his emotions. "Say her name –"

"I won't man," I croaked out, sitting my ass back down, feeling like the biggest bastard on the face of the earth. "I'm sorry," I added, wiping the blood from my lip.

He stared at my face for a long time before exhaling heavily and nodding.

"I did some digging," he finally said, and just like that, the mask he wore slipped back into place and he was easygoing Lucky again. Drinking his feelings away and burying his pain with a smile. "Tommy was dead on the money when he said the Ring of Fire was up and running."

"I never doubted it," I replied, keeping my voice down.

"He's got a new guy in training," he told me. "The next big thing apparently. Fucking lethal. Kills without a hint of remorse. Trained from a pup. Sound familiar?"

Just like me...

"Too familiar –"

"What's familiar?" Teagan's voice filled the room, causing me to break off mid-sentence as I swung around to see her.

The second my eyes locked on her standing in the doorway wearing my black t-shirt I was hard as fucking die cast metal. "I don't have any clothes here," she added, cheeks reddening, as she pulled the shirt further down her thighs.

"You want a napkin, Messina?" Lucky chuckled. "You've got a little something on your mouth."

"Funny," I grumbled, unable to take my eyes off the woman standing in front of me. I didn't stand up because I knew my legs were shaking like a fucking teenage virgin and I didn't trust myself to not fall flat on my face.

I was in big trouble with that woman.

TEAGAN

I woke feeling more sated than I had in years.

Memories of what happened last night with Noah caused the smile on my face to spread into a demented grin.

Stretching out on the luxurious king-size bed, I reached out and patted Noah's side – where his big body had left an impressionable dip in the mattress.

When I found it was still warm, I rolled over and snuggled up in a ball for a long time until the icky feeling that came with a hangover got the better of me.

Dragging myself out of bed, I padded into the bathroom and climbed into the shower. Turning the knob, I closed my eyes as the piping hot water cascaded down on me.

Sighing in contentment, I thought back to everything that happened last night – post club of course. Everything before that I shoved to the back of my mind.

Those memories had no place in my happy little bubble.

Those memories could fuck right off.

He let me back in last night. I knew I had a hell of a lot of work to do to break down the barriers caging off Noah Messina's heart; but last night, for the tiniest moment, I had achieved the unachievable. I had worked my way back into the place no one else had been before me and no else had been since.

"I will always want you, Teagan... There will always be a way back for us..."

Last night his words had floored me.

This morning didn't change that.

I was reeling in emotions, having heard his truth, and I wanted nothing more than to drag him back to bed and pin him here with me.

I knew today wouldn't be all rainbows and kittens – the loud male voices coming from the other room assured me of that – but we had hope.

For the first time in years, Noah and I were both on the same page.

We had the same goal.

Each other.

That was enough to make it work.

Even when he morphed me into a raging bitch and I drove him batshit crazy. He still loved me and there was no question that I was still head over heels in love with him.

I was a stubborn woman, but I loved him enough to know that I couldn't be without him again.

That knowledge made me swallow my pride and take the blame.

He was worth it.

There was no greater feeling than being that man's sole focus, having his undivided attention.

Remembering the feel of his touch on my skin caused me to groan loudly. I knew that there would be many more nights of screaming and fighting and heartbreak, but there wasn't another person on this planet I would rather break my heart loving.

We needed to make this work somehow, because the alternative, the thought of being without him again, well that just wasn't an option.

When I was finished showering, I dressed in the only pieces of clothing I had at my disposal; Noah's black t-shirt and a gray pair of his Calvin Klein's, before making my way out of the room.

Everything inside of me clenched the moment I set eyes on Noah, lounging on the coach, bare chested, dressed only in the black suit pants he wore last night. He looked so comfortable in his own body, so content in his own skin as he sat legs spread, arms sprawled over the back of the chair, hanging on every word Lucky, who was towering over him, said.

I knew they had been fighting. Their raised voices were what had woken me. And Noah's reopened cut on his lip was bleeding but I didn't say anything.

Those two had a strange bond, and I wasn't getting in the middle of it. Besides, they looked fine now.

"...Trained from a pup. Sound familiar?" Lucky said dryly.

"Too familiar," Noah growled.

"What's familiar?" I asked.

Real tactful, Teegs.

Both men turned simultaneously at the sound of my voice.

"I don't have any clothes here," I added sheepishly when I caught Noah staring at my legs.

"You want a napkin, Messina?" Lucky chuckled. "You've got a little something on your mouth."

"Funny," he shot back, not taking his eyes off my body.

"What's familiar?" I asked again, tugging on the hem of my shirt as I approached the couch, heading straight for my man. When I was an arm's length from him, Noah grabbed my hand and pulled me down on his lap. Nestling his face in my neck, he pressed a kiss to my throbbing pulse and growled. "You smell like me."

I stifled a moan as his kiss triggered every nerve ending in my body to spring to life. "That's because I used your shampoo," I whispered, using my hair as a curtain to cloak us in privacy. Noah replied with a low growl of approval.

Shifting beneath me, I felt his erection spring to life against my ass and I was instantly wet. Seemingly unaffected with his friend's presence, Noah continued to nip and suckle on my neck and I, in return, continued to squirm on his lap.

"Donut?"

Lucky's voice penetrated our perfect moment, causing

Noah to rip his mouth away from my neck, and me to bite down hard on my lip in frustration.

"She doesn't want any fucking donuts, Lucky," Noah growled, breathing hard, his eyes never leaving my face.

"Actually..." Springing off Noah's lap, I reached forward and retrieved the gorgeous looking pink iced donut Lucky was offering. "This is so good," I moaned between mouthfuls, pausing when I noticed Noah's cocked brow. "What?" I mumbled, lowering myself down on the coffee table in front of him. Eyeing the bag full of donuts, I snagged another one. "I haven't eaten in days. I'm starving."

Both men watched me with amusement flickering in their eyes, so much so that I started to feel a little embarrassed.

"So, how did you guys meet?" I asked, trying to turn the attention away from me. "The MFA, or the gym or something?"

That question caused both men to smirk at each other before bursting out laughing in unison.

"Or something," Lucky drawled in a teasing tone before glancing over at Noah and winking. "We've been roommates for a long time," he added with a mischievous glint in his eye. "Isn't that right, *roomie*?"

"Am I missing something here?" I asked heatedly, feeling confused and out of the loop.

"We shared a cell, Thorn," Noah said, smiling indulgently at me.

"Oh."

I didn't have a clue what to say.

Here I was, sitting in a hotel room, half naked, with two ex-convicts.

"That's...." I was going for nice, or cool, or anything besides, "fucked up," but that's what came out of my mouth.

"I like her," Lucky chuckled. Moving over to the couch, he sat down beside Noah and grinned. "You're a strange, little woman."

"She's my strange, little woman," Noah said in a warning tone, elbowing him in the ribs. "Remember that."

Lucky threw his head back and laughed. "I think I'll

remember," he said, clearly amused. "Considering she's all you talked about for the past seven years."

Ouch.

Swallowing hard, I wiped the corner of my mouth with my thumb, forcing my expression to remain bright and not expose how much that comment stung.

"May I?" I asked, gesturing to the tray of coffees beside me.

"Be my guest," Lucky said and I quickly snagged a cup and took a long sip. The froth-foamed coffee hit exactly the right spot and I moaned in appreciation.

Noah sat back on the couch, considering me with a caged expression.

To be quite honest, he looked mildly bored, and a little apprehensive.

Like who I was now wasn't what he expected.

The thought caused my appetite to evaporate in record time.

Wiping my mouth with the back of my hand, I forced myself to look at him. "What's wrong?"

Noah didn't reply for a long time.

Instead, he sat forward on the edge of the couch and rested his elbows on his knees, clasping them loosely between his open legs. His thick thighs made a serious impression on those pants, stretching the fabric and quickly I came to the conclusion that Noah was too big for his clothes. They fit him, but he was too built to be constrained in suits. He was too big and muscular. That man was born to lie naked on a bed.

"I'm leaving tonight, Thorn." His voice was steady, his tone was calm, but his eyes gave him away. His brown eyes were full of unease as he watched me watching him, gauging my reaction.

"You are?" I heard the disappointment in my own voice and it made me want to kick my own ass. "So soon?"

Noah nodded, emotionless. "I've got a meeting first thing tomorrow morning with the disciplinary board." Clearing his throat, he plucked an invisible thread from his pants before adding, "I'm in deep shit, baby. Someone recorded the incident outside the bar last night."

"And what? They want to fire you?" I demanded, outraged. I was trying really hard to rein it in and be a grownup and logical when all I wanted to do was kick the floor and wail like a demon; rant on about how bad of an omen I seemed to be to this man. "They can't fire you," I carried on saying, not waiting for him to reply. "You're Noah fucking Messina. The MFA would be nothing without you." Shaking my head, I venomously rejected the notion of Noah losing his job because of me. "You're too valuable to them."

"See?" Lucky chimed in. "I really like her. Girl's got good sense."

Cracking his neck from side to side, Noah let my words sink in for a moment before saying, "Maybe so, but I have to attend."

"This is bullshit," I managed to squeeze out, though my chest felt like it was constricting inside of me. My throat felt like it was closing up. The walls around me were closing in and everything was moving in slow motion. We were just getting back on our feet and he was leaving. Karma was playing a mean trick on us.

I couldn't sit still.

My eyeballs were burning, not a good sign.

Climbing clumsily to my feet, I began to clean off the coffee table. "Well, I suppose you were leaving next week anyway," I rambled, forcing myself to sound happy for him. "With the tour kicking off and all." Scooping up the trash in my arms, I forced myself to walk across the room and dump the contents of my arms into the waste bin. "You were never staying here long term."

"I was hoping I would have more time to do this," Noah said cagily, and for a huge man like him, his nervousness was adorable. "But I...fuck!" His voice broke off and he drummed his fingers against the arm of the couch, clearly struggling with something.

"What Noah is *trying* to say is how would you feel about

accompanying us back to the states?" Lucky interrupted with a smug grin.

"Dammit, Lucky," Noah growled. "I was handling it."

"Oh please," Lucky snickered. "If I didn't say it now, you'd still be here tomorrow trying to find your balls."

Jerking to his feet, Noah walked towards me with his hands held up in front of him, as if he was trying to capture a flight risk bird or something. "Thorn, just hear me out before you say no –"

My feet were moving towards him faster than my brain could catch up. I barreled into his arms, and like always, Noah caught me. "Hell yes," I squealed, wrapping my arms around his neck and my legs around his waist. "Absolutely."

"Wait...what?" Setting me down on my feet, Noah took a step back, hands still planted firmly on my shoulders, and gaped at me. "For real?"

"Why wouldn't I want to?" I said, grinning. "A vacation with you sounds like music to my ears."

"Well...because you like to fight me on just about everything?" He replied, confused. Suddenly his head snapped back to me. "Hold up. A vacation?" He shook his head. "Thorn, no, that's not what I –"

The sudden and urgent rapping on the hotel door drew my attention away from Noah and I skipped over and put my hand on the door handle to open it.

"Teagan. No!" Noah hissed, grabbing my arm and dragging me up against his chest.

"What?" I shrieked, totally freaked out by his sudden movement. "I can't answer the door now?"

"No," he snarled angrily. "You *can't* answer the door now." Walking us over to the couch, he pushed me down on the seat and towered over me with his hands on his hips, chest heaving. "You don't open doors to strangers, Thorn," he spat, glowering down at me. "You fucking got that?"

"What's going on here?" I demanded as a trickle of fear ran down my spine. That fear spread further when Noah wouldn't meet my eyes. "Noah," I hissed. "I want to know what the hell is going on here?"

Running a hand roughly through his hair, Noah hissed a string of curse words before glancing at Lucky. He tipped his chin and Lucky immediately rose from the couch and moved towards the door.

The tension was running off Noah in waves as he stood with his back to me, blocking my view of the door. His stance reminded me of a lion braced for trouble.

Adrenalin, fear, and lust flooded me as I watched this man stand guard over me.

For what reason, I had no idea, but I didn't have time to ask, because the minute Lucky opened the door Hope's voice filled my ears.

"Where is she?" She demanded as she stormed into the suite and headed straight for Noah. Noticing me peeking around his huge frame, Hope made a beeline for me. "Why the hell haven't you been answering your phone?" Grabbing my arms, she dragged me off the couch, enveloping me in a hug so tight I could hardly breathe. "Well?"

"I left my purse and jacket at the club last night," I managed to choke out, patting her back. "Can you ease up on the love? I'm kinda suffocating here."

Instantly, Hope released me and took a step back.

Only then did I notice the tall man accompanying her.

"Jordan?"

I shook my head and gaped at the man who had broken my best friend's heart.

"What are you doing here?"

"Never mind us. This is about the two of you," Hope countered swiftly, as she eyed Noah who was standing slightly apart from me. "What the hell have you gotten her into this time?" She demanded, glaring up at him with a murderous expression. Taking a step toward him, Hope raised her hand and slapped Noah across the face.

"Hey," I snapped. Scrambling, I dived between my boyfriend and my best friend. "Don't put your hands on him," I warned her as I kept my back to Noah and glared at Hope. "Noah hasn't gotten me into anything," I added, forcing myself to remain calm even though a reckless streak of protectiveness was coursing through my body. "I'm here because I want to be."

"I'm not talking about you being here, Teagan," Hope shot back, furious, eyes locked on Noah. "I'm talking about the fact that our apartment was trashed last night." Shuddering, she added, "While we were sleeping."

"What?" I whispered, covering my mouth with my hand.

"Your room, Teagan," Hope squeezed out, turning her attention back to me. "It was covered in red roses, all over the floor, the bed, and on your pillow there was...ugh." Covering her face with her hands, she sank down on the couch and groaned. "I don't even want to say it."

Noah stiffened behind me. "Are you okay?" He demanded, moving around me to check his niece. Crouching down on his haunches, Noah looked her over and asked, "Were you harmed?"

"I'm fine," she replied shakily. "Whoever broke in last night wasn't looking for me and I think you know that."

"Did you call the cops?" Noah demanded. "Hope, tell me you didn't call the –"

"Of course I didn't," Hope shot back heatedly. "I'm not stupid."

"Okay." Noah sagged in visible relief. "Okay."

"There's more, Teagan," Jordan said in a quiet voice, stepping toward us.

He seemed to be having an internal battle with himself, as he looked at Hope with a torn expression, but the hungry expression Lucky wore as he stared unabashedly at Hope seemed to be the game changer for Jordan.

Finally, he exhaled a shaky breath and sat down beside her. When Hope turned her face into his neck, Jordan's face twisted in pain as he inhaled through his nose and wrapped his arm around her shoulder. Glancing up at us through thick, sooty lashes, Jordan squeezed out, "There was a bullet on her pillow," he told Noah.

"A bullet?" I gaped at them. "But why?" I forced my mind to think back to everyone I had pissed off. Yeah, it was a pretty long list, but nothing I had ever done fortified death threats. "Why is this happening to me?"

Immediately, Noah was in front of me. With his hands on my shoulders, he forced me to look at him. "Breathe," he said in a calm tone, brown eyes locked on mine. "You're safe now. I swear to god, you are safe, baby."

"I didn't realize I *wasn't* safe," I shot back, chest heaving. "What's going on, Noah?"

The sound of a phone ringing cut through the air, distracting him.

Growling, Noah slid his hand into his pocket and pulled out his phone before putting it to his ear. I watched as his eyes flashed with anger. Whoever was on the other side of that call had tripped a switch in Noah, because he threw his head back and roared "Fuck," before stalking off in the direction of the bedroom, with Lucky hot on his heels.

The minute the bedroom door slammed shut behind them, I flew into a blind panic.

"Why is this happening?" I shrieked, pacing the floor. "Why?"

"I don't know, Teagan," Hope, who had gotten to her feet, said as she rushed over to me and wrapped me up in a hug. "But I would take it as a clear message."

"A message about what?" I shrieked. "Oh my god. Yesterday there was a rose and a note."

"A note?" Hope's brows furrowed.

"Yeah," I choked out. "It said *Tick tock.*"

"You don't open doors to strangers, Thorn. You fucking got that?"

"What the hell have you gotten her into this time?"

I gasped as awareness smacked me straight in the face.

NOAH

"*D*id you think we were going to sit back and watch you and that slut have everything after destroying our world?"

JD's familiar voice filled my ears and my blood ran cold. Every ounce of fear and anger I was feeling escalated at a rapid pace.

Conscious of Teagan watching my every move, I stormed into the bedroom and out of earshot. Lucky followed after me, closing the door in his tracks. I appreciated it. Teagan was already terrified. I didn't need her to hear this conversation.

"Leave her out of this," I warned him, pacing the room. "I fucking mean it, asshole. This is between you and me."

"And where would the fun be in that?" He sneered. "No, I'm enjoying this little game of cat and mouse. But I have to say, I don't blame you for losing your head over her." Chuckling, he added, "I'm going to enjoy breaking her in."

"You'll never get within sniffing distance of her," I hissed with a death grip on my phone. "And if you try, I will kill you."

"Big words, little brother," he chuckled. "I wonder if you can back them up."

"Oh, I can back it up," I snarled. "Face me like a fucking man and I'll show you just how well I can back it up."

"Did she like the gift?" He added, taunting me, fucking

driving me batshit crazy. "I have to say, it's not like her to stay out all night. But then again, she was always stupid when it came to you."

"What?" I deadpanned.

"I know all about your little thorn, Messina," JD laughed. "Where she lives. The gym she works in. The friends she hangs out with. Hell, I even know what time she leaves her apartment each morning and returns each night. I've had eyes on her for years now, you stupid, little prick. She looked real good in that little white dress last night..."

"Why now?" I demanded, chest heaving. "If you've been watching her all these years, then why make your move now?"

"Where would the fun have been in taking her before you two kissed and made up?" He laughed, cruelly. "You know how I like to play with my kill. I'm going to take her from you. You'll never see it coming, and when I do, she's going to wish she was dead."

"This isn't about her and you know it," I managed to grind out, jaw clenched. "This is about me. So fucking come at me. Leave her out of this."

"On the contrary," he countered. "My father held a particularly nasty grudge against the little bitch for taking his prized fighter away."

"She didn't do shit, JD." Running my hand through my hair in frustration, I hissed, "I was never staying with your father."

"In fact," he continued, ignoring what I had said. "His dying wish was for me to drain that little bitch's body of blood while you watch helplessly."

"Try it and I guarantee you I'll be waiting for you, asshole," I snarled. "No one is going to touch her. So you can send your army. Fucking bring it. Because I will take every one of you motherfuckers down."

"Clock is ticking, Messina. I'll be seeing you two real soon," he said and then the line went dead.

"He was in her goddamn house," I roared, flinging my phone across the room. "He's been watching her all this fucking time, Lucky." I choked out, sinking down on the bed. "How the hell am I supposed to tell her?"

"I don't know," he replied calmly. "But she can't be left in the dark, Noah. Not about something like this." Walking over to where my phone was, Lucky bent down and retrieved it. "Listen," he told me as he tapped at the screen. "I'll go over to her apartment and pick up some stuff. Stay with her. I'll meet you both at the airport in an hour."

"Make sure you bring a photograph of her mother," I told him. "There's one on her nightstand."

Lucky nodded once before putting the phone to his ear. "Hey man, it's me. I need a favor..." I heard him say before moving towards the window.

"Noah!" Teagan's voice boomed through my ears as she marched into the bedroom. "What are you hiding from me?"

I couldn't look at her face.

It was too fucking painful.

There was only one thing I could think of and that was Teagan making it out of this mess alive.

If I had to die in the process then so fucking be it.

TEAGAN

"*N*oah!" I roared as I stalked through the suite toward the bedroom with my heart hammering in my chest.

Stopping outside the bedroom door, I inhaled a deep, calming breath and braced myself before pushing it inward.

"What are you hiding from me?" Clamping my hands firmly on my hips, I drank in the sight of Noah, sitting on the edge of the bed with his head bent and hands hanging loosely between his legs.

Lucky was standing by the window talking low and fast into his phone.

When he noticed my presence, he nodded to Noah and walked out of the room, phone still welded to his ear as he barked orders to whoever was on the other line.

"What's going on, Noah?" I repeated. Him being unable to look me in the eye was my first warning of trouble. The swell of obscenities he muttered under his breath was my second. "I'm no wallflower, Noah," I added in a shaky tone. "And I'm not stupid. I know you're hiding something from me."

"I'm thinking here, Thorn." Jerking off the bed, he stalked over to the window. With his arms braced against the sill, Noah hissed, "Give me a minute. *Please.*"

"No," I shot back, marching toward him. "I will *not* give you a minute." Grabbing his arm, I forced him to look at me. "I'm being threatened. Some freak filled my bedroom with roses and put a bullet on my fucking pillow," I screamed. "So talk to me, dammit."

Noah's eyes flashed with anger and for a moment I thought he was going to explode. "I'm so fucking sorry for dragging you back into this," he choked out.

"Dragging me back into what, Noah?" I whispered, terrified.
"JD is back."

"No." The moment those words came out of Noah's mouth I began to shake. "I thought that was over." Tears filled my eyes. The ground fell out from beneath my feet as I spiraled into a full-blown panic attack. "Please tell me this isn't true."

"This is my fault," Noah choked out, eyes wild with fear and anger. "He's using my feelings for you against me, making you a target..." his voice broke off and he groaned like he was in physical pain. "Making you the only fucking target."

"He's coming for me?" I whispered in a small voice.

"You think I'm gonna let him get near you?" Noah demanded, pulling me into his arms. "Not a chance, baby. You're safe. I fucking promise you, I will not let anything happen to you," he snarled, holding me tightly. "Why the hell do you think I want you on that plane with me?" Leaning back, Noah looked into my eyes. "I've been trying to figure out how to get you on there since I found out he was back." He shuddered and pressed a kiss to my forehead. "I need you with me, Thorn, so I can keep you safe. If anything bad happened to you because of me, it would *kill* me. I can't be responsible for that."

"Is that why you came back for me?" I whispered, stepping out of his arms, my blood turning to ice in my veins. "Why you want me to go back to the states with you – out of duty?"

"What?" Noah blanched and shook his head. "No. Of fucking course it isn't," he growled. "I want you to come so I can keep you safe."

"See, there's that word again," I muttered, taking a step back. "Safe." Wiping my cheeks, I looked up at him and said, "I don't want you to want me with you for those reasons."

Capturing my waist with his hand, he dragged me back to him, slamming my body to his chest. "Is needing you alive and fucking breathing not a good enough reason for you now?" Glaring down at me, I could feel his heart hammering in his chest. "Fine. Then how about the fact that I've only loved one person in my whole entire fucking life and that person is *you*." Knotting his hand in my hair, he drew me closer. "Or the only time I've ever felt happiness was when I was in your presence, and I would gladly do a hundred lifetimes in prison if it meant you were *safe*. If it meant you were *alive*," he added gruffly. "Do you want me to write my feelings down in blood, Thorn? Because I can tell you I love you, but unless you cut my heart out of my chest and hold it in your hands, you're never going to understand just how fucking much." Exhaling heavily, Noah's eyes flared with heat and raw passion. "Is that a good enough reason to want you with me?"

"More than enough." I could feel the change inside of me. It was acceptance of myself and of him. I was letting go of the pain of the past. I wanted to see this through with him.

Noah had fought for me. He was my freaking solider and I never wanted to be apart from him again. I needed to be with him more than I needed my next breath. That's how important he was to me. That was how much I loved him. My heart had never beat so fast before. It was like it was leading me toward him, and I let it.

Wrapping one arm around his neck, I cupped his cheek with the other. "I'll follow you anywhere. I made a mistake by letting you go once, Noah," I told him. "I won't make the same mistake twice."

I was giving up everything for an uncertain future with the only person I was certain I wanted to be with.

I was stepping into the unknown with Noah, taking a gamble and risking my future on the man they called The Machine.

His enemies wanted me dead.

I should be running in the opposite direction.

But I couldn't fight my fate, and he was my future.

I realized that now.

And I would follow him to the ends of the earth.

Even if that meant trusting him not to let me lose myself in the process.

Even if that meant putting my life in his hands.

NOAH

*C*upping her face between my hands, I pressed my forehead against hers and sighed. "I love you," I told her. "So damn much. I will do whatever I have to do to keep you safe." I pressed my lips to her head and exhaled heavily. "So are we good now?" I hoped like fuck we were because I didn't need Thorn getting cold feet on me.

Not now that JD had upped the stakes. That bastard was suicidal. He had to be to break into my woman's home and put a fucking bullet on her bed.

I appreciated the ammo, though.

I planned on using that exact one on him when I blew his fucking brains out.

"We're good," she assured me, breaking through my thoughts. Resting her cheek on my chest, she sighed heavily. "This is permanent, Noah. Isn't it?"

"Like a sharpie." Hooking my hands under her arms, I picked her up and walked her over to the bed. "Now get dressed. We'll leave for the airport from here."

"But I don't have any clothes."

"Wear mine. Take whatever you want." Sitting her down on the bed, I pressed a kiss to the top of her head, inhaling the smell of her, before pulling back. "I need to have a quick word with Jordan."

"But what about my stuff?" She exclaimed as she knelt on the bed. "My passport and my clothes. My pictures of my mother," she blurted out. "Everything I own is back at the apartment."

"Lucky's already taking care of it," I assured her. "He'll meet us at the airport. Everything's been taken care of."

"So when you said come with you..." her voice trailed off and she grinned. "You didn't mean a vacation?"

"I'm not giving you back," I warned her, unsmiling. "See this through with me, Thorn, and I'll make you happy. I will sort everything with JD," I promised her – I fucking vowed. "And then we can have it all, baby."

NOAH

"You should go say goodbye," I told Hope when I walked back into the sitting area of the suite. "She's coming with me."

Hope shook her head and groaned. "Noah, I swear to god if you hurt her again –"

"I won't," I interrupted quickly, shutting her down. "Now go say goodbye."

I waited until Hope disappeared into the bedroom before turning my attention to Jordan.

"You need to get her out of here for a while," I told him in a low tone of voice. "I don't care what you have to do," I added. "Woo her. Take her on a holiday. I don't care. Just keep Hope out of that building until I say otherwise."

"Jesus Christ, Noah," Jordan groaned. He stood up and walked over to the window. "I'm not...I can't be here," he whispered with his head bent as he clutched the windowsill. "I'm supposed to be...fuck!"

"Listen to me, dipshit," I snarled, stalking over to him. Grabbing his shoulder, I swung him around to face me. "I know you've got some fucked up reason for walking away from her, but I also know that somewhere inside that stone heart you still love her. And the only reason I'm not kicking your ass right now is because I need you fucking mobile," I added, resisting the urge to break his fucking jaw for breaking Hope's heart. "I don't give two shits about your daddy issues or who's waiting for you back home. You make my niece your *only* priority."

Jordan stared at me for a long moment before nodding stiffly. "I'll keep her safe," he finally said, jaw clenched.

"Good." I nodded. "Glad we're on the same page." *Glad he finally found his balls...*

"But if anything happens to Hope because of you, you won't have to worry about your enemies," he hissed, stepping closer. "I'll kill you myself."

I snorted. "If anything happens to Hope because of me, you'll be one of a long list of people ready to kill me." Sighing, I added, "She's not a target. She just happens to live with the *only* target."

"I'm ready," Teagan called out as she strolled out of the bedroom arm in arm with Hope.

I turned around to see her and my heart slammed against my chest. She was swallowed up in a pair of my sweatpants and a hoodie, looking so small and vulnerable that the protective instinct inside of me roared to life.

"Are you sure about this, Teegs?" Hope asked her.

"I'm sure about him," she replied before walking straight into my arms. "I'm sure about you," she whispered, wrapping her arms around my waist. "Whatever happens," Teagan said, eyes locked on my face. "I'm not walking away from you again. I will be right by your side. I'm yours, Noah Messina. I'm in."

Fuck me, she was really with me on this.

I looked down at her and smiled. "I know."

This woman was my best friend.

She knew me inside and out.

She knew it all.

The good, the bad, and the illegal.

And for some fucked up reason she loved me anyway.

I couldn't let her go again.

I fucking couldn't.

TEAGAN

TWO WEEKS LATER

*L*ike I had predicted, Noah wasn't fired. He got a slap on the wrist and a huge fine for his part at Krash Bar that night, but that was it. My man was too important to the company. He was indispensable.

He proved that tonight when he packed out the Odyssey Arena with an army of adoring fans. Fifteen thousand people were on their feet, screaming his name, myself included from the front row.

JD had been quiet since we returned to the States.

No roses, no bullets on pillows or unwanted phone calls, but I wasn't stupid. I knew he was still out there somewhere, waiting for his opportunity.

So did Noah, which was why I was being chaperoned tonight by his newly hired bodyguard, Lewis, who was currently sitting beside me.

I understood the dangers that came with being stalked by a sadistic mob boss determined to kill me – and make it painful – which was why I didn't protest having a bodyguard.

I also knew that the only one that stood in his way of making good on his promise was my fallen angel.

My savior.

My fighter boyfriend.

But I wasn't going to dwell on JD tonight.

In fact, I was determined to put that creep to the back of my mind.

Tonight was all about Noah and I planned on savoring every second of it.

The cage, the metal bars, the scent of sweat mixed with tobacco and alcohol was poignant as I watched Noah make his way to the cage.

His entrance song *Can't be touched* was blaring through the speakers, causing the momentum to soar.

A line of security guards with their arms crossed over their burly, bigger than life chests were all that kept Noah from being mauled by his overly zealous fans.

"Ladies and gentlemen, for your pleasure, for one night only, we have a knockout fight," the announcer called excitedly. "That's right, folks. MFA veteran, and three times former heavyweight champion-Roy the wringerrrrr Wicks. And going against him tonight, a crowd favorite, it's your very own bad boy from the wrong side of the tracks. Noah the Machine Messsinaaaaaa!"

When he entered the cage, Noah bounced lightly on his feet; a challenge for a man who was 6'4" in height and 245 pounds of pure muscle.

Ignoring his opposition, who was already in the cage and trying to taunt him, Noah rolled his shoulders and twisted his neck from side to side, loosening out.

When the match official called both men to the center of the ring to touch gloves, the screaming and cheering went through the roof.

The bell rang and Noah curled his lip up and smirked.

And then he attacked.

THANK YOU SO MUCH FOR READING!

Noah and Teagan's story continues in
Tame
Available now.

Please consider leaving a review on the platform you purchased this book.

<u>Carter Kids in order:</u>
Treacherous
Always
Thorn
Tame
Torment
Inevitable
Altered

OTHER BOOKS BY CHLOE WALSH

Treacherous – Carter Kids #1
Always – Carter Kids #1.5
Thorn – Carter Kids #2
Tame – Carter Kids #3
Torment – Carter Kids #4
Inevitable – Carter Kids #5
Altered – Carter Kids #6

The DiMarco Dynasty:
DiMarco's Secret Love Child: Part One
DiMarco's Secret Love Child: Part Two

The Blurred Lines Duet:
Blurring Lines – Book #1
Never Let me Go – Book #2

Boys of Tommen:
Binding 13 – Book #1
Keeping 13 – Book #2
Saving 6 – Book #3
Redeeming 6 – Book #4

Crellids:
The Bastard Prince

Other titles:
Seven Sleepless Nights

ABOUT THE AUTHOR

Chloe Walsh is the bestselling author of The Boys of Tommen series, which exploded in popularity. She has been writing and publishing New Adult and Adult contemporary romance for a decade. Her books have been translated into multiple languages. Animal lover, music addict, TV junkie, Chloe loves spending time with her family and is a passionate advocate for mental health awareness. Chloe lives in Cork, Ireland with her family.

Join Chloe's mailing list for exclusive content and release updates.
http://eepurl.com/dPzXMI

Printed in Great Britain
by Amazon